CAPE D

REVENGE AND REM

WIL

A NOVEL

M. E. ROSTRON

Michael E Rostron
Blaine, WA

Michael E Rostron
5545 Hillvue Rd.
Blaine, WA/98230
www.mikerostron.com

Cover design and maps by Kenzie Mahoskey

Book Layout ©2017 BookDesignTemplates.com

Cape Decision/ M. E. Rostron. -- 1st ed.
ISBN 978-0-578-42622-8

SE ALASKA
Pacific Ocean
SKAGWAY
HAINES
Lynn Canal
GLACIER BAY
JUNEAU
Tenekee Springs
Frederick Sound
CHICHAGOF IS.
ADMIRALTY IS.
Stephens Passage
SITKA
BARANOF IS.
KAKE
Chatham Strait
KUPREANOF IS.
PETERSBURG
WRANGELL
ZAREMBO IS.
ETOLIN IS.
KUIU IS.
Clarence Strait
PRINCE OF WALES IS.
REVILLAGIGEDO IS.
KETCHIKAN
Thorne Bay
Dixon Entrance

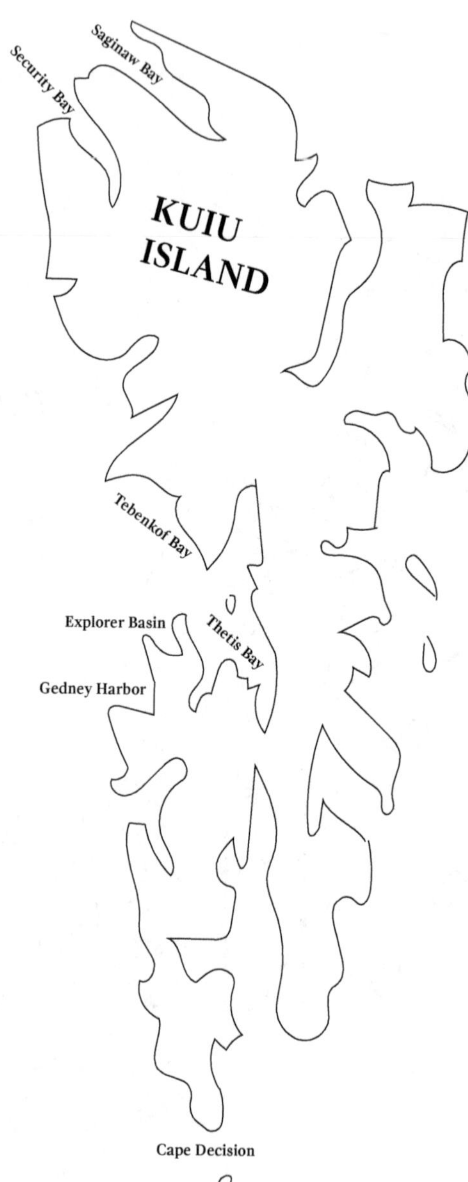
Saginaw Bay
Security Bay
KUIU
ISLAND
Tebenkof Bay
Explorer Basin
Thetis Bay
Gedney Harbor
Cape Decision

Egg Harbor
Alikula Bay
Aats Bay
Gish Bay
Windy Bay
CORONATION IS.

Nothing inspires forgiveness quite like revenge.
—Scott Adams

PROLOGUE

Juneau

January in Juneau, Alaska, normally the coldest month of the long dark winter, but the heavy wet snow from the previous night was rapidly melting away in the strong warm southerly that had already shaken most of the tree branches free of their white flocking. On the streets and in their driveways early morning commuters scraped slushy snow from idling autos. The meteorologists had consulted their computer simulations with the diligence of diviners, but the augured cold snap had not materialized.

Karen Stuckrath watched the television weatherwoman—a sleek sibyl who spun her skein of portents like some modern day Moira—diagram the positions and relative strengths of the fronts which rolled and crested like waves in the ocean of air above their isolated northern outpost.

Karen's daughter and husband both left the house early weekday mornings to attend Juneau High School, where Cindy was a student and David taught history. After she watched David maneuver the old Subaru wagon out of their icy driveway—bordered this time of year by four foot high snow berms, Karen leisurely drank her morning coffee while she simultaneously watched the morning news and scanned the daily paper. Several weeks earlier she had given up her office job with the Alaska Marine Highway System—the ferry network that linked the communities of the southeastern part of the state. She planned to take a few months off before going back to school to pursue her life-long interest in pediatrics. The early hours had become her favorite time of day. With her son, Marshall, attending college in faraway Fairbanks, she enjoyed the still somewhat novel luxury of a solitary and unhurried morning.

The phone rang. Instinctively, she sensed trouble.

"Mom... I really screwed up... It's serious... I was so stupid! I need a lawyer right away."

"Are you in jail, Marshall?" Karen asked. Her hands shook, but she kept her voice as calm as she could manage.

"They let me go back to the dorm. They said I'll be indicted in a couple of weeks. You better tell Dad. I really messed up... I'm so sorry!"

After she calmed him down, he told her what had happened. Like many college students away from home for the first time, Marshall Stuckrath had found the temptation of fast food and weekend beer bashes too hard to resist. Before long he had put on a few pounds. With a regional wrestling match looming, he needed to drop some weight quickly. A fellow student suggested an easy solution; he knew a guy who would sell Marshall some powder that would suppress his appetite and help him quickly shed the extra weight.

Unfortunately for Marshall the seller was being monitored by local and federal investigators. When they arrived at the rendezvous Marshall and the dealer were arrested by the local police and an officer from AKNET, an organization of local, regional, and federal drug investigators.

David and Karen had never had any dealings with the legal system beyond a couple of traffic tickets, and were nearly as shocked and panic-stricken as their son. They engaged a lawyer, Tom Larson, who came highly recommended by a friend whose own son had managed to beat a pot possession charge with Larson's help. Larson got a change of venue from Fairbanks to Juneau so that Marshall could stay with his family. The lawyer reassured the Stuckrath's that because it was their son's first offense, he would most likely be charged with a misdemeanor. They could expect a fine and some public service, plus mandatory substance abuse counseling.

But Larson's assumptions were wrong. The state charged Marshall with felony possession of cocaine. If convicted he faced possible prison time, and lifetime stigma as a felon. He would be ineligible for educational loans or grants. He would have trouble traveling to other countries. Some careers would be closed to him. A stiff price for a single indiscretion.

"Our first priority must be to get this charge reduced to a misdemeanor," the lawyer explained.

"We will be up against a new prosecutor who I am not familiar with, and for some reason she is out to make this particular case a feather in her cap—and it doesn't stop there. Unfortunately I have more bad news. We've drawn the worst possible judge in Alaska for drug cases. Judge Henry Daise has said publicly on several occasions that anyone who is convicted of drug charges in his court will spend time in prison. No exceptions. So far that is what has transpired in all of his cases that have not been appealed. This is going to be more difficult than I anticipated."

Larson recommended Marshall enroll in a three week long substance abuse treatment program at a well-known facility in Washington state. This could count as time served if he were sentenced, and would also show the court he was serious about no longer using drugs.

So Marshall, with the permission of the court, flew south and went through the regime in the treatment facility. It cost the family thousands of dollars, and Marshall was disappointed to miss winter term at college, where he was just starting to feel like he fit in. As they had hoped, the prosecution agreed to reduce the charges to a misdemeanor in return for Marshall waiving his right to a jury trial. Marshall's sentence would be determined after a hearing in front of judge Daise.

"This is definitely a step in the right direction," the lawyer said, as they conferred in his office a few days after Marshall returned from the drug treatment facility.

"I'm frankly surprised the state still wants to take this into Daise's courtroom. We should have been able to negotiate a sentence too, but the worse case scenario should be a few weeks in a half-way house—probably right here in Juneau—and a fine, more drug counseling, and most likely a significant amount of public service work. I doubt Marshall will be able to make it back to Fairbanks in time for spring term, but hopefully he will be able to jump through all the legal hoops in time to go back to college in the fall."

Marshall felt miserable, and David and Karen were not comforted. The costs were mounting, and too much seemed uncertain.

"It's a hell of a lot more involved and expensive than I had ever imagined. It's been so long since we had anything to do with illegal drugs. I remember when pot was legal in both Alaska and Oregon," David protested.

"You haven't been paying attention—that was way back in the seventies," Larson responded. "Since the Reagan administration things have really changed—and obviously not for the better. Drugs are the modern day version of the witch hunt, or McCarthyism."

"It sure as hell seems that way!"

"Believe me, I deal with these kinds of cases constantly. A powerful group of reactionaries have turned the harassment of drug users into a major industry. The reality is that I'm just another one of the cogs in the machine."

Larson was not surprised by David's naivety. He found it depressingly all to common in his clients—even the well-educated ones.

"I had no idea before Marshall's problems how many people make their living arresting, processing, counseling, testing, investigating, and imprisoning users —it just goes on and on! What a fucking Byzantine mess! It's like we're characters in some Kafka novel!" David raged.

David had been exasperated, offended, and frustrated with Marshall's pretrial ordeal. He had been angry with his son at first, but soon decided the incident had been blown grossly out of proportion. He cursed the legal system that seemed bent on thrusting his family into its insatiable maw.

Karen's misgivings about the whole legal process only intensified the more she learned. The daughter of a friend had been convicted in a similar possession case, spent months in jail, treatment centers, and half-way houses. She emerged shaken and emotionally brutalized—a diminished and timid shadow of her former self.

Another local teen-aged girl Karen knew of was arrested and given the choice of a "correctional facility" or going undercover. After her status as a snitch was discovered, the high school students where she was sent to spy became enraged, first hazing and threatening her, before finally ostracizing her completely. In desperation the girl attempted suicide and very nearly succeeded. Only the efforts of a sympathetic psychiatrist had kept her from re-incarceration, once she could be of no further use to the drug investigators.

"Maybe we should just take Marshall to Canada,"

Karen suggested. "Since he was born there he has dual citizenship."

Marshall had been delivered in Whitehorse, Yukon, where medical costs were a fraction of what they would have been in Juneau.

"I don't think Canada would allow Alaska to extradite him. He's never been in trouble there, and I doubt the Alaska court would spend the money and effort to try. They must have many more important cases."

Finally verbalizing to David what she had been mulling over for the last several days made it suddenly clear to Karen that this was in fact exactly what they should do.

"I don't think that is such a good idea. He would have a warrant hanging over him if he ever decided to come back to the states. We could be charged with helping him escape. How will it help the children if one or both of us goes to jail? Our best bet is to go along with the plea bargain and hope judge Daise hands down a reasonable sentence. Marshall will probably get off with no jail time, a fine, and some public service work, like Larson says."

"The problem with you, David, is you just have too damn much faith in the rationality of people and the legal system," Karen shot back. "You've been a history teacher for so long you've totally lost touch with the present!"

"You know that's not fair, Karen. And I'm not the one who is being irrational!"

"Can't you recall how it was back when we were young, during the Viet Nam war? The paranoia—the drug busts—people getting beat up at peaceful protests—fights between the hippies and red-necks? Don't you remember the people back then who spent years in jail just for smoking pot... Have you forgotten all that? Do you think those people—the ones who beat up protesters and persecuted pot smokers—have just gone away, or mellowed out, or changed their attitudes? These are those same people—older, just as mean-spirited, and now in positions of power! I hope for Marshall's sake you are right. But what if you're wrong?"

"Have you talked about Canada with Marshall?"

Her intensity frightened him. Karen was a she-wolf defending her cub.

"Of course not. I wanted to see how you felt about it first, but I should have known!"

At that moment she realized she did not trust David's judgement in this crucial matter. A terrible thought crept into her mind. She tried to put it aside but it was no use. What if David had learned the secret she had hidden for so long about Marshall? But she realized that it could not possibly matter to David, even if he did know. And she was sure he did not. His view of the situation, she understood, arose from his basic nature. He was so rational, calm (part of what had initially attracted her to him), and methodical—and he was right about most things—but not about this. In her heart she knew it. Marshall was in real danger, and David refused to acknowledge it.

"Well now you do know how I feel. I don't think moving to Canada is an option," David continued, trying not to make it sound as though he was giving his wife an ultimatum.

"I'm willing to take him to Canada, even if you don't have the balls," Karen answered. Her face was ashen, and her clenched fists shook.

In all the years of their mostly peaceful and harmonious marriage Karen and David had never found themselves at such an impasse. Her simple statement was an accusation, and a challenge. They were seated at the breakfast bar, their coffees growing cold. David would be late for work he realized, and he could not stop himself from feeling the attendant anxiety, though he knew it should not matter compared to the ramifications of the decision they were contemplating.

For an instant David had a vision of Karen as she had appeared when he first met her. So young, strong, and beautiful. Back then—two decades earlier—she had been self-confident and precocious. They had both been politically and socially progressive—even radical—unafraid and clear-eyed. How had he lost that spirit himself? How had he become so cautious, fearful, and conventional? It had been a slow incremental process, he knew. The accretion of so many things. Of course not only the things, but the whole desire for stability and security that went along with raising a family and providing for them.

Karen's willingness to change the rules and completely uproot their life in order to save Marshall from what she saw as a too risky legal process destroyed the peace in their home. Night after night they fought over Karen's stubborn desire to escape with the boy. Their bedroom—where they struggled to keep their voices low so the children would not hear—became a battle ground. They were never able to resolve their differences. David steadfastly clung to the belief that all would work out for the best if they followed their lawyer's advice. Karen continued to insist that leaving the country was Marshall's best chance. She refused to believe his act was in any way criminal, or that he owed society any restitution for his attempt to buy a small amount of stimulant.

David became steadily more depressed, and although he tried to maintain a positive attitude around the children, his work suffered. He half-heartedly taught his classes and trudged through his routine at the high school. The feeling he was somehow failing at protecting their son persisted and grew as it got closer to Marshall's sentencing date.

The strain began to affect their family life in varied ways. Most of their friends and family were supportive, recalling their own experimentations with drugs, or other youthful misjudgments and mistakes. There were a couple of notable exceptions.

David's older brother wrote a particularly nasty letter to Marshall, accusing him of letting down the entire family and worse. The irony was that he himself abused pills and booze, and had a long history of ruined relationships caused by his years of alcoholic excess.

Luckily he had never been arrested. When Marshall showed his father the letter from his uncle, David responded in a totally uncharacteristic way, with a blistering phone call that ended with David threatening his older sibling with a good beating if he ever saw him again. A Juneau acquaintance informed David this would have never happened had he raised his children as good Christians. David gave that person an explicit description of the part of his anatomy his opinion was best suited for.

He was losing it. His normal restraint and good manners seemed to be falling away, leaving only a raw core of anger and frustration. Around his colleagues at work he became unusually combative, and over-sensitive to the slightest of perceived animadverts. He dreaded his classes, and he was habitually late and unprepared.

In contrast Marshall seemed to be taking things in stride, trusting that his parents and their lawyer were giving him the best advice, and with youth's characteristic optimism, hoping for a light punishment from the court. His only complaint was that he was missing winter term at college. Karen suspected (and was correct) that it might have something to do with a new girlfriend in Fairbanks. He spent his free time much as he had during his last winter in high school; snowboarding and skiing at the local ski slope, hanging out with friends who had not themselves gone off to college, and working out at a local gymnasium. The only noticeable change seemed to be his greater sensitivity to his parents Though he had always been dependable and good natured, he was even quicker than usual at volunteering to help with the household chores, as if in apology for the suffering he was causing the family.

During his time in the substance abuse rehabilitation facility Marshall was forced by the staff to go through a twelve-step type of program and urged to admit he was a drug addict, who had no control over his cravings. Some of the people at the treatment center were seriously addicted to heroin, cocaine, or alcohol. Others were there as part of a court mandated treatment resulting from a drug conviction. A few more, like Marshall, attended voluntarily or because their legal advisors or family thought it best. For the worst cases, it was rehab or inevitable death from an overdose.

The problem for Marshall was the constant pressure to admit he was an addict. Marshall knew he was not addicted to drugs. He had simply wanted a quick way to loose some weight. The films and testimonials of the inmates had certainly taught him the potential dangers of drug use, and he accepted that wisdom, but the staff wanted more. Using psychological techniques, peer pressure, and thinly veiled threats they tried to convince him his past experiments with alcohol and marijuana—actually less extensive than usual for his generation—were part of a more serious problem. Marshall had a combative and stubborn streak, which resulted in a series of clashes with those in charge of his 'rehabilitation.' In the limited conversations with family that the facility allowed he explained the situation to his father.

"If I don't cooperate they'll give the court a bad report, and I could end up in jail. But if I do what they want, I will be lying to myself and everyone. I know I'm not addicted to cocaine or anything else—except maybe sports," he told his father.

"I know you aren't either, but we are going to have to play the game by their rules if you want to stay out of prison. Go along with them and do what they ask. You just have to get through this as best you can. We love you, and this will all soon be behind us," was all David could offer as advice. He felt he must trust in their counsel's greater knowledge of the legal system in which they had become ensnared.

In the end Marshall cooperated. The facility recommended Marshall to an Anchorage substance abuse center for a six to twelve month treatment regime. Their lawyer was infuriated.

"This would mean up to a year in a facility with a good percentage of hard core drug addicts," he explained to the family.

"It's just not acceptable. I told the management that if they do not retract this part of your son's evaluation, I will stop sending any more clients to their facility, and will recommend another institution to my colleagues. That would result in a significant loss of revenue to them."

"So I see. This is all about the money, isn't it?" David said.

"I'm afraid you are largely correct. Drug treatment and counseling are big business. A lot of people's jobs depend on a constant stream of drug cases to keep their operations running. Obviously I make a great deal of my income from cases like these. I'm not saying some of the treatment facilities don't do some good, but the system is self-perpetuating, and certainly was not designed for cases like Marshall's."

At the hearing Marshall pleaded guilty to a misdemeanor 'attempt to possess.' Judge Daise sentenced him to sixty days in the penitentiary, with credit for the twenty-one days he had spent in the substance abuse facility, and treated him to a generic lecture on the evils of illegal drug use. The bottom line; thirty-nine days of incarceration.

Tom Larson and the Stuckrath family were shocked at the harshness of the sentence, but the lawyer reassured them that Marshall would actually only spend a few days in Lime River, the state penitentiary in Juneau, before he would most likely go to a half-way house where lodgings would be more relaxed, visitor hours much more flexible, and chaperoned trips outside the institution would be permitted.

In their limited visiting time allotments David, Karen, and Cindy Stuckrath did their best to cheer him up, but Marshall looked shaken and frightened. He complained that one of the prisoners had it in for him. He told his family he was going to ask for a different exercise time. David and Karen assured their son that they would talk to his attorney and see what could be done. There was little else to say. The truth was they were completely powerless to help him.

Marshall never made it to the half-way house. He was stabbed to death on his fourth day of incarceration in a fight with another prisoner.

CHAPTER ONE

Clarence Strait

David Stuckrath considered the ragged line of white foam of surf breaking on the rocks less than a quarter mile to the east. *Close enough*, he thought, and brought the tiller over. His tacking maneuver was clean. The boat came about smartly as he winched in the jib sheet. The cutter *Lethe*, under reefed mainsail and jib, charged away on her new heading, her starboard rail periodically dipping into the frigid water as the boat heeled to the opposite tack.

Lethe's progress had slowed considerably in the last hour, as the rising southwesterly wind and contrary tides conspired against her. The steep four foot seas were so close together that her bow split an oncoming wave before the previous one had time to clear her stern, only thirty feet back. David ducked into the cabin, checked the barometer, and listened to the weather station on his VHF radio, momentarily letting the wind vane steer the boat. The barometer was falling rapidly. The robotic radio voice continued to warn of the approaching storm. White streaks of foam blowing from the tops of the waves and the howling in the rigging confirmed the weather station's observations that the wind had already risen to force seven on the Beaufort scale—well over thirty miles per hour, and what sailors refer to as a "near gale."

Better shorten sail again, David decided. He still had plenty of daylight left to make port, he reflected, even with the reduction in speed which would result from substituting the much smaller staysail for the working jib. He moved the tiller again, and *Lethe* obediently put her bow up into the wind. He reset the self-steering gear, and carefully moved forward to the pin-rail where the halyards—the lines which raised and lowered the sails—were coiled neatly over stout oaken pins. David's rubber deck boots sloshed in the water that coursed over the deck. He let go the jib halyard, but the jib sail stuck half way down, flapping and snapping on its wire stay. David cautiously inched out on the jutting bowsprit to haul down the stubborn sheet of flailing fabric. He hung on with one hand and laboriously doused the unruly bundle of canvas.

As practiced as he was at this activity, it was intense and wet work. Several times the bowsprit dipped him to his thighs in the cold waters of Clarence Strait. He swore as the water filled his boots, but his exclamations were mere mutterings in the cacophony of sea and wind. With effort and more foul language David bundled up the jib and lashed it down to the bowsprit netting. He still had the job of raising the staysail, but at least he could do that from the relative security of the foredeck. He carefully worked his way back to the pin-rail, where he tied off the gyrating jib halyard and hoisted the small staysail. Once back again in the cockpit, David sheeted in the staysail and *Lethe* surged ahead.

That's better, he thought, noting that his speed had decreased only slightly, while the heeling angle of the boat was half what it had been. David remembered the old sailor's adage—"when you start to think about reefing, it is time to reef," and knew he had taken in sail none too soon. The wind had increased noticeably even in the few minutes it had taken him to make the sail changes, and this was only the leading edge of the storm.

With the boat reasonably comfortable and balanced for the present, David fine-tuned the wind vane steering mechanism, then descended the companionway stairs into the cozy cabin. Inside it was strangely quiet, in contrast to the noise of the wind and sea outside on deck. He poured coffee from his thermos into an insulated cup with a tight fitting lid, glad he had thought to brew a pot earlier that evening, before the weather had deteriorated. As he climbed back into the cockpit with the warm brew in hand, he heard the radio squawk.

"Mayday, mayday, mayday! This is motor vessel *Legal Eagle* requesting aid. I am unable to start my engine—heading towards Ernest point! Is anyone out there?" The man followed this with his latitude and longitude coordinates.

David listened with alarm.

"Shit, I'm practically on top of him!" he exclaimed loudly, though he was alone on his boat.

David found his binoculars and scanned the rugged western shoreline of Onslow Island. In the waning late August evening light which filtered weakly through the thick cumulous cover, he could just make out a boat perhaps two miles southeast of his vessel—not far from the rockbound coast he had just changed tacks to avoid. No other boats were in sight. David quickly started *Lethe's* small diesel engine and changed course again, coming back to his original tack and bearing. With the engine at maximum and the reduced sails still pulling, he made for the distressed boat at his best speed. He hoped it would be fast enough to get him to the caller before the other boat encountered Ernest Point or the jumble of partially submerged rocks and reefs that stretched south from there.

"*Legal Eagle*," he radioed. "This is sailing vessel *Lethe*. I'm about fifteen minutes away from you. I have you in sight. Prepare to be taken under tow," David said, trying to sound as calm and professional as possible, even as he felt the effects of the adrenaline circulating in his body. He had never before attempted to take a boat under tow in such conditions.

As he motor-sailed towards the stricken boat the coast guard station in Ketchikan picked up the hail, and advised all boaters in the area that it would take them at least thirty minutes to get a rescue helicopter on the scene. They further informed all area mariners that a storm warning for force nine to ten winds was now in effect for at least the next twenty-four hours. That meant they could expect gusts to sixty miles an hour or more—conditions that could produce twenty foot breaking waves and blinding spray in Clarence Strait, and could threaten even the largest vessels. The Coast Guard requested that David keep them advised of the situation. With the storm building and the prospect of other emergencies arising, they did not want to commit their helicopter unless absolutely necessary.

Chuck Riggs, a resident of tiny Spruce Cove village about ten miles south, a fishing boat twice that many miles away, and a yet more distant cruise ship all reported their positions and also offered help, but David's vessel was the only one within immediate range. It dawned on him that he was the the sole person near enough to have any chance of saving the man's boat, and perhaps even his life.

As he drew closer David could see it was a fairly typical craft for the area—a boxy-looking power boat slightly under thirty feet long—beamy, with an elevated steering station, which now only served to give the wind more purchase. The light displacement boat bounced and lurched in the violent seas, in stark contrast to the easy motion of David's deep-keeled heavy cutter.

On his second toss he was able to get a line to the desperate man. By this time the rocks of Ernest Point were uncomfortably close, looming threatening and unforgiving just off their port bows. The man had wisely donned a survival suit, David observed—a bulky, bright, and buoyant insulated neoprene outfit that might keep him alive for a short time in the near freezing waters of the strait. Looking like a large Gumby character in his garb, the man made the line secure about a deck cleat, and signaled with a wave of his orange glove. David took up the slack as gently as he could, then, turning sharply away from the craggy coast of the island, he headed out into the exposed white-capped expanse of Ernest Sound, another deep fjord intersecting Clarence Strait from the northeast. Here the seas were even steeper and more confused than before, and with the extra weight and drag of the *Legal Eagle* their speed slowed to less than three knots. It would be dark before they made Spruce Cove, David worried. The harbor entrance was tricky, but it was the closest secure anchorage. Still, David was familiar with the harbor from previous voyages, and felt confident he could manage as long as he could make out the entrance lights.

The little diesel droned steadily. The *Legal Eagle* saltated behind him, at times nearly vanishing in the troughs of the building waves, but the tough nylon line stood the strain. David radioed the Coast Guard once again, informing them he had the boat under tow, and that no one appeared to be injured. He gave them his estimated time to Spruce Cove. Squinting into the flying spray, he steered as direct a course as he could for the entrance, still obscured in the fading light and blowing spray. The boat shuddered as the train of waves broke relentlessly against her starboard bow, drenching the foredeck and cabin, while the rising gale ripped the foaming crests from the seas and blasted his face with stinging spindrift. But the distance to the safe haven of the harbor closed steadily.

A few miles south, in the calm security of Spruce Cove, Chuck Riggs and Mike Schwindel listened to the radio exchanges in Chuck's comfortable kitchen. The old wood-burning range did double duty, heating the room and warming their coffee. They were both well acquainted with the owner of the sailboat *Lethe*. They too were long-time residents of Southeast Alaska, with many years of boating experience between them in the treacherous waters of the archipelago, known to locals as the Alaskan "Panhandle"—a vast and complex maze formed of hundreds of forested islands interlaced with intricately branching networks of fjords and their radiating offshoots—a labyrinth nearly four hundred miles long and one hundred miles wide, where bears and deer still outnumbered humans. The tiny hamlet of Spruce Cove was situated in the southern part of the region, on a peninsula of the nearly impossible to pronounce Revillagigedo Island, in one of the wildest and least populated regions of North America.

"I think we had better get the skiff ready just in case," Chuck pronounced.

"I was just about to suggest the same. They're not out of trouble yet. David's a pretty capable sailor, but he's not going to make much headway pulling that boat in these conditions," Mike replied. "We should take your skiff. My inflatable won't be much damn good if we need to help tow."

"They'll have a rough time of it when they get close up to Spruce Island. It's going to be like a mixmaster out there with this tide and wind combination—and that wind is building fast," Chuck added.

Chuck filled a thermos with hot coffee. The two men put on their foul weather gear and went down to the husky wooden dory that served Chuck as his waterborne pick-up truck and fishing platform. They put in an extra five gallon container of fuel, and a long coil of heavy line. Chuck attached his waterproof portable VHF radio in its protected location under the small control console, and they motored across the quiet harbor. Once underway Chuck hailed *Lethe* on the VHF, and told David he would be standing by to help if necessary. When they got to the entrance of the cove, they hugged the north shore of tiny Spruce Island—a mere spit of forested rock barely separated from the mainland, where they were protected from the worst of the storm and sea's turbulence.

Chuck and Mike could just make out the faint running lights of *Lethe* and *Legal Eagle* in the distance. The two men sipped coffee from the metal thermos, and waited while the powerful outboard engine held them off the rocky shore in the lee of the islet. They knew the seas were especially confused a half mile or so to the southwest of another group of islets, where the two boats would have to make their turn into the narrow entrance channel leading into the cove. That group of steep-sided and half-awash rocks blocked any direct route, and there was no protection from the raging southern gale until well past the area. For a short time David's boat and its disabled tow would be beam on to the worst of the wind and waves. If anything went wrong, the tide and wind would deliver one or both boats directly into the stony embrace of those guard islands. Chuck and Mike watched and waited, hoping their assistance would not be needed.

A tense hour passed before David finally discerned the red and green navigation lights that marked the entrance to Spruce Cove. After he determined he was properly lined up for the run through the channel, he carefully turned his boat to the east, a maneuver which put L*ethe* and *Legal Eagle* broadside to the mounting wave train. It could not be helped. There was no other route to the protection of the harbor. He watched the tow line loosen then snap taut as the Bayliner jumped to follow his turn in the chaotic seas. David did not envy the powerboat owner. It appeared it was all he could do to hang on and keep from being thrown to the deck or out of the boat as it tossed wildly some sixty feet behind Lethe's stern.

Just a couple of hundred yards more and we've got it made, David thought, relaxing slightly as he successfully completed the turn. The lights marking the narrowest part of the channel were very close now. He could see dimly Chuck's skiff ahead off his port bow, and the lights of a cabin in the harbor beyond. He felt a sharper jerk, and turned just in time to see the tow line go slack, and drop into the water. The hefty rope had not failed, but had torn the mooring cleat of the *Legal Eagle* from its deck. David turned hard to intercept, but he knew he had no chance of making up the distance before the crippled vessel must inevitably strike the outlying rocks, where the crashing surf would surely smash it to bits.

All seemed lost, but as David watched helplessly from the cockpit of his sailboat, Chuck Rigg's skiff shot past him, recklessly smashing through and over the breaking waves, the bow of the craft pointing nearly vertical at times as it rapidly closed with the disabled powerboat. Chuck expertly maneuvered his craft close, ramming hard up against the *Legal Eagle's* hull to keep it off the rocky islets, while Mike quickly got the line to the power boat's owner, who attached it to the closest tie point at hand, a cleat on the stern bulwarks of the boat. Chuck's skiff turned and accelerated hard, her bow rising clear out of the water from the sudden load, as the towing line was pulled bar taut. It was not at first apparent if the skiff would be able to tow the larger boat stern first against the wind and current, but after several tense seconds it became evident they were making incremental but steady progress away from the threatening rocks of the leeward islets. With agonizing slowness, the outboard engine screaming at full throttle, the skiff drug the Bayliner backwards into the calm waters of the harbor as David followed closely behind.

The contrast when at last they made the lee of the barrier ridge of the bay was remarkable. In a matter of a few score yards the wind diminished from gale force to nearly zero as the stormy open waters of Clarence Strait were left behind, and they entered the secure womb of Spruce Cove harbor.

"We'll take care of things! Get some rest and we'll see you in the morning!" Chuck Riggs shouted to David over the din of the outboard.

"Thank you!" the man in the survival suit called, waving his orange rubber mitt at David from the stern of the Legal Eagle.

The skiff turned towards Chucks's home and private dock, the disabled boat now dragging docilely behind through the smooth water, while David continued on straight toward the public pier he knew to be located directly ahead, although by now it was barely discernible in the fading light. He had not been able to make out the face of the hooded figure on the deck of the powerboat in the dim light, but something about the voice sounded familiar. No matter, he would meet the man tomorrow.

Now that the excitement was over and his adrenaline had dissipated, David realized he was completely exhausted, and wanted nothing more than to crawl into his bunk and close his eyes. Weary, wet, and chilled from his efforts, David barely found the energy to secure the boat and undress, before falling quickly and deeply to sleep in his snug berth.

CHAPTER TWO

Aftermath

After Marshall's funeral Karen withdrew from all social activity, only leaving the house to shop for groceries. She refused any effort David made to comfort her. It had been her impassioned argument they could have saved Marshall's life had they followed her plan, and taken him to Canada. Though they did not speak of it, the allegation hung between them—an opaque cloud of unvoiced accusal and guilt.

A few days after the funeral Karen moved into the guest bedroom. She replaced her morning coffee with vodka and juice, spending her days drinking and sobbing quietly in front of the television. David walked out of their home for the last time a few weeks later, and moved on board their sailboat.

From the time of Marshall's arrest David had barely managed to continue his marginal teaching efforts. After Marshall's death he fell apart completely, missing days at a time, and barely functioning in the classroom.

"I can't have you here in your condition. It's not fair to the students," the principal explained.

David had taught at the high school for nearly two decades, and the principal, who had been there nearly as long himself, was as much a friend as David's colleague and boss.

"I want you to take the rest of the school year off. Let's see how you feel about things next fall. You need to decide if you want to continue on here. I am sorry David—I really am... I wish I could do something to help. You need to see someone—a professional grief counselor. Give it a chance, David."

David respected the man and knew he was right, but he no longer cared the least bit about his job, the school, or anyone in it. His mind was a deep black chasm.

Their daughter Cindy, a senior in the same high school her father taught at, was essentially abandoned to her own devices. She quit going to school, although she was only a few credits away from graduation and was salutatorian of her class. She moved into a seedy apartment with a boyfriend a few years older. Several teachers contacted her, begging her not to throw away her chances for scholarships and college.

"Fuck college!" she told one of them. "Leave me alone. And fuck your stupid society too. I would rather live my life as a bum or a whore than contribute one bit of my energy to your corrupt system!"

The well-meaning teachers soon gave up, hoping that time and maturity would eventually alleviate her grief and anger.

Attorney Larson, genuinely shaken by events,

quit Juneau and Alaska in disgust, telling his partners he wanted to work in a place where they did not treat young non-violent offenders like vicious criminals. His featured article in the Juneau newspaper concerning Marshall's case resulted in a reprimand from the Alaskan bar, whose previous president had been judge Henry Daise. The lawyer exposed AKNET and the state courts for wasting time and resources on "easy pickings" while ignoring the big-time distributors of drugs, and exposing the lives and futures of the young to unacceptable hazards from a legal system more devastating to them than the drugs themselves.

Abandoning Juneau and his family, David began his forlorn voyage along the Southeast Alaskan coast. He did not feel he could be of any help to his wife or daughter. For all he knew they would be better off without him. If he had taken his son and run to Canada as Karen had wanted Marshall would be alive now, regardless of the complications which would have ensued. Karen had most likely been right in thinking the Canadian government would not have allowed an extradition of one of its own citizens for an offense that would have netted a fine and some counseling under their more humane system. He had played by the rules just as he'd taught his children to do, with ruinous results for his family. He had been absolutely and fatally wrong. His daughter would fend for herself or not. He had not protected his son—why should he think he could protect her? She was seventeen—the same age he had been when he had left home. She could make her own way.

She might even be better off without him.

He felt even worse about Karen, but how could he ever face her again? He had failed a father's most basic duty. He had not safeguarded his family. Even worse, he had lied to himself and Karen. When the lawyer had insisted the best strategy was to plea bargain and to decline a jury trial, his gut feeling had been to reject the prosecution's offer. At least with a jury, he had reasoned at the time, they should have been able to find one or more citizens who were themselves parents, and would surely have refused to send a nineteen year old freshman college student to jail for the attempt to buy a minuscule amount of stimulant. But in the end he had gone along with the lawyer's advice and against his own intuition and his wife's wishes. That decision had cost his son his life.

He squandered most of the summer sailing aimlessly up the fjords and among the islands of the Panhandle, spending weeks alone in a series of isolated anchorages, only sailing back to the nearest towns when he ran low on supplies, especially alcohol. Eventually though he began to drink less, and came to the realization there was nothing to hold him in Alaska anymore. The overwhelming circumstances of his son's death negated any of the positive experiences of the years in Juneau. At the same time, as the summer wore on the immensity and grandeur of his surroundings seemed to put his own small existence into perspective, and the opaque paralysis of the previous months was gradually replaced with a growing glimmer of possibilities and purpose. Slowly, but steadily, David's instinct for self-preservation reasserted itself.

After many weeks of no contact with family or friends, he finally called his daughter and asked if she needed anything. She sounded somewhat more positive on the phone. She wanted out of Juneau. David wrote her a check and mailed it in Wrangell.

He called a friend in Juneau and asked how Karen was doing. Then he called Karen herself. She had put the house up for sale and had a good offer. She needed him to sign some papers. She was seeing a therapist and drinking less, she said.

"Where will you go when the house sells?" he asked.

"I'll probably stay with my sister in Oregon for a while, I guess. After that—I don't know. Anyway, Cindy is leaving too. I want to be close to her. At least she is speaking to me again." Her voice sounded small and tired, and there was an irritating delay in the satellite link.

"I spoke with Cindy too. She seems better—less bitter at least."

"I'm not sure exactly where she is going, and I don't think she is either, yet. Just away from here, like all of us. I'm glad you called her, David. You know she still needs you."

"I still need you," he said, after an awkward pause. He could sense the effort it was taking her to hold the tears back.

"I can't. I just can't," she finally said, after an

even longer silence.

He knew then she still had not forgiven him for refusing to take the boy away, and for agreeing to the plea bargain. Perhaps she never would.

"What will you do?" Karen asked.

"I haven't decided. I'm going south too, eventually. Maybe I'll spend some time in the Gulf or San Juan Islands," David answered, but he really had no plans beyond sailing farther south before the start of winter.

They said good bye, and agreed to stay in contact. It was a start, David hoped. It was the first thing he had hoped for since his son's death.

CHAPTER THREE

Conrad

The storm driven rain stung his cheeks as Conrad Slocum climbed the steep switchbacks of the trail leading to the summit. His hiking boots made deep tracks in the muddy path which wound through the darkly forested flanks of the ridge. Grasping at wet shrubbery, he lunged the last few yards and was rewarded with a panoramic view of the west side of Cleveland Peninsula. Far below him to the northwest was the small settlement of Spruce Cove, its scattering of run-down buildings, and the ruins of the old cannery pier. Beyond were the gray spindrift streaked waters of Clarence Strait. Inland to the east a small green-carpeted valley separated his ridge from a much taller rise. He could see that the rough, little-used trail disappeared into the valley before reappearing on the flanks of the next hillside. It appeared to be a moderate hike with the reward of an even better vista at its end, and Conrad had been cooped up so long in his boat that he looked forward to the strenuous trek.

He had arrived at Spruce Cove the evening before, after an arduous twelve day trip north from

Seattle. Gale force winds and heavy seas at Queen Charlotte Strait and again at Dixon entrance had battered his forty-five year old wooden gaff cutter and tested his stamina, but the leading edge of the same storm system that had slowed David Stuckrath's passage south and resulted in his detour to save the *Legal Eagle* had driven Conrad the opposite direction—north through Clarence Strait in an exhilarating downwind run from Ketchikan to Spruce Cove. He had spent his first comfortable night in many days securely moored in the protected harbor. Conrad had awakened very early that morning, refreshed, rejuvenated, and eager to feel land beneath his feet.

He descended quickly through towering cedar and hemlock stands, then tramped for thirty more minutes through a marshy bottom land dominated by dense green tangles of false lily-of-the-valley and skunk cabbage before the trail turned upward again, rising in tight switchbacks through progressively more open forest, until the path ended on a rocky outcrop just short of the higher peak. The view from this hilltop was well worth the effort—more spectacular even than the scene from the lower ridge. The rain had temporarily slackened, but the wind buffeted Conrad as he stood, perspiring and catching his breath, at the crest. His commanding view included much of the strait; Ernest Sound, Etolin Island, Behm Canal, and a good portion of the peninsula, some of the least disturbed wild country in Southeast Alaska—or the world for that matter. Everything within his sight represented only a small slice of the seventeen million acre Tongass National Forest, by far the largest in the United States. Two thirds of that was glacier covered wilderness. A small percentage was old growth lower elevation forest, and half of that had been logged in the years since World War II. But once one penetrated beyond this narrow coastal strip most of the land was uninhabited and untouched by man. Even the native tribes of the area had historically kept to the coasts and major river valleys, where they could count on a reliable runs of salmon and easier transportation by water between settlements. It was the kind of place that made man's puny efforts look insignificant, ultimately no more than minor transitory disturbances to a vast wilderness that only constant effort could barely keep at bay.

Through his binoculars Conrad picked out his boat from the cluster of others huddled against the old wooden dock in the cove. An albicant cloud of wood smoke rose from one of the houses nestled in the trees at the water's edge. Something, perhaps a seal or sea lion, raised a ripple in the water as it swam near a single fishing boat anchored placidly mid-bay. The tranquil scene in the harbor contrasted strongly with the furious roar of the gale at his elevated vantage point.

A pair of eagles circled high above him, and he raised his binoculars to get a better look. After a time he lowered the glasses and began to scan the nearby slopes and ridges, hoping for a glimpse of one of the mountain goats that were known to inhabit the higher elevations of the peninsula. Having no luck with that, he studied the forested lower slopes. As his restricted circle of view transited a partial clearing in the forest cover, where an old landslide had deposited a jumble of boulders and destroyed a section of the old growth forest, he noticed a tawny smudge of color which, with a quick adjustment of the focus, coalesced into the form of a mountain lion. He was startled to see the animal here, unaware the species ranged so far north.

If Conrad could have somehow followed the wanderings of this particular animal, he would have discovered it was a young male from interior British Columbia. Hemmed in by the established territories of mature dominant males, it had wandered over one hundred miles, following the Unuk river drainage through the coastal mountains and crossing the length of Cleveland peninsula to arrive here, where the lack of humans, rugged terrain, and the presence of the Sitka white tailed deer—preferred prey for the puma, made the area a perfect habitat. The big cat, P. *concolor*, went by many names: cougar, puma, catamount, American lion, panther, mountain screamer, and at least thirty-five more. Native cultures from Patagonia to Alaska gave their names to the beast and included it in their legends and myths.

From his perch near the peak Conrad was able to observe without being detected by the animal. The tumult of the storm had disguised the sounds of his climb. He was upwind, and his scent had likewise not given him away. The rain began again, an insistent wind-driven sideways fusillade. He pulled his well-worn but still mostly water-proof raincoat from his backpack and moved behind a convenient rocky knoll, where he could watch the cat from a more sheltered position.

The animal was stalking something. It was slowly traversing a clearing, slinking from boulder to boulder, apparently hiding its movements from prey lower down the slope. The cat was clearly visible through his high quality military spec binoculars. He could even see its tail twitch, like a house cat stalking a bird, but he was unable to see what it was that had so captured the cougar's attention. A few more minutes passed. At last the catamount crouched, stiffened, and launched itself down the slope in a single leap that spanned more than thirty feet. A large deer burst into a clearing with the lion astride its back. In an instant the cougar's powerful front legs jerked up the muzzle while its jaws gripped the nape of the doomed animal's neck. The animal fell, its spine snapped and bitten through. It had all occurred in a few seconds. The cat drug its kill to a sheltering recess under a nearby boulder and began its feeding.

Conrad marveled at the efficiency of the animal. He envied its savage focus. It was hard not to contrast his own life to that of the cougar's. *Both of us are killers*, he mused, *but there the kinship ends*. In the many years of his government service he too had been death's agent, *but never so intimately, or with such honest motivation*, he thought. It was as though the two animals had perfectly performed the choreography of an ancient and deadly dance. A dance as old as both species.

His institutionalized murders of supposed enemies of the state were impersonal and ignoble by comparison. The main instruments of his deceitful trade had been, for the most part, the pen or computer terminal, and for many years now vassals of a lower station than his had done most of the Agency's dirty work. Most commonly he had caused the death of the Agency's adversaries by simply passing information to the right person, and the actual killing had been done by another.

He had become merely an epigone. He possessed nothing of the nobility of his childhood heroes—the knights of the early labor struggles, the men and women of the resistance movements of World War II, or the indefatigable Nazi hunters of the Mossad. His actions for the Agency were ultimately inconsequential. His orders came from higher up the chain, and he obeyed, for the most part.

There had been a time when he had been different, more honorable. Or had he only been more naive then? But that had been many years ago, and those deaths had not been ordered, let alone condoned by his superiors.

Conrad had never been a particularly patriotic individual. Espionage was his job. It paid well. He liked the travel, and he was not tied like so many to an oppressive work schedule. Much of the time his occupation involved keeping the flow of information about advanced weapons and the weapons themselves from proliferating. This was a cause Conrad did believe in. It wasn't so much that he thought his country should be the only one with the deadly technologies; his opinion was more that the fewer countries acquired the weapons, the better mankind's chances were.

Conrad had certain skills, linguistic abilities, and social contacts that made him especially valuable to the Agency, and allowed him to take liberties other agents could not. The Agency was well aware of his family's left wing background and of Conrad's youthful participation in certain radical causes, as well as his tendency to sometimes act without first consulting his superiors. In spite of these heresies, and because of his unique set of capabilities, experience, and field knowledge, Conrad had managed to establish himself as a sort of semi-independent operative, given more or less free rein as long as he accomplished certain tasks. Even so, Conrad was well aware this relative freedom came with a price. Ultimately, he was not sure that there was any way he could ever quit the Agency safely, or retire from his position even if he wanted to. Once in, it seemed—in for life.

Since at least the early eighties he had grown steadily less convinced of the value and even the rectitude of his work. He had seen plenty of corruption and the futility and damage of the many covert actions and declared or undeclared wars; the destruction and waste of lives in the Middle East, South America, Asia, and Africa. He knew of fellow agents who practiced mental and physical torture to wring confessions from suspects.

With every passing year he became less comfortable with the motives and methods of his colleagues and superiors. He had reason to believe some in the Agency were in collusion with those who were profiteering from the arms trade.

Eventually the time came when the entire game sickened him, but not wanting to disappear himself (like a few others who had mysteriously vanished, or had sudden heart attacks and strokes), he had thus far been careful not to give anyone at the Agency any indication of the true extent of his doubts and reservations. Outwardly he was still an effective and (mostly) obedient employee of the vast well-monied organization that employed his talents, but he knew he would need to make himself less reliable and effective if he hoped to eventually escape into civilian life. The trick, as he saw it, was to ease himself out of the organization without alerting any of his superiors or fellow agents of his real motives. He began casually mentioning his retirement plans during informal chats with other agents. He volunteered less often for risky or uncomfortable duty, and he began to take advantage of some of his accrued leave time, as was the case with this Alaskan trip.

But this voyage was no vacation. Although he had tried to escape his vassalage, if for only a few weeks, the Agency had managed to hijack even that effort. Still, he would bend the assignment to serve his own objectives, which he refused to postpone any longer.

CHAPTER FOUR

Karen And Conrad

David Stuckrath first met his future wife, Karen Truman, on a torrid afternoon in a cheap Kabul hotel. She was with her then lover, a navy man who had escaped from the brig and gone AWOL from his unit in Viet Nam. Her long hair, greasy and dusty from days on the road, was bound in a messy bun, and her clothing wrinkled and grubby. She had a headache and wanted a hot bath more than anything in the world.

Before meeting her boyfriend, who had come to her father's clinic for treatment of his dysentery, Karen had been living with her parents in Nepal, where her father was a doctor for the World Health Organization. She had run away with her lover, traveling through northern Pakistan and via the Khyber Pass to Kabul, where they had rented a room at the fleabag backpacker hotel. For David, it had been lust at first sight.

Ultimately, some time after her boyfriend was killed that eventful summer, Karen had found her solace with David. After the traumatic events associated with the Afghan coup d' état of 1973 they eventually returned to Northwest, their home turf. In Seattle the couple worked at various menial jobs, saved a little money, and eventually married. David went back to school to earn his teachers certificate and a masters degree in history, while Karen worked as a waitress to keep food on their table and a roof over their heads. Fresh out of college, David accepted a teaching offer from Juneau High School, and they moved to Southeast Alaska.

David took to Alaska immediately. He enjoyed teaching for the most part, and the summer months off each year gave him time to pursue his other interests. He made alterations and improvements on their modest home, turned the garage into a woodworking shop, and began practicing the woodworking skills that would eventually enable him to complete their sailboat. For recreation he fished, hiked, and enthusiastically supported their son Marshall's growing involvement in school sports.

Karen's attitude to their new home was far more ambivalent. She was happy for her husband. Their life was comfortable and they had made some good friends, but the long winter darkness oppressed her. The brief riotous green outburst of foliage following the endless gray winters that characterized the all too attenuated summers only seemed to aggravate her discontent.

For Karen, Juneau was schizophrenic and dismal—split between the claustrophobic downtown section of narrow streets perched precariously on a slender strip of land between the frigid depths of Gastineau Channel and precipitous glacier-capped slopes—and the ugly strip-mall sprawl of the newer districts to the north of the old town. The old and new sections of the city were separated by a few miles of featureless freeway which connected the old city core to the ferry and airport. In between was an eastern extension that included some run-down trailer courts, a junk yard, and a bleak subdivision that bordered the intimidating razor wire fencing of the Lime Creek Correctional Center.

When their daughter, Cindy, started school Karen found a job with the state ferry system, which at least got her out of the house, but it did not completely dispel her ennui and acedia. She suspected her lassitude was from sunlight deprivation, but the weather was so often wet and gloomy it was difficult for her to muster the will to spend any time outdoors, or to catch what stray glimmer of sunlight might occasionally break through the omnipresent cloud cover. When Karen's father called one bleak November day to tell her that her mother had been injured in a fall, Karen was quick to offer her help—motivated as much by her desire to escape Juneau for a few weeks, as by the wish to help out her parents.

For a month she took care of her mother's needs during the day while her father was at work. In the evenings she often did the grocery shopping or helped with other errands. One such evening, while downtown, she stopped in at a local hotel lounge to have a drink before catching the bus back to her parent's house.

Conrad Slocum had long ago cut his hair and beard, and was dressed neatly and conservatively in slacks and a sports jacket, but even so she had no trouble recognizing the man at the other end of the bar. Conrad, who because of the nature of his employment never spent much time in any one place, still kept up an apartment in Seattle, it being the familiar city of his youth, the place where his boat was berthed, and otherwise convenient to his needs.

His invitation to dinner led to more drinks, and ultimately to his apartment. For the remainder of her time in Seattle she managed to meet him nearly every day. For Karen, the time was both exhilarating and nerve-wracking. She had no desire to leave her husband, but the sexual chemistry between them was irresistible. By the time she boarded the jet back to Juneau she knew she was pregnant.

Conrad drove her to the airport her last day in Seattle. He did not seem overly surprised at her revelation, but he was often inscrutable, to all who knew him.

"I'm going to have this baby," Karen told Conrad as he deftly threaded the car through the dense freeway traffic.

"Well, that is your decision to make."

She had told him of a doctor's prognosis years earlier that she would probably never be able to have children, due to complications of a childhood infection. She and David had even discussed the idea of adopting, but nothing had ever come of it.

"I'm going to let David think it is his," she went on, "but I want you to know as much as possible about our child—or at least as much as you want to know. You always get a holiday card from us every year anyway. I'll send you family pictures and Christmas greetings like I do everyone else, but yours will be special. It must be our secret. It would only hurt David needlessly. This can never happen again."

They drove on silently for a time. Conrad took the airport exit.

"What are you thinking?" Karen insisted.

"Seems like a reasonable plan for an awkward situation."

She looked steadily at him, and touched his face fleetingly. Conrad could only glance briefly at her. Traffic was thick as they approached the airport.

"I just need some sort of reassurance, I guess."

In reality she was not so sure she could pull it off, but Karen sensed the life growing within her, and already a protective instinct urged her towards caution and security. David could be depended on, and he loved her—she was sure of that. She loved him as well, though their early passion and youthful intensity had mellowed much over the years. Conrad was another matter. He was not a man who could be tamed, even by love—of that she was sure as well. Yet their relationship too, interrupted and intermittent though it had been, was one grounded in mutual trust and respect, and this latest episode was only another permutation of what was essentially a true friendship, complicated by a strong mutual sexual attraction and all too convenient circumstances.

"Of course it makes sense," Conrad continued.

"David is a good man. He deserves you if anyone does. You know I could never be much of a father. I could suddenly leave in the middle of the night, and I might not return for months, or never. Most of the time I can't tell anyone where I'm going or when I will return. You made the right decision when you chose David in the first place, but I haven't been able to get you out of my head since Kabul. Let me know as much as you can, but don't take any risks."

"Who knows if I'll make it to term anyway, but I can't keep myself from hoping."

Karen boarded the flight to Juneau with an impossible mix of emotions, but the trip had at least served its original purpose. Gone was the boredom and depression that had clouded her previous time in that northern outpost, replaced now by a new feeling of excitement and anticipation. Far from pining over Conrad, she found new joy and meaning in the smallest of domestic pleasures, and the time of her first pregnancy was one of the most joyful she had ever experienced.

Marshall was born nine months later in the Whitehorse, B.C. hospital. Karen was as good as her word and better. She supplied Conrad with frequent reports of Marshall's growth and development. By the time the boy entered high school Conrad was as proud a father as David. The difference was that Conrad could not brag to anyone about his son's accomplishments, or gleefully display the pictures of Marshall's first steps, his grade school class photos, the nearly perfect report cards, the newspaper clippings of his athletic triumphs, or the handsome young man in the midst of mid-air snowboarding acrobatics. Yet during all his years with the intelligence agency, and throughout his many travels, he observed with a silent pride the growth of the boy—his only known offspring—into a man.

He had seen his son on just one occasion, when Marshall was ten years old. Karen and David had taken the children south for Christmas with Karen's parents. Normally Conrad did not spend the holidays in Seattle, whose long damp winters he had over the years found increasingly unpleasant. But coincidentally that year he happened to be in town, enjoying a few days of free time before his next assignment. Karen invited another couple to join them for an evening downtown, and the group got together for dinner and drinks.

Karen was still a very attractive woman, though she had gained about a pound for every year since their affair, and a few fine lines had appeared around her mouth and eyes. Conrad was relieved to find the previous intensity of his feelings for her had mellowed to a comfortable if perhaps overly familiar camaraderie. He was pleased that David and Karen had made a good life for themselves and their children in Juneau. Karen, in spite of the potentially awkward collocation of her husband and past lover, appeared happier and more relaxed than he remembered her from ten years earlier, when her passion for him had seemed even at the time to be motivated as much by depression, boredom, and desperation as by her true temper. Karen's real feelings, if deeper than friendship, had never been revealed in her communications to him over the passage of a decade, and remained mysterious to Conrad.

In any case Conrad was far more excited by the possibility of seeing his son than in gaining more insight into Karen's state of mind, and she colluded with him to arrange a meeting with the boy. During the dinner conversation she revealed that David would be escorting their daughter, Cindy, to the zoo the next morning, and that she had promised Marshall a trip to the museum to see the dinosaur fossils, which the boy's sister had little interest in.

"Would you mind if I joined you tomorrow?" Conrad asked, on cue. "I have the morning free, and I've always been kind of a nut about dinosaurs myself."

"That would be great! We'll be there right at ten. I think you will be surprised to see how much Marshall knows about the subject," Karen replied.

Her eyes met his. She held her gaze an instant longer than he found comfortable. For a moment Conrad feared another sort of artifact might be exhumed, but the conversation took another turn and the phantom fossil faded.

The next morning Conrad was waiting at the museum entrance when Karen and the boy arrived. Karen looked Seattle sophisticated in a black dress suit and low heels. Marshall wore a newly acquired Mariners baseball cap and hooded sweatshirt a size too big for his thin frame. He was tall for his age, but in every obvious way resembled his mother, having inherited her fair complexion, and auburn hair. They spent the next two hours touring the museum. Marshall, like many boys his age, was fascinated most with the menacing grimace of Tyrannosaurus Rex and the behemothic Brontosaurus, but Conrad was pleasantly surprised that his son also spent some time studying the exhibits on the ecology of the Cretaceous era, and the displays explaining and illustrating the concepts of continental drift.

"He does resemble you in many ways," Karen remarked. The boy had run ahead to marvel at another skeleton, while they tarried by the pterodactyls.

"I'd say he looks a lot more like you...that hair and those freckles," Conrad objected.

"It's more his deportment and confidence—and of course your widow's peak and forehead too."

She reached up playfully to ruffle his hair. Her hand hesitated slightly in its retreat from him, as if it had memories of its own, and slightly brushed his cheek before landing with a flutter on the display sign in front of them. Except for the brief formal hug they had exchanged at the restaurant the day before, it was the first time she had touched him in ten years. Her spontaneous contact brought back a torrent of suppressed memories and emotion.

"I wonder why you never got married", she continued, seemingly oblivious to his agitation.

"Because I could never find another woman to compete with your memory," he replied roguishly, regaining his composure somewhat.

"If I did not know you so well, I might actually believe you. You're still a wonderful liar, but thanks anyway. I've got a couple of girlfriends I would love to introduce you to."

"I appreciate the sentiment, but I'm sure I can do well enough on my own."

"Is that so? I couldn't help but notice you didn't bring anyone to dinner yesterday, and you are the only one of our old group that has never married. Maybe you really could use some help."

Conrad was spared more discussion of the subject by the excited voice of Marshall calling them over to the next exhibit.

"What do you want to be when you grow up—a paleontologist?" Conrad asked, mostly for the joy it gave him to hear the sound of his son's voice in reply.

"Oh, I don't know... Maybe I'll be a scientist—or a baseball player. I can't decide. Can I be both?" The boy's voice was high and clear, unaffected as yet by the inevitable rush of testosterone that would soon morph him into a gangly adolescent.

The adults laughed sympathetically at his confusion.

"Of course you can be anything you want to be," his mother answered.

"Your dad is a teacher and a carpenter, and Conrad is a sailor like your dad when he's not working."

"What are you when you work?" the curious child inquired.

"I guess you would say I am a kind of detective," Conrad replied.

"What kind of detective is that?"

"Marshall, it's not polite to pry," Karen chided.

"No—it's okay. He's just curious. I'm what they call an investigator. I find out all I can about the bad guys and give that information to my bosses so they can put them in jail—but I don't wear a badge or a uniform like a policeman does. Now, how about some lunch. Are you hungry?"

The boy seemed satisfied with Conrad's answer, and the prospect of food distracted him from any further questioning.

That lunch was the last time he saw his son. Somehow a suitable opportunity never again occurred. Over the years Karen continued to send him the photographs; a clean-limbed adolescent posing stiffly in a suit with his first prom date; his braces glinting as Marshall stood grinning proudly in front of a beat-up Jeep, paid for with his own sweat by working the summer of his junior year for a local contractor; the report card grades—nearly all A's; the clippings from the Juneau newspaper sports section documenting his athletic accomplishments. Conrad saved them all in a battered old leather suitcase his grandmother had given him when he had left home for college for the first time.

Conrad had been disappointed when Marshall accepted an athletic scholarship at the University in Fairbanks, Alaska. He had hoped the boy would choose the University of Washington in Seattle, or even Karen's old alma mater, the University of Oregon, so that he would at least be able to see his son when he was in the area. He had even offered to help the young man find housing if he didn't want to stay in a dorm. He would always regret he had not made more of an effort to extoll the attractions of college life in Washington and Oregon. The boy might still be alive today had he only been able to convince him to come south instead.

He got the news of Marshall's death months after the fact. For most of that year he had been on assignment in the Middle East. His cover had made it too dangerous to communicate with anyone back in the states. His few old friends, including Karen and David, were familiar with his periodic disappearances, so he was surprised at his homecoming by the increasingly desperate phone messages, emails, and letters from Karen.

At the post office, where he rented a box to cover his frequent absences from Seattle, he picked up his accumulated stack of mail. There was a parcel from Karen. A small portion of the boy's remains had been carefully packed in a sturdy plastic container. The package also contained several Juneau newspaper clippings, including Marshall's obituary, and a brief letter.

The note read:

Dear Conrad, I have been trying to contact you for many weeks. I even called the state department. No one will admit you work for them, let alone tell me how to find you. I know your grief will in some ways be worse than mine. I at least have friends and family who I can turn to. David and I have separated, but we still have our daughter and our memories of Marshall, and of the good times to-

gether. I can't imagine how it must be for you, not even being able to admit to anyone that you have lost a son.

We have already had our funeral. This package contains a portion of our son's remains. Keep them, or scatter them as you see fit.

When you think of Marshall remember he could not have been more loved. When you think of me understand I have never had any regrets or doubts. I hope you feel the same way. Please call or write if you need to.

Love always, Karen.

CHAPTER 5

Conrad's Mission

The day Conrad learned of the events leading to the death of Marshall he had walked the streets of Seattle for hours, fighting down the urge to catch the first plane north. His immediate emotional reaction was rage. He felt as though he had been plunged back into the middle ages—that he was fighting on the wrong side for a corrupt regime that was willing to sacrifice its own children to a self-perpetuating prison system, bloated with a population of persons convicted of consensual crimes.

He vowed his son's death would not go unavenged. It was a trivial matter to access the Agency computers and gather all the information he needed concerning the case particulars. He had already killed or caused death for less compelling reasons, he reasoned. Officially sanctioned killing was at least an implicit part of his employment. His plan for Grant Tadlock, the murderer of Marshall, was simple: the man would die by his hand, and the sooner the better. He was ambivalent about the sentencing judge, who certainly could not have expected such an outcome, but at the very least he must find out the true character of a man who would commit a promising youth to prison for such a minor offense. In this bitter state of mind he had taken advantage of his accrued leave and planned his trip to Alaska.

"I understand you have vacation plans for a sail north on your boat next month," the supervisor said, after the two men exchanged only the summary greetings that minimal civility mandated.

"I haven't been north of the Gulf Islands in a few year—thought I might get up at least as far as Juneau if time and weather allow," Conrad replied.

"I wonder how you would feel about combining your pleasure trip with a little investigative work?"

"I suppose if that is my new posting assignment there is not much I can say about it, now is there, Dick?"

Supervisor Richard Head recognized the intended insolence, but gave no sign of irritation. He had endured many years of teasing over his name, and had learned long ago to ignore it. In any case, with his emaciated frame and sickly constitution—a result of his lifelong chronic asthma and a constitutional aversion to exercise—he had never been capable of contesting any insult, at least physically. The fact that he had risen so far in the Agency was due more to his obsessive dedication to the service and his special connections (an uncle was a senator), than any real aptitude. Still, Richard found interactions with Conrad to be especially galling, knowing that the supervisory position he currently held had only been offered to him after Conrad had first turned it down.

"Of course you can object. You've been an important asset to the Agency for years now, and you have earned the right to cherry pick assignments to a certain extent. It's no secret you have some influential friends quite a bit higher up in the food chain. Still, as you are headed up north anyway, I wonder if you might do a little nosing around while you're there. Naturally your expenses will be covered, including all costs you might incur during the four weeks vacation time you have scheduled, and you will have your extra travel per diem to boot. In short, you will be amply rewarded for a very small amount of time and effort."

It irked Richard that Conrad had so much pull within the agency. Even though he technically outranked him, he knew Conrad's connections higher up would usually see the man got his way. Although Richard's uncle had pulled the political levers to get him his present position, the senator had no say in the actual day to day operations of the regional Agency office. Richard hated the fact that he could not order Conrad outright to take the assignment.

Conrad knew this meant he would be expected to be at the Agency's beck and call during his vacation time, and normally that would have rankled, but it immediately occurred to him the assignment might be useful as cover should he encounter any problems with local authorities, or need access to law enforcement information.

Although he did not yet know the details,

Conrad was aware the Agency had been assisting the DEA in investigating several fishing boats they suspected of drug smuggling in the various fjords and channels that opened into the Pacific from the Southeast Alaskan coast. Richard soon provided those details. Large amounts of cocaine and methamphetamine had lately tuned up in Ketchikan, Alaska and Prince Rupert, Canada. The authorities were pretty sure the contraband was not coming in on the airlines, which they insisted were well monitored. On the other hand the fishing industry was not what it had been, and desperate fishermen, with boat and permit payments to make, were not always adverse to hauling the illicit freight.

With this new assignment in hand, and still feigning resentment over the imposition (it would have looked suspicious had he cooperated too agreeably), Conrad left the office and the unpleasant presence of his titular superior.

Minutes later Head buzzed the Director on the inter-office phone, requesting an audience.

"I am well aware of your attitude towards Slocum," the head of the field office said brusquely, before Richard could utter a word.

"Believe me, I appreciate your restraint and professionalism for the most part. The fact remains that agent Slocum's rare constellation of abilities have been of great benefit to us in the past, and are likely to continue to be for some time yet."

The director, Carson Septumas, was a huge ruin of a man; corpulent, florid, and twenty years Richard's senior. He was famous in the agency for his exploits in various middle eastern countries during the decades of the fifties and sixties, before age and obesity had rendered him more useful behind a desk than in the field.

"The man is simply not trustworthy. For Christ sakes, his grandmother was a Wobbly! His mom is a known socialist—probably a damned communist too. We know she was in communication with Slovo during the sixties and seventies!"

Richard gasped for air at this exclamation, and reached into his pocket for his atomizer. He had felt the asthma attack coming on earlier, but had refused to let agent Slocum see his weakness.

"I shouldn't have to remind you that a lot of people opposed Apartheid—not just communists. I opposed it during those years too. So am I suspect as well?"

Carson shifted his substantial mass in his leather armchair, and watched as Richard took two quick shots of Albuterol. Carson's back ached and he needed to stand. The extra pounds had become a more noticeable burden the last few years. He was being disingenuous with his subaltern at any event. He had worked actively for the defeat of the ANC, SACP, and other anti-Apartheid groups on occasion as part of the U.S. effort to support the status quo in South Africa during those years. Though he was ethically opposed to the separation of races, he had been against the participation of communists and socialists in the struggle, and had experienced no moral reservations in working for their destruction.

"The fact is, you are asking for the impossible, with Agency resources stretched as thin as they are these days. You want two agents full time, and access to a helicopter for the duration of agent Slocum's Alaskan expedition? You must be aware of the costs involved, especially in that remote area. Just what exactly do you expect to discover that is worth such a diversion of resources?"

"I haven't changed my opinion about the Davis case. Someone tipped him off and I am sure it was Slocum, or someone Slocum knew. If you look at his record, every drug case he has been involved in has resulted in a less than satisfactory resolution. Besides, if Slocum does manage to find the smugglers, he will most likely need help to make the arrests—assuming he even tries," Richard replied disdainfully.

"Yes, yes," Carson waved a fleshy hand dismissively, choosing to ignore Richard's disrespectful tone.

"It's no secret he has a less than stellar record with domestic drug investigation cases, but that is not the point. Agent Slocum was recruited for his abilities to investigate entirely different matters as you well know. His command of Pashto and Farsi, as well as his connections and abilities with respect to central Asian matters in general are practically unparalleled in the organization. In any case I think you are underestimating Slocum's abilities. I doubt he will need the resources you request when it comes to making an arrest."

This was all true, but somewhat beside the point. Carson Septumas' experiences as a young intelligence agent working in risky circumstances overseas made him inherently more sympathetic to agent Slocum. He respected and admired Conrad far more than this wheedling asthmatic underling, whom he had always regarded as an example of the general deterioration in the quality of personnel at the Agency. In the past Carson did not think a man such as Richard Head would have ever been accepted, let alone promoted to even his present low level management position. Moreover, he found the agency's new emphasis on terrorism and drug trafficking to be less compelling than the cold war struggle that had formerly been its main focus.

Although it was common knowledge in the Agency that Slocum detested drug investigative work (he had not tried to hide the fact), Carson did not think he would purposely compromise a case. Still, subaltern Head had his supporters, and his uncle the senator was a particularly loud-mouthed advocate of the drug war. Although it irritated him to do so, he must accommodate the man to a certain extent.

"What about Jack? He's still up in Juneau."

Agent Jack Dolon was one of the few friends Richard had in the Agency. They had attended college together for a time, and supervisor Head had been responsible for agent Dolon's recruitment. He was an experienced and gung-ho operative known for his aggressive field tactics and expertise in crime scene investigation.

"Jack's already busy on that other matter, as you well know, but I suppose we can spare him for a day or two when the time comes, if necessary."

Carson was only too aware of the mutual animosity that existed between Conrad Slocum and Richard Head. He disliked having to constantly referee the inevitable jealousies and pecking order issues that existed between the other agents under his command. He resented this whole assignment. His feeling was that the Agency's resources and manpower were being wasted on a trifling matter of little real importance to the country's security. The Director heaved a heavy sigh.

"I'll brief Jack on the situation. He'll have a launch at his disposal. More than that I cannot promise now, but keep me posted. I will do what I can."

His back on fire, Carson laboriously rose from his chair, signaling that the meeting was over.

CHAPTER 6

The Inside Passage

For several weeks before he began his trip north Conrad labored to prepare his boat for the voyage. There were the usual items: inspecting the anchoring tackle; replacing worn lines and checking sails; changing the engine oil; and stocking up with the provisions and spare parts for the journey up the sparsely inhabited "Inside Passage," the intricate inner sea route to Southeast Alaska.

There was also a more serious item to attend to —changing the name of his boat. This was not a decision to be made lightly, and a rechristening must be done correctly if bad luck was to be avoided, according to ancient maritime tradition. Conrad had not changed the name of the boat when he bought it, because he liked the name, *Frondeur*, and like many sailors, believed a boat should not be rechristened without compelling reasons. Now circumstances had changed, and he felt the need for a break with the past. He had earlier settled on the new name, *Tisiphone*, and set about getting rid of any and all traces of the old name, as tradition also demanded. Besides the boat itself, his dingy, life preservers, and fenders were repainted with the new moniker.

On a misty spring afternoon under an argent sky Conrad relaunched his boat, which had been hauled out for cleaning and a new coat of bottom paint, as well as the other work. He invoked the ancient sea gods and goddesses and poured a glass of his finest rum into the harbor waters and over the bow of his boat before taking a stiff drink himself. He shared the rest of the bottle with some appreciative Greek sailors from the island of Ithaca, who were more than happy to take a break from doing maintenance on their freighter.

That evening Conrad had dinner and drinks with an old friend from his college days who happened to be visiting in Seattle. Afterwards, although it was after midnight, Conrad felt restless and not the least bit sleepy. He stopped by the marina, where his newly rechristened sailboat was now back in the water at its regular slip. He hoped a walk along the wharves and the fresh marine breeze might help him sleep.

The gate to the dock was always locked after sunset. He punched in the combination and turned the handle. His boat was nearly at the end of the last finger—almost a quarter of mile from the main gate. One of the overhead lights was out—a not uncommon occurrence in the marina, where maintenance was notably slack. Even though his boat was just barely visible in the distance, he had the sense all was not quite right. He was sure he had heard something out of the ordinary.

Conrad approached his boat cautiously. As he edged closer, he could see the bow of an unfamiliar inflatable boat tied to the dock on the far side of *Tisiphone.* What he had heard was a mass of air bubbles breaking the surface of the otherwise still water next to his sailboat. Conrad quickly took cover behind the yacht in the neighboring slip, and waited. The diver soon surfaced in an eruption of effervescence and hauled himself onto the dock, where he took off his diving apparatus. After quietly placing his tanks, mask, and flippers into the inflatable craft, the man paddled some distance into the darkness before starting the small outboard and motoring away.

Conrad had no doubt of the diver's purpose in the harbor, and who had sent him. It was obvious that someone at the Agency, probably supervisor Head, or even Septumas himself, wanted to keep track of his activities and had ordered some sort of tracking device planted on *Tisiphone's* hull. He had done the same to automobiles as part of his typical surveillance activities. It seemed it was not enough that Septumas had already issued him a special cellular phone which was supposed to work even in the areas of little or no coverage, which included much of the Inside Passage and Southeast Alaska. He was aware that the phone used GPS satellite technology to keep tabs on his movements. Apparently the Agency wanted further assurance that they could find him if need be. He knew if he complained they would most likely feign ignorance or, if pressed, that they were only "monitoring him for his own protection" and as a backup to the cell phone. Conrad was glad to have had the good luck to have observed the diver—not that it would change any of his plans, but it was always good to be reminded that he must never relax his vigilance where the Agency was concerned.

As he walked back to his apartment Conrad reflected that his long relationship with the Agency had rarely been comfortable, and much of the time his duties chafed. His original agreement, made so many years ago in Kabul—to provide intelligence to contacts at irregular intervals without actually being an official employee—had been the slippery slope to eventual full-time operative status. His relationship to the Agency had become a careful ballet, where one misstep could have meant his disappearance. The pas de deux had been initiated by Paul Sherman, who certainly knew more about Conrad's motivations than anyone else in the Agency, and valued his contributions more than many. Without the patronage of Paul, Conrad doubted he would still have his present position, and there was more than a passing chance he might have been fired or "gone missing in the line of duty" by now.

Richard Head was essentially correct in his observation that Conrad was suspect because of his generations deep family connections with left of center politics and causes. The facts about Conrad's family background were known to Paul and others in the Agency, but Conrad had become much too valuable a resource to cut loose. Further complicating the issue was the close emotional relationship which had evolved between Paul and his protege. To Conrad, raised by women, Paul had become almost a surrogate father, and that relationship was largely reciprocated by Director Sherman, who had never himself married or had children. There were those in the Agency who were at least somewhat aware of their friendship, but Paul Sherman had for so long occupied such a position of prominence and power no one dared challenge his judgement in retaining the services of agent Slocum.

Additionally, Conrad knew, the Agency had a long history of using persons of dubious loyalty for their own sometimes unfathomable ends. Ironically, Conrad could never be sure if his actions, at times motivated by his own desires, were not in fact beneficial to the Agency whether or not he intended it.

Conrad had never for a moment renounced the moral and political ideals that had motivated a large part of his actions since that fateful day some four decades earlier, when he had delivered a much deserved beating to the school yard bully who had called his family commies and traitors. Although he still remained loyal to the same causes that had so inspired his mother and grandmother, he had consciously chosen for himself a role that was essentially that of a double agent or agent provocateur, doing what he could without compromising his position. Conrad had walked this tightrope for years, but the day would come very soon when Paul must retire, and without Paul Sherman's backing Conrad doubted he would survive long in the Agency, or perhaps at all.

A few days later, when at last he left the security

of the marina and began his voyage north, Paul's stormy state of mind had been mirrored by the unsettled and blustery weather he had encountered for much of the passage. The first part of the voyage he had made good time. The southerly winds had seldom been less than force five, and at times six or seven—a strong breeze to near gale, with winds of more than twenty knots and often higher. He had pushed the boat and himself hard, putting in fourteen and even sixteen hours some days between anchorages.

Several days out of Seattle he was half way across Queen Charlotte Sound, an area completely exposed to the open Pacific, and notorious for rough conditions. A few miles off aptly named Cape Caution in steep fifteen foot seas the strain finally got to him. He had not felt well that morning in Port McNeil, but the forecast had called for worsening weather with a gale warning predicted for that evening, so he had headed out into it, hoping to make most of the crossing before the winds and seas got even worse.

Conrad normally did not experience motion sickness, but he had felt queasy all morning. He wondered if the greasy hamburger and fries he had indulged in the evening before were to blame. After days of eating nutritious but boring ship's fare (when sailing he often lived for days at a time on rice, beans, cheese, dried fruit, and nuts), he had not been able to resist the luxury of hot food and service at the burger joint in the northern Vancouver Island town. The seas grew steadily as the south wind gained intensity. He hunched lethargically in the cockpit while the wind vane steered the boat. Going below only made his nausea worse.

The fourteen ton yacht climbed each foam-topped ridge and crashed into the following trough. Down in the wave hollows it was nearly calm, and the mainsail shivered and went slack until part way up the next wave, when the wind slammed into the sail again, heeling the boat twenty degrees and more, and giving it the momentum to coast through the next trough.

He had too much sail up for the conditions, he knew, and he was trying to muster the will and energy to put a reef in the main, when the sail gave out with a loud crack. A weakened seam had finally given way under the strain of the repeated abrupt wind loads. This event at least provided the shot of energy Conrad needed to shake him from his apathetic torpor. It took much longer than it should have—exhausting effort in his weakened condition—but he finally managed to get the mainsail furled. He continued on under staysail and storm jib. Repairs would have to wait until his next anchorage. He had no spare mainsail. By that evening he was in more protected waters east of Cape Calvert. He was just able to find the energy to drop anchor in Safety Cove, before climbing fully clothed into his berth, where he alternately shivered and sweated away much of the restless night.

Towards morning he finally slept soundly, and awoke feeling somewhat better, but still shaky. Safety Cove was well protected from the prevailing winds. It was a popular anteroom for those boats waiting for better conditions to get across Queen Charlotte Sound heading south. Several other boats bobbed at their anchors, but it was a spacious anchorage and no one crowded him. He didn't feel at all sociable in any case. After a light breakfast he sat about repairing the torn mainsail. He spent most of the day at his sewing, taking the opportunity to reinforce any other suspect areas that might cause future problems. His heavy-duty sewing machine, which could be foot powered, had served him well over the years, and Conrad had used it to construct several of the headsails for *Tisiphone*, his gaff rigged Ingrid cutter.

From Safety Cove to Prince Rupert, his favorite stretch of the Inside Passage route to Southeast Alaska, the weather moderated substantially. He made good time sailing and motoring through this mostly uninhabited and spectacular stretch of the convoluted Canadian coastline, but conditions steadily worsened as he crossed Dixon Entrance just south of Ketchikan, another notorious open expanse of water exposed to the Pacific Ocean's storms and seas. Here he was again vulnerable to the full force of the elements, with no moderating island barriers. This time he made the rough passage without incident.

After the Dixon Entrance crossing there followed a wild and exhilarating run from Cape Chacon north to Cleveland Peninsula, but more ominous weather forecasts for his route through the upper reaches of Clarence Strait had finally convinced him to seek shelter in Spruce Cove until conditions moderated.

As Conrad cautiously retraced his steps down the slippery switch-backed trail above Spruce Cove, he was grateful for the rare vision he had been granted. In his present state of mind the scene he had just witnessed had already taken on a deeper significance, and seemed to him to be a sign, if not from the gods (for he was a life-long skeptic), something undeniably more than mere luck or happenstance—at the very least a synchronicity that invited an allegorical interpretation. Like the mountain lion he would strike stealthily, quickly, and without mercy. The rage he felt would cease to eat at him. No one would be saved. The dead could not be brought back, but he could and would take on the responsibility of becoming an agent of the fates.

In his view the anguish and distress that impelled him, caused by the premature and senseless death of the boy, Marshall Stuckrath, was mirrored by some larger imbalance in nature itself. It was for this reason he had been granted the rare vision, he mused, as he carefully negotiated the rain-slicked path. (He dared not risk a fall or injury so close to his goal.)

On this deeper level—a more primitive and animistic stratum, he allowed himself to experience the healing wave of emotion the epiphany had granted him. Only a handful of people in the world could have been witness to such a scene, and his initiation into that select group was further illumination of the significance and rectitude of his purpose here—not that he would have admitted to anyone a need for any such symbolic justification of his actions. Conrad was astute and grounded enough to know that most would question his interpretation, even his sanity, and he realized that in some sense he was only trying to rationalize his implacable decision, and to allay whatever lingering doubts he might still have about his course of action. Conrad was aware that some might judge him a sociopath, but only because his personal code of ethics did not always conform to the currently fashionable morality—yet killing could always be justified if those in power desired it. What was war but a form of mechanized murder, ordained and sanctified by the state? He would fight his own war—one with a far more compelling and intimate justification.

As he made his way down the muddy track that ran down to the harbor and back along the shore to the dock, his coat streaming water from the steady rainfall, Conrad realized the anger and emptiness that had possessed him for months had now been replaced with something far more sufferable—a feeling of calm purpose.

From his first knowledge of Marshall's fate he had known what he must do, but beyond that had been only darkness. Now came the first glimmers of an understanding that there might yet be something worth striving for, and perhaps even the potential for some sort of meaningful life lying just beyond the calamity of the imbalance, as the meadow viewed from the mountain top, or the calm harbor after the stormy passage. All was essential, and all part of the order of things. For the first time since learning of the boy's death he found a kind of inner peace in accepting his role in the necessary and inevitable rebalancing. He would surely kill the man who had murdered Marshall—as surely as the cougar must kill the deer to survive—and the offering of the dead boy's killer to the fates would satiate a different, but just as insistent hunger.

An observer privy to Conrad's history might conclude he had killed before, if only in the role of an agent or soldier for the state while following orders, so this mission was perhaps not out of character, but to Conrad the essential task of ending the life of Marshall Stuckrath's killer had now acquired the additional nature of a sacred duty, if it was still no less an act of personal vengeance. That was the difference. This time it was personal, and Conrad was prepared to risk everything he had, everything he had worked for, and even his life it came down to it.

That night in Spruce Cove he slept as he had not in months—a sleep so deep and refreshing that he did not even wake to the sounds of the three boats coming into Spruce Cove after the rescue of the Judge Daise.

CHAPTER 7

Spruce Cove

In spite of his strenuous adventures in Clarence Strait the night before David Stuckrath was up at six the next morning, which was actually later than normal for him when he was on the water. As he drank his first mug of strong coffee David listened to the weather channel on his VHF radio. The wind was out of the southwest at a steady thirty-five knots with some gusts to over sixty. No improvement was predicted for at least another twelve hours. It didn't matter. He was in no hurry to leave, and he had no particular destination in mind.

The previous morning he had left Wrangell after two weeks in that small fishing town. It had rained nearly constantly. He spent most of the days reading and brooding in *Lethe's* compact cabin. In the rare dry intervals he hiked the local trails and made periodic forays into town for his necessities. The nights when he grew bored with drinking alone he usually spent in one of the smokey Wrangell bars in idle conversation with unemployed loggers, rubber-booted fishermen, and chain-smoking bar-stool doyennes. It was not his usual routine, but nothing was routine these days for David except sorrow—not since that devastating day—and when people got too nosy, or the bartenders started to water his drinks, it was easy enough to loose the dock lines and sail away.

In the diffuse early morning light he gazed through a portlight at the smoke rising from Chuck Riggs' house as he sipped his strong brew, somewhat inspissated from its overlong simmer. Chuck would have been up for at least an hour he knew—would have already split the kindling for his ancient wood-burning cook stove, fed the chickens, and gathered the eggs from the shed he had built many years before out behind the old house—the house he had occupied for more than twenty years.

Chuck was the caretaker of Spruce Cove. He was in his seventies; a sinewy individual with a weather-beaten face that reflected a life lived in the outdoors. Chuck could easily keep up with most people half his age. No one knew exactly what his duties were as the caretaker of the cove, but he was famous for the quality of his home-made spruce tip beer, his legendary fishing abilities, and especially for his hospitality. What David did know was that Chuck had worked for the company that owned most of Spruce Cove through much of the nineteen fifties and sixties. For those years of service he received a small stipend and the title of caretaker. Other than the boards from the rotting buildings, and perhaps some scrap iron from the old mining and cannery operations, there was nothing to steal in the cove. Most people who knew Chuck assumed he was there just so the company could maintain its claim on the acreage. Certainly Chuck had never denied anyone he liked the use of the derelict buildings, but there had not been a company boat or float plane in the cove for many years.

The company had operated a salmon cannery in the cove, and before that the land had been owned by a mining concern. The mining corporation had built most of the town at the turn of the century. It had prospered for a time, but a tunnel collapsed and men died. In any case the price of gold and silver had gone down and the cost of labor up, so the corporation sold out and moved on to South America where lives and labor were cheaper.

Ninety years earlier the town of Spruce Cove had boasted an impressive three story hotel, a post office, two general stores, several saloons, a brothel, and even two churches. After the mine was sold most of the occupants left, but a few stayed on until the cannery went into operation. The new owners utilized some of the buildings for seasonal cannery worker housing, continuing to maintain the structures after a fashion, but eventually the cannery operations were moved to Ketchikan.

All that now remained of Spruce Cove were a handful of moldering houses, a tangle of iron and timbers that had been the cannery factory, the ruins of the hotel, and some decomposing sections of the original boardwalks. Many of the buildings, including the churches and brothel had been torn down over the years to repair and modify the few habitable houses that remained, or to patch up the boardwalks and docks. This work was done by a series of squatters, dreamers, and hermits who had occupied the cove in the years since the cannery had closed.

Spruce Cove was a near perfect, albeit Lilliputian natural harbor. To the north and south, the direction of the prevailing winds which funneled down Clarence Strait a good percentage of the year, were the forested ridges which entirely protected the cove and the vestiges of the town. Even now, as the south wind roiled the strait the little bay was perfectly calm; only the tops of the evergreen trees higher up the slopes bending in the gusts hinted at the storm's intensity outside. The old jetty, which had at one time stretched nearly a half mile into the bay was now just a skeleton of broken timbers and rotten planking. At low tide it stood more than a dozen feet over the bay. It had at one time supported a narrow gauge rail system which transported first the ore and then canned salmon to waiting tenders tied along side. Patches of moss and lichen grew on the wooden surfaces of the jetty, and rusted bolts hung down at random angles. Here and there, for a few feet, sections of the jetty were relatively intact, only to give way to missing segments where the old iron rails hung precariously into the gaps.

Over the years commercial fisherman and Spruce Bay residents had salvaged parts of the old jetty and built a much smaller float, which they had attached perpendicular to the original pier. There was room here for perhaps a dozen boats. For much of the summer this wharf was in high demand, with boats rafting up to each other and crowding the little anchorage. But this late in August only a few vessels, including *Tisiphone* and *Lethe*, were moored there. Out in the cove, not far from the guest wharf, the forty foot fishing boat *Bad Attitude* swung easily from her anchor. Chuck Riggs' skiff was tied to his own small private dock further down the shore just below his house.

David climbed out to the cockpit and took in the crisp morning air, coffee mug in hand. He eyed the other boats sharing the security of the guest dock. At the far end of the dock was *Legal Eagle*, the boat he had rescued the night before. The light of day showed it to be an older Bayliner model something-or-other. David was no expert on and had no interest in powerboats generally, unless they were old or built of wood. Another boat on the other side of the dock was also a pedestrian-looking fiberglass power boat similar in size and appearance to the *Legal Eagle*, while still another, the gleaming motorsailer yacht *Elixir*, more than sixty feet long, was so meretricious—at least in David's opinion—that it seemed garishly out of place in the otherwise harmonious scene.

He turned his attention to the remaining two craft at the wharf, both of which appealed much more to his sensibilities. The first was a low slung gaff-rigged double ender. The name, *Tisiphone*, stood out black against the bright white hull. David immediately recognized it as the classic "Ingrid" design—a wooden cutter with a great long bowsprit, even longer main boom, and separate top mast, strongly rigged and obviously capable of blue water voyaging. David smiled appreciatively and toasted the boat with his raised coffee cup.

The other vessel, a wooden gaff-rigged yawl with a shorter bowsprit, was much smaller and decades older, but with an even more distinguished pedigree. Both it and its owner were well known to David. The *Black Hawk* was a nicely maintained vintage Seabird Yawl that would have been right at home when Spruce Cove was a mining town nearly a hundred years earlier. Perhaps that very sailboat might have stopped here in the years before the first world war, when the town had experienced its brief prominence.

David knew the boat had been built in the early part of the century in Vancouver B.C. Its current owner was an old friend, Mike Schwindel, who had lovingly restored the boat back in the late seventies. An itinerant shipwright, house carpenter, and a jack-of-all-trades, he was known throughout Southeast Alaska as much for his unpredictability and intransigence as for the superior quality of his work. He was what many would call a "strange bird," but David had always enjoyed his company. They had first met in the early nineteen eighties when David had been researching and dreaming about the possibility of building his own boat. Mike had been appreciative, opinionated, irritating, and helpful in equal measure. Mike would always be connected in David's mind with the happiest time of his life. The time before everything came crashing down.

The years that David had devoted much of his free time to the finishing of his boat were also the years of his son's growth into manhood. Marshall had worked along side his father on the project whenever he had time away from his other activities. It seemed to David the boat and the boy grew together to a kind of beauty and perfection of form and purpose.

David had purchased the Cape George 31 fiberglass hull from the estate of a man who died before he had been able to complete the boat. The interior was only roughed out, and the boat had lacked rigging, sails, and deck fittings. It was essentially just a shell, with all the time-consuming and painstaking work yet to complete. Marshall had been thirteen then, with the shadow of a new mustache, and the brash confidence of an up-and-coming star wrestler in his weight division, as well as one of the best middle distance runners in his class. Together father and son had constructed a temporary building of two-by-fours and plastic sheeting to house the hull. There, in addition to the piles of parts, supplies, and tools, were Marshall's training weights, and a chin-up bar.

Marshall always took his training very seriously. David had found his son's initiative remarkable, recalling his own largely aimless teen years. Most days after school, while many of his friends watched television or played video games, Marshall would change into his sweats, run three or four miles, then work out with his weights. Following dinner, if there was no home work, and on weekends, he liked to join his dad in the boat shed.

Marshall had even come up with *Lethe*, their name for the boat. This was the topic of much lively family discussion until Marshall had suggested the solution. David's wife, Karen, thought they should adopt a name from a historically famous boat; their daughter Cindy, a year and a half younger than her brother, and obsessed at the time with the famous dancer, wanted "Isadora." David had favored a name from Greek or Nordic mythology, and Marshall thought the boat should be named after something related to Alaskan geography or history. Ultimately Marshall came up with the choice after noting the river "Lethe" in the Valley of Ten Thousand Smokes, a remarkable stream in the Katmai National Park that had cut a gorge through the ash of the huge 1912 eruption, which had nearly buried the town of Kodiak.

At the launching, three years and many hundreds of man hours later, his daughter poured the whisky on the boat and into the sea, and he allowed both children a shot of the same (Cindy choked and spit much of hers out, but Marshall managed his—a little too easily, David remembered thinking at the time). Later that evening, after a successful shakedown cruise from Auk Bay a small group of friends helped them celebrate the occasion.

That same year, as a high school junior, Marshall won the regional wrestling title in his division. For the next two years, when Marshall was not working, going to sporting events, or off with friends, they sailed often on summer evenings and weekends, learning together how to get the best performance from the boat. They even managed to find time for a few longer voyages, exploring the waters of Lynn Canal, Stephen's Passage, and Frederick Sound. On two yet more ambitious outings they had ventured as far south as Prince Rupert in British Columbia, and all the way north to Skagway, thus spanning the entire length of Southeast Alaska.

In those days—a few months by the calendar, but a lifetime ago—they had still been a family. Frequently, during the warmer months of the year, when Juneau enjoyed eighteen or more hours of daylight, the four of them went out together on leisurely evening sails. Often they would observe humpback whales spouting only a few yards distant from their small craft, sail through pods of sleek Orca, or laugh at the antics of the porpoises, which would sometimes swim figure eights around their much slower sailboat.

But those days were gone forever. David sailed on from anchorage to anchorage, without purpose, knowing only that he would never forgive himself for having allowed Marshall to fall into the hands of the obscene legal system which he held responsible for his son's death. The irony of his boat's name did not escape him. He would never drink from that stream of forgetfulness. All that summer the murky currents of Acheron and Erebus swirled around him and carried him in his frail craft to where he did not know or care.

CHAPTER 8

Old Friends

David saw the hatch of the *Black Hawk* slide open. He watched Mike Schwindel emerge wearing his trademark Greek fisherman's cap and woolen navy peacoat, an unusual combination in this part of Alaska where most men favored baseball or stocking caps and the ubiquitous halibut jacket. Some guys are hat guys and some guys are not. Mike was definitely of the former persuasion. David had never seen him without headgear, and it was rumored that none of his girlfriends or his two former wives had ever observed him bare-headed either. Whether this was because he was mostly bald and slightly under medium height, or simply a style statement no one knew. The hat and his mutton chop sideburns moderated his otherwise leptocephalic visage, and gave Mike a vaguely continental appearance.

"Hey David!" Mike called when he saw him. "Good to see you! ...any coffee in your galley, old boy—I'm down to my last dregs."

"You're in luck. Climb aboard. ...can't have you getting the DTs now can we?"

While Mike made himself comfortable in the

little cabin, David poured him a cup and started water heating for another pot.

"This seems like a ballroom compared to the *Hawk*," Mike commented, his eyes taking in the snug quarters.

Although *Lethe* was herself pretty small by yacht standards, with a beam of nine and a half feet and a main cabin that only measured about a dozen feet long, she had considerably more interior room than the *Black Hawk*—barely eight feet wide at maximum, with quarters that were even more constrained. Mike could not help but note that both David and the interior of his boat had a disheveled and unkempt appearance, which was completely out of character for his friend, who was normally meticulous in both boat maintenance and personal hygiene.

"When you gonna rig this thing as a proper gaff cutter?" Mike asked, between sips of coffee.

"Don't think I haven't thought about it. Maybe when my mainsail wears out. I've got to admit I like the look of that Ingrid and your yawl nestled up together—makes my boat look comparatively tall and awkward with the Marconi rig," David replied.

While peering out at the other boats, he noticed the muted glow of light shining from *Legal Eagle's* portlights a few yards away.

"It looks like our neighbor is awake too. He must have gotten a pretty good scare yesterday," Mike commented, following David's gaze.

"It was pretty sloppy out there last night—still is.

It was all Chuck's poor skiff could do to drag that piece of shit in here. Of course it might have been a little easier bow first," Mike chuckled.

"He was lucky twice. I barely managed to get to him in time. He would have broken up on Ernest Point."

Mike looked intently at David, then took an old, well-chewed briar pipe out of an inside pocket. He took his time with the ritual, fussing over the packing and tamping of the tobacco. Finally he lit the pipe, puffing strongly at first and filling the small cabin with the curling strands of smoke. It did not occur to him to ask whether David minded, though he knew David had never been a smoker. The pipe stem was curved, and as Mike puffed the herb to life he resembled a sea-going Sherlock Holmes.

"It is pretty obvious you don't know who you rescued last night," Mike said, after his pipe was properly stoked.

"Hell, I was half dead—almost asleep on my feet. I just went straight to bed. I figured I'd meet the guy today... I wouldn't have recognized anyone in that chaos out there last night anyway, most likely."

"Shit, no way to break this easy, David. It's ironic as hell—I can hardly believe it myself—but I gotta tell you; the guy you drug off the rocks last night is judge Daise, the same asshole that sent your son to jail." Mike's cheeks hollowed deeply as he pulled on his pipe. He sat back sharply, waiting for David's reaction.

David said nothing immediately. He remained expressionless, except for a just detectable reddening of his face. David was a youngish-looking fifty, with a thick head of brown hair just beginning to gray. (Some of his friends had noticed how much of that had appeared in the last few months.) He had a symmetrical and intelligent face that was attractive and friendly without being exactly handsome. His eyes, normally periwinkle, darkened abruptly to a deep Prussian blue at this sudden revelation.

"Now look, David, I know you pretty well, and I remember some of the things you said after the trial, and later after Marshall died. I know you blame Daise in part for Marshall's death, but I hope you won't do anything stupid. Judging by the weather forecast we're all going to be stuck here another day at least—maybe longer. You're not going to get out of here without some sort of confrontation with Daise, and I wouldn't blame you for taking a crack at him. Come to think of it, I wouldn't have faulted you if you had just let him eat those rocks out there last night. Who would have known, right? I can't say what I might have done in the same situation, had I known who it was—but of course you didn't."

They were both silent for a time while Mike puffed steadily on his pipe, continuing to watch David closely.

"Well, I had no idea who was on that boat—it could have been a family aboard for all I could tell. Do you think he knows who towed him in?" David finally responded.

"I doubt it. We didn't mention your name as I

recall. We were all so wet and tired we couldn't even manage proper introductions before we headed for our bunks. Chuck invited him to his cabin, but he just wanted to hit the sack. I only realized who he was this morning, when I remembered meeting him and his family a few years back, up in Elfin Cove."

The sound of steps on the wooden planked dock, followed by a rap on the side of the cabin announced the arrival of Chuck Riggs, the Spruce Cove caretaker. David rose and slid open the hatch.

"Hey, I thought I'd better come down and wake you tourists up. ...didn't see much action down this way. ...good to see you again David—got any more coffee there?"

Chuck negotiated the narrow companionway ladder and found a seat next to Mike at the little drop-leaf table that occupied most of the main cabin. David poured him a cup of black coffee from the fresh pot. He had been in Spruce Cove often enough to know Chuck liked his brew black in the morning and spiked with whisky in the evening.

"I just wanted to make sure you guys know you are expected at lunch today, twelve o'clock sharp."

After a cautious sip of the hot brew he continued awkwardly:

"Say David, I don't know how to put this so's it doesn't hurt, but I gotta say something now or I'm gonna tiptoe around it the whole time you're here. When a man gets to be my age time is too precious to waste on ceremony anyhow. I'm sorry about your son.

I've never forgotten the first time you brought him into Spruce Cove—seeing him swim in the bay—like the water was eighty degrees instead of fifty. I liked the way he handled that kayak too. Man, he was a natural on the water—so young—God damn it anyway! I'm so sorry David."

Chuck suddenly looked his age and more as he gazed into his coffee mug. The three men were silent. Outside the tide was changing and they could hear the gurgle of the water along the hull as the tidal current speed increased. The yacht strained against its spring lines. The inflated plastic fenders squeaked against the old wooden pier.

"I guess you don't know who we drug in last night either, eh?" Mike finally said, addressing Chuck.

"No, he said his name was Henry—never seen him before—didn't get his last name. I'm not sure if it's my memory or hearing going. I just invited him up for lunch at the house before I dropped in here. He wants to thank everyone personally that helped in his rescue last night. Well, everybody here is invited anyway—even that crazy son-of-a-bitch Sam anchored out there. I just finished aging a new batch of stout, and I'm countin' on you folks to help me get rid of a little venison too."

The peninsula and surrounding islands supported a large number of deer, and their population was robust enough the state allowed hunting year round, and liberal harvest limits in most areas. During the winter when the salmon were not available, Chuck, like many subsistence hunters in Southeast Alaska, relied on venison to supplement the seafoods that were his more usual summer fare.

"The guy's name is Henry Daise. Judge Henry Daise," Mike said.

"Not the same one who...?" Chuck's eyes widened. "Hell, that is some coincidence!"

"It's a small world up here in the Panhandle. Coincidences are routine, and everybody knows everyone else's business—or thinks they do," Mike commented.

There was another awkward lag in the conversation before Mike deliberately and inelegantly turned the conversation to the state of the weather, the season's salmon runs, and the other visitors in the cove.

"So who owns that nice looking Ingrid?" David asked, seeming to accept the conversational gambit.

"I don't know," Chuck replied. "He got in yesterday afternoon. He's a pretty early riser too. I saw him walking along the shore this morning about five—looked like he was heading up the south ridge trail."

"Yeah, but we know who the real early riser is in Spruce cove," David said, smiling.

Chuck nodded and sipped the last of his coffee before continuing.

"I never could see any reason for stayin' in bed when it's light out. Look David, I'm thinking I should go tell the judge he's not welcome for lunch. I've personally got nothing against him, but I consider you a friend, and I don't want any trouble, or for anyone to feel uncomfortable," Chuck said.

Chuck finished his coffee and stood to go. He felt a sudden uncharacteristic rush of claustrophobia in the tight cabin quarters.

"No—it's okay. You know I don't really give a damn if he is there—might even be interesting. He might recognize me, and he might not. I don't know how many cases he presides over a year—must be at least dozens—maybe hundreds. Karen and I were not in the courtroom long. They had already made their little back room deals. That hearing was just a formality. Our lawyer advised us not to have any contact with the judge or the prosecutor. No, I doubt he would recognize my face, but maybe it is time we got more acquainted."

David's expression was impenetrable. Mike, who knew David as well as anyone, looked at him closely but said nothing.

"Now look David, I think I have some idea of what you might feel, but like I said—I don't want any trouble. If you guys have issues that need to be settled I'd appreciate it if you would do it somewhere else besides my house. I just thought I'd be neighborly and get everyone together to pass the time until this storm lets up some. Maybe have a few beers and play some cards. I got no beef with the judge, and the last thing I want is a bunch of cops or the press comin' down here like a noisy flock of crows."

"I think you mean a murder of crows," David replied sardonically.

"Now don't jump to conclusions, Chuck," Mike

interjected. "David isn't the type to go and make a scene, and he is perfectly well aware the judge is not the one that prosecuted or killed Marshall."

"Mike's right. What makes you think my manners are so bad that I would compromise your hospitality, Chuck? I wouldn't want to profane your home—that would certainly be in poor taste—after all, we are all civilized people here, right? I'm not going to take a swing at the judge, or come up to your house with a shotgun. It's all completely legal and no one is responsible, and if something goes wrong nobody is to blame because everyone is just doing their job. Does that sound familiar? It should to you Chuck. After all, I seem to remember you telling me what it was like to talk to captured Nazi officers at the end of the war."

Mike was taken aback by this outburst. Although David spoke in a conversational tone and without much visible emotion, the implications of his statements and their confrontational nature were obvious and completely out of character. In all his years of acquaintance and friendship with David, Mike had never seen him behave this way.

"Aw, come on now David, we both know Chuck feels terrible about the whole thing. But dammit Chuck, you don't help things by suggesting that David would do something stupid! For Christ's sake, David just now found out it was Daise he hauled in last night. Do you expect him to go over and exchange pleasantries with the man that put his kid in the slammer where he ended up getting killed? What?—should he invite him over for a tea party—give him a kiss on the cheek? Anyway, let's just drop the whole subject, goddammit," Mike continued, trying his best to defuse the situation.

"Well, I apologize if I spoke out of turn. Maybe I'm just getting old and insensitive," Chuck replied, rising to leave.

"Anyway thanks for the coffee. I can understand if you don't want to come by for lunch with the judge there, David, but I hope you do stop by sometime before you leave. You know the door is always open to you as long as I'm here, and whatever is in the soup pot is yours too. I gotta get back and get things organized, at any rate."

Chuck ascended the companionway ladder, glad to be back in the open and out of the too close boat cabin. He regretted his earlier words, and David's accusation stung, but he could excuse it as the bitterness of a bereaved father. He had plenty to do before lunch in any case, and it struck him that he really had no reason to think David Stuckrath would behave badly. Still, as he made his way back up the shoreside path to his house he felt uneasy. It occurred to him that he should go back to the judge's boat and let him know his concerns, but he quickly thought the better of it, realizing David would probably see him and might take even more offense. The fact was the situation was out of his control, and the two men would inevitably meet either in the harbor or at his house, and there was nothing he could do or say to make the situation any less awkward.

"You were pretty hard on the old man," Mike

said after Chuck left. "He really is a well-meaning old coot, and I know he feels terrible about Marshall."

"Fuck him. Chuck likes everybody. He'd give his life savings to anyone that asked, if he had any. He's no fucking judge of character, that's for sure."

"Well that at least explains why he likes us," Mike deadpanned.

David laughed in spite of himself.

CHAPTER 9

Judge Daise

Across the the small bay at Chuck's pier Henry Daise's body was reminding him of his adventures the preceding night. Every muscle and joint seemed to ache. He finished his breakfast and cleaned up the small galley. Some of the doors and drawers in the cabin had flown open during the storm. He had been too tired the night before to pick up the mess, but he was pleased to find no serious damage to the boat. The caretaker, Chuck Riggs, had graciously invited him to lunch, and he looked forward to the diversion of a social gathering while the storm continued to rage outside the tranquil little harbor. It was somewhat embarrassing to realize how close he had come to disaster the night before, but he rationalized it could happen to any boater, and he would have behaved no differently had he been in his rescuer's position. He would get the names of the men who had come to his aid and find some small tokens of his appreciation when he returned to Juneau.

Henry Daise wanted to find a way back as soon as possible. He hoped to hitch a ride on one of the other boats in the harbor when weather conditions improved, otherwise he would have to charter a plane, as he was aware there were no regularly scheduled flights from Juneau or anywhere else to Spruce Cove, nor did the Alaska State Ferry stop here. Had it not been for the storm and his bad luck with the engine (it had still refused to start when he had tried again earlier that morning) he would be in Juneau now.

The judge had a court case to prepare for Monday morning, and by chance his oldest daughter, Linda, was in town—an infrequent occurrence these days. Unfortunately they had quarreled, and she had refused to join him on his voyage. After his close call the previous night he was contrite, regretting that the spat had robbed him of precious time they could have enjoyed together. Now that she had moved south, that time was increasingly rare. He wanted to get back to Juneau before she left. Daise did not like the idea of her getting on the plane before they had a chance to make up.

The fact that his daughter was an attorney with a very different point of view about the handling of drug related cases had initiated their most recent conflict. It seemed to him this scourge of civilization had caused him more grief than anything else he could name. Even in his own family, where no one consumed anything other than moderate amounts of alcohol, the subject had been the cause of much infighting since at least his daughter's college years. He was proud of her reputation as an aggressive public defender; everyone, even drug users had the right to a competent legal advocate, and he had no illusions about the fact that mistakes were sometimes made by investigators, enforcement officers, and district attorneys. It was her argument that the drug laws caused more damage than the drugs themselves which infuriated him, and had caused their latest bitter exchange. He regretted his words now, and wanted nothing more than to get home as quickly as possible to repair the rift.

Daise's doleful thoughts mirrored the dreary day's outlook. The rain, falling steadily, had managed to find a small crack in the seal of a fitting located just above the galley table. A slow but steady patter of cold droplets pooled in a plate of breakfast leftovers. For some reason he found the leak especially annoying. The recalcitrant engine, and now water dripping in the cabin. Daise looked forward to attending the gathering at the caretaker's house. Perhaps it would distract him and improve his mood, and he could use the occasion to see if any of the guests might be heading north tomorrow, when the weather was predicted to moderate.

CHAPTER 10

Conrad And David

After his strenuous and invigorating hike Conrad hung his wet rain coat and damp clothes near the small diesel cabin heater to dry while he fixed himself a late breakfast in the comfortable quarters of the old wooden cutter. Conrad was a tall man with a good physique improved by years of strict attention to a regime that included yoga, weight training, martial arts, long distance hiking, and scuba diving. He spent much of his free time while in Seattle hiking the numerous trails of the North Cascades, or sailing and kayaking the San Juan and Gulf Islands. At forty-nine he considered himself only slightly past his prime; perhaps not quite as nimble as he had been in his twenties and thirties, but with more stamina, strength, and situational awareness. He had close-cropped hair revealing a slight widow's peak, and dark eyes set deeply into a sun and wind-bronzed face that sported several days worth of stubble.

The main cabin of his sailboat was a sheltering womb of glowing varnished Yellow Cedar and Douglas Fir. His particular version of the much loved Atkin design had been built of ancient first growth timber in the mid-fifties by a logger and shipwright in British Columbia, who had subsequently sailed with his family throughout the Pacific, before selling the boat in the nineteen eighties to a retired couple who used the boat only for occasional outings on Puget Sound. The last owners had let the boat go some, and Conrad had got the Ingrid for a good price. After a year of work and several thousand dollars invested, *Tisiphone* was now in better condition than at any time since her launching.

Conrad was a minimalist sailor. He had replaced the old four cylinder Perkins with a one lung Saab model which could be started with a cranking handle, thus lessoning his reliance on electricity. Two solar panels provided the small amount of electricity he needed. He used a GPS, depth meter, and electric running lights, but did without radar, refrigeration, or pressurized water. More often than not, he used his kerosine lamps for inside illumination. When the wind died or in tight quarters he preferred to use a home-made sculling oar or a pair of long sweeps, rather than the engine whenever possible. For offshore sailing he usually removed the propeller to cut down on drag. He had nearly doubled the standard sail area of the production model Ingrids by rigging her as a top-sail gaff cutter. In light winds he could set over two thousand square feet of sail, which could be quickly reduced when the wind increased. He seldom used the little engine, filling the fifteen gallon diesel tank a couple of times a year.

Conrad had learned his sailing skills as a boy growing up in Seattle, where he had sailed the local lakes, the inland seas of Puget Sound, and the Strait of Georgia. (A Bellingham biologist had proposed the name "Salish Sea" to encompass all the region's salt water in the late 1980's.) Since the early nineteen seventies Conrad had owned a succession of sailboats before buying the Ingrid, and he had honed his sailing and navigation skills on a variety of small and large sailing craft, much of the time, as now, without the help of additional crew.

From his sailboat, berthed at the end of the wharf, Conrad had a good view of the other visiting vessels. He immediately recognized one of them, the cutter *Lethe*. He had been fast asleep during the rescue of the *Legal Eagle* the previous evening He was surprised and disconcerted to see David's boat moored here in Spruce Cove. He watched as first Mike Schwindel and then Chuck Riggs visited David. A while later, after he had finished his breakfast and cleaned up the galley, he saw the Chuck leave and head back up the wharf to the small group of rotting wooden houses that still managed to stand in the way of the relentless rain forest, which was slowly but inexorably taking back the town site. Conrad walked down the dock in the chilly rain the short distance to David's boat. He expected David would be shocked to find this specter from his past here in this obscure corner of the world.

Back in the early nineteen seventies, he, like David, had sported a full beard and fashionably long hair. But Conrad's generic hippie affectation had been a disguise convenient to his employment that summer in Kabul, where he had first met David Stuckrath and Karen Truman. In those days Karen had been the sun about which several lovestruck men orbited. Conrad had always believed she had made the right choice in marrying David instead of one of her other suitors.

In those years David Stuckrath had been a Peace Corps Volunteer fresh out of college working in the tuberculosis eradication efforts, and teaching English to Afghans in Kabul. Conrad had a small import-export business, and also taught English part time. Additionally, he had begun working secretly as an informant for the intelligence gathering agency that still employed him. He had met David one day on the USIS premises, where David sometimes went to see the occasional movie or to check out books from the small library. They had hit it off immediately and were soon spending time together hanging out at bars and teahouses, and exploring the bazaars of Kabul.

Conrad's job had not been very demanding. His assignment was to get to know some of the young Afghans in the local communist party, gather what information he could about them, and report to his contact which of them seemed to be leaders or potential leaders among their peers. Some time earlier the Peoples Democratic Party of Afghanistan, or the PDPA, had split into two main factions, the Parcham and Khalq parties. He had been able to establish contact with several young members of the more urban Parcham group, but had not had much luck gaining access to the Khalq faction, which was dominated by Pashtuns. This group was more rural and tribal, with fewer social connections to Westerners. It was his first assignment and was not rated as very important or dangerous by his superiors, but Conrad had been ambitious in those days, and hoped to exceed the expectations of his superiors. Eventually he made himself indispensable to them.

Conrad taught English privately to a few Afghans, but in his case teaching was both part of his cover and helpful in extending his local social contacts, as each student gave him entry into their extended family. The Afghans were curious about the Westerners, and his students never failed to invite him into their homes, where he was treated as an honorable guest. His students were chosen for their political connections. Conrad had a natural gift for language, and had rapidly become fluent in both the Dari and Pashtun tongues. The Pashtun language was harder to learn, but as luck would have it his new friend, David, was among a handful in his Peace Corps cycle learning that language, and he too had a gift for acquiring language skills quickly.

Conrad had not had any scruples about using their friendship to help him establish social contacts with several influential Pashtuns, one of whom happened to be a close relative of Taraki, leader of the Khalq party. David provided the young Afghan with alcohol, and a safe place to drink it in return for hashish. Partly because of the information Conrad was able to gather during drinking sessions with David and the Afghan, he was able to give the Agency critical information about a planned coup before it was carried out in July of 1973 by Mohammad Daoud. This early success assured Conrad's future in the intelligence bureau.

Shortly after the coup David left the Peace Corps and returned to Seattle, where he and Karen were married. Conrad had continued his life of travel and intrigue with the Agency, but though they had gotten together only a few times over the years, Karen—even before their tryst that fateful Seattle winter—had always kept Conrad apprised of the Stuckrath family activities through her regular cards, letters, and photographs, which arrived like clockwork around holidays and family birthdays.

Absorbed in their conversation, Mike and David did not hear Conrad approach the boat. They were surprised by the abrupt knocking at the companionway hatch. David slid the hatch open and stared amazed into the face of his old companion.

"Hey David, aren't you going to invite a poor guy in out of this damned rain?" Conrad said.

"I'll be damned! You are the last person I expected to see here—what a pleasant surprise! What the hell brings you to this corner of the world, of all places?" David exclaimed, as Conrad negotiated the steep companionway ladder. Conrad and David embraced, and Conrad shook hands with Mike Schwindel, introducing himself, before taking a seat.

"Whoa! Slow down David. I'll start by having some of that coffee that smells so good. I own *Tisiphone*, the Ingrid over there," he added, pointing towards his yacht.

"That boat—no way! I thought you sailed a Pearson Vanguard?"

"Hell, that was two boats ago. I guess I haven't been very good about staying in touch lately," Conrad replied.

Although Karen had kept up her regular correspondence since their time in Afghanistan, Conrad had rarely reciprocated.

Their talk turned quickly to sailing, the storm, and the like. Mike complimented Conrad on his taste in boats, and they spent some minutes extolling the virtues of the Atkin designs, noting that David's Cape George Cutter was also a modification of a design by the same revered naval architect.

"Yeah, I guess I'm a member of the AAA club; Alden, Alberg, and Atkin. It seems most of my boats have been designed by one of those three. After the Alberg Vanguard I salvaged an old Alden Malabar Jr. That was a great sailboat, and convinced me I would rather work with wood than fiberglass. I was perfectly happy with it, but the Ingrid was such a good deal I couldn't pass her up—but she is definitely a lot of boat for one man."

"Well, this is quite a coincidence—you two old friends meeting up here," Mike observed, re-lighting his pipe.

"Maybe not as much of a coincidence as you might think. I'm on my way to Juneau and hoped I might run into David somewhere up here. I heard about your loss—about Marshall... I don't know what I can say. I suppose there is nothing to say or do, but I just want you to understand I know the details, so don't feel like you have to explain or talk about any of it with me, unless you want to. Anyway, it's good to see you again after so long."

Conrad had indeed planned to visit David, but not so soon, or in this place. He hoped this would not complicate or interfere with his plans, and speaking at all with David of Marshall taxed even Conrad's great reserves of self-control.

"Shit! ...just too many fucking coincidences, one right after another! I bet you can't guess who we pulled in from the storm last night," Mike interjected. He told Conrad about judge Daise's rescue the previous night.

"Look you guys," Mike continued after a time. "I'm going to leave you two to get reacquainted while I run up and give old Chuck a hand with setting things up for his little party. The coffee was great, but I'm about ready to switch over to something a bit stronger. Are you planning to come too, David?"

"I haven't really decided yet. I don't know if I can keep myself from saying something to Daise, especially if I start drinking—which I most certainly intend to do," David replied.

"Why the hell shouldn't you say something to him! He is, after all, the person who made the decision to send Marshall to the penitentiary!" Conrad exclaimed.

The other two men were taken aback at the unexpected vehemence of Conrad's outburst.

"Well, when you put it that way, I guess he did have a choice. Other sentences were certainly possible."

Mike puffed thoughtfully on his pipe before elaborating.

"Who judges the judges anyway? Daise was in charge of sentencing of course, but why rub salt in David's wounds? It's usually best to accept the past and get on with life—but that is just one man's opinion, and perhaps not the most intelligent of men. It was nice meeting you Conrad. I hope I see you up at Chuck's place later."

"Sure, that sounds like a good way to spend the afternoon, and I could definitely use a change in diet," Conrad replied.

"David, you know you can always count on me for whatever I can give, even if it's only cheap talk and cheaper booze," Mike continued, slapping his friend gently on the back as he turned to climb up the companionway ladder.

"I know I can, and thanks Mike," David replied.

A spatter of rain drops wetted the galley counter and cabin sole before Mike slid the hatch home. For a moment the two remaining men were silent. Then David spoke quietly, repeating Mike's offhand comment: "...who judges the judge... I wonder...?"

Conrad said nothing, only observing David closely.

For the next hour they caught up on each other's

pasts. They marveled that through entirely separate paths they had both ended up as committed sailors with similar types of boats. From long habit Conrad extracted much more from David than he volunteered in the exchange. Had he stopped to think about it, David would have been surprised at just how little concrete information Conrad actually revealed about himself and his activities since they had last seen each other, years earlier during one of Mike and Karen's infrequent Seattle outings. On the other hand, David's awareness was not entirely focused on their conversation. Mike's words had suggested the faint outlines of an idea that began to stir at the edges of his consciousness. At some point in their meandering conversation the idea coalesced into a definite plan.

"Sometimes I wish I was a man of action like you," David blurted out suddenly.

"What do you mean?" was all Conrad could reply to David's non sequitur, which had come out of nowhere while Conrad had been telling of his own stormy passage north from Dixon Entrance to Spruce Cove.

"What I mean is; people who know me well might say that it would be totally out of character for me to take any real risk, even for a cause I believed in strongly—even if I did not care about the consequences to myself."

"I don't agree. You sail, and in cold dangerous waters. A lot of people might call that a hazardous activity."

"Maybe, but what I mean is that I never leave my comfort zone. Sailing can be learned incrementally, and unless you get caught out in a storm or make a stupid mistake, you are pretty safe, or at least you feel pretty safe, and that is what matters."

"I don't think many people like getting out of their comfort zones. You are no different than myself or anyone else in that respect. It's just that people's comfort zones are all different. You know that old sailor's adage—there are two kinds of boaters; those that have already been aground, and those that will be. If you sail long enough you will eventually find that storm or make that mistake, or maybe I should say that situation will find you."

"Maybe it has. Maybe that storm or uncharted rock has found me at last," David replied.

Conrad waited, but David seemed unwilling to explain his cryptic comments.

"I am curious as to why you seem so obsessed with the actions of the judge. What about the man who actually murdered Marshall?" Conrad queried, when David did not elaborate further.

"You mean Grant Tadlock? You are not the first person to ask me that question, and at first he was the one who was the focus of my anger. I hated the man and wished nothing more for him than a slow and painful death—but not anymore. I now think judge Daise bears more responsibility ultimately for Marshall's death."

"Why is that?" Conrad prompted.

"...a couple of reasons, mainly. First, although

Marshall was as good and loving son as any father could wish for, he did have his faults like all of us, and one of them was a quick temper. He got in trouble a few times in school for fighting when he would have been better off working things out in some other way, or going to the teachers or principal. As much as Karen and I tried to teach him the futility of violence for solving problems, he seemed to have a breaking point beyond which he simply would not be pushed. In jail, instead of keeping quiet and enduring the inevitable hazing that takes place there, he refused to take it. In the end that led to his death."

"You honestly believe it was Marshall's fault?" Conrad asked, genuinely shocked at David's attitude.

"I am not saying that, exactly. It did seem that sports helped. Marshall had a lot of energy, which needed a constant outlet. Once he got involved in school sports he rarely had any problems with aggression. I don't mean that he started fights. He just would not be threatened or pushed around verbally or physically without taking action. He refused to be intimidated, and on occasion he got into trouble for protecting other kids from bullies. It was just an integral part of his personality—something I would think you could understand, based on what I know of your own history, Conrad."

"All right, I get that, but you said there were two reasons why you don't hold Tadlock totally responsible. What was the other one?"

"I learned some things about Grant Tadlock's family history. It was a childhood marked by abuse and inhumane torment. He came from a family of alcoholics and child abusers. He was in the streets and on his own by the time he was twelve years old. The man never had a chance."

"So you believe that it was inevitable he would become a murderer?"

"Not necessarily inevitable, but likely under the right circumstances. In the confines and atmosphere of the penitentiary Marshall's refusal to take shit from anyone was what finally caused Tadlock to explode. Tadlock had a history of petty crime, and he had been involved in a few violent episodes, but I don't think it ever came to anything more serious because he was at least free to come and go—to get away from the situation as long as he was not restrained. Once he was confined I think it was just too much like being back home as a child without any control, and he just completely lost it when Marshall, who was bigger and obviously pretty fit, would not back down. He saw that as a personal threat and just blew up."

Conrad had no patience for such psychological justifications as excusals for bad behavior.

"Regardless of Tadlock's motivation or personal history, where is the justice for society in your way of thinking? Tadlock was responsible, and it is Tadlock who should pay the price, although I suppose it would also be just to imprison his parents as well. Why call Daise to account for it, who was at least doing what society expects of a judge? It sounds like you are blaming your son for his own death, and letting Tadlock off because he had a difficult home life. That is simply bullshit!" Conrad insisted.

"I went to school with a kid whose father beat him so badly he was hospitalized, and social services had to put him in a foster home. Then his foster father abused him sexually on a regular basis until he ran away from that situation. That kid grew up to become a prominent businessmen, raised a lovely family without resorting to buggering his own children, and started a charity for abused teenagers."

"Well, without getting into the whole nature versus nurture arguments, I understand your point. I'm no simple Pavlovian. I don't mean to blame Marshall, of course. Perhaps I'm only rationalizing. But how does it help society if every such case resulted in a vendetta? We would end up with a wild west where family feuds carried on for generations."

"I am here to tell you that is really the case, one way or the other. Mostly it is just those with wealth and power who call the tune and we dance to it. You will never convince me that Tadlock should not pay the ultimate price for his actions. One can understand him to a certain point, and one can feel compassion for his circumstances, but sometimes a rabid dog just needs to be put down! Sometimes a primitive sort of justice must take precedence over the law or sympathy. We can always forgive and feel empathy for the dog, even after we have done what is necessary and prudent to ensure it never bites again."

Following this diatribe Conrad stood slowly,

stooping slightly, his six foot three height several inches too much for the curve of the cabin ceiling where it arched over the settee. He motioned towards a portlight.

"It looks like that fisherman is coming in to take advantage of the caretaker's hospitality too."

David's earlier statements about judge Daise, Grant Tadlock, and Marshall's temper had fazed him, and he realized he had come perilously close to revealing the reason for his presence so far north. He meant to distract his old friend.

Through the gray drizzle they made out a bulky hooded form hunched over the buzzing outboard of the *Bad Attitude's* skiff, which curved towards Chuck Riggs' dock, blazing a spumy trail through the otherwise placid bay.

"That's Sam Thornton. I know him pretty well. His son was in one of my history classes a couple of years ago. He got into some trouble at school and I helped him out a little. We've been pretty good friends ever since."

"Helped him out—how?" Conrad asked.

"Basically the school wanted to expel his kid. I told the principal that if they did, they could find another history teacher. They finally agreed to let the boy stay in class, but only after Sam, his son, and I agreed to several conditions. In any case it all worked out. His son finished high school, and Sam is the kind of guy that never forgets a favor. For the past couple of years I have never lacked for fresh salmon or halibut. I don't see him too often because he fishes out of Petersburg these days, but he never fails to bring me a few fish and to ask if there is anything I need every time he gets up to Juneau. I had barely tied up last night before he hailed me on the radio and invited me over for some crab and beer. He's a hard man to say no to, but I was just too damned tired. After Marshall died he was one of the first people to call on us."

"Jesus David, you just explained to me how you never take any risks, and now you tell me about risking your job to save some fisherman's kid from getting kicked out of school!"

"Just as I said before. I did not leave my comfort zone. The risk to me was really pretty minimal. I had tenure, and I knew the principal and superintendent well enough to know they only needed a little pressure to bend the rules some for one student. I just had to make them believe I wasn't bluffing."

"Were you?" Conrad asked.

David smiled slightly and answered: "I never could bluff—maybe that's why I usually loose at cards."

"I think I will go on up to this caretaker's place and check out his legendary hospitality for myself. I'm curious to meet the judge you rescued last night, whom you seem to hold in such low esteem."

"I might join you all later too—judge Daise be damned. Why should I be the one to mope down in the harbor by myself while everyone else is having a good time? The whole situation might make for a livelier party after all."

"David, I want you to pretend you don't know me if you do decide to show up," Conrad said, abruptly.

"Sure, but why?"

"No reason really. Just as a favor for an old friend, if you don't mind," Conrad replied.

"Okay, if that's what you want. Are you on some kind of assignment up here? Sorry—I should know better than to ask. Anyway Mike knows that we're friends."

"Yes, I am on assignment up here, and the fewer that know the better." (At least this statement was accurate, though it certainly was an equivocation.) "I'll go talk to your friend; maybe I can convince him not to let on. He seems like the discreet type."

"You know, I brought Marshall here a few times. He loved this place. We always had a great time on the boat. He would have loved yours—would have been up those ratlines in no time. He scared the shit out of Karen, jumping from the spreaders into the bay, but I knew he had it figured. Hell, I used to jump off bridges myself at that age. Sometimes I still can't believe he is really gone."

Conrad embraced David awkwardly in the tiny cabin before climbing the the companionway ladder. His eyes were moist, and the rain was not the cause.

David watched Conrad walk down the dock and along the trail that circled the bay just above the high tide limit. His gaze continued even after his old friend disappeared up the path that branched off to the caretaker's house. After a while he stood up and went to one of the bins above the v-berth. He took out a well-worn sweatshirt and put it on. Just a couple of months earlier it would have been uncomfortably tight around his middle, but it now fit his leaner frame well. It had belonged to his son, Marshall, and it bore the polar bear logo of his college track team.

"Who judges the judge," he repeated out loud, though he was alone.

CHAPTER 11

Lunch At Chuck's

Chuck's house set on a knoll at the end of the old boardwalk that had once been the main boulevard of Spruce Cove town. Other wooden walkways, now mostly missing or in poor repair had originally served as the transportation grid for the village, which had never included provisions for the automobile. Chuck's residence was more substantial than most of the other homes constructed during the earliest mining era, having been built to house the supervisor and his family. It was a rambling two story structure, with a generous porch and four gables aligned roughly to the cardinal points.

His guests negotiated several wooden steps and a short gravel trail that led from the boardwalk to the main entrance of the house. After entering a small vestibule and shedding their coats and boots, they proceeded directly into what had originally been a formal dining room, now used by Chuck as a library, office, and general storage area. The entire room was lined with shelves. A heavy oak desk salvaged from the company's office years earlier squatted under the weight of books, magazines, and miscellaneous heaps of paper. The shelves sagged with yet more books and periodicals. Stairs on the back wall rose to the second floor and three seldom visited bedrooms. A doorway opened into a generous kitchen, which contained the original wood burning cooking range—a massive piece of wrought iron filigree and porcelain, and Chuck's proudest possession. Although Chuck had propane periodically delivered from Ketchikan, he preferred cooking on the venerable old stove. He used the propane to run a small on-demand water heater, which in turn was plumbed into coils of copper tubing that ran through the old range. This arrangement provided him with adequate hot water for his frugal needs.

The old town had never progressed to the point of having completely modern indoor plumbing. Soon after the settlement's founding most of the homes and businesses were plumbed to running water, supplied from a wooden pipe system leading up the hill a short way to the head of a small stream. Although the pipe had supplied water to nearly every building in the town's heyday, no waste system had ever been installed. A privy was located a few steps away down an overgrown path leading from Chuck's back door. The original water pipe had rotted away years earlier, and Chuck had replaced it with a plastic pipe and garden hose system which worked for most of the year. When the pipe froze he laboriously hauled his water in five gallon plastic buckets.

The spacious living room occupied the north side of his house. This comfortable space was dominated by large windows overlooking the crescent bay. From here Chuck could observe any boats entering or leaving the harbor. He enjoyed the play of light on the water, and the panoramic view of the picturesque remnants of Spruce Cove village and the surrounding densely forested ridges.

In order to accommodate the expected guests Chuck had moved a small oak table he normally kept in the kitchen to the main room, as well as two beat-up card tables. The chairs were an assortment of old patched and repaired relics of the mining and cannery years. Other furniture consisted of a pew salvaged from one of the original churches, a couple of rustic end tables built by Chuck of salvaged lumber, and a threadbare sofa—laboriously brought in by boat from Wrangell many years earlier as a gift to Chuck from a grateful fisherman who had been the recipient, like so many others over the years, of Chuck's legendary hospitality.

Seated on the pew, the esteemed sofa, and at the improvised tables, were several of the dozen or so year round residents of Spruce Cove. Bill and Sharon Craften, both in their late twenties, had moved into one of the abandoned houses a few years earlier. Bill had discovered the place while crewing on Sam Thornton's fishing boat. Lanky, with blonde hair tied in a pony tail and a bushy beard, he could have stepped right out of San Francisco in the sixties, and had in fact had been raised for a time in a commune, the son of a free-thinking couple from Oregon. Bill was a willing and energetic worker, always ready to give Chuck a hand whenever any maintenance chore came up that was too much for him alone. Sharon was attractive, quiet, and hardworking; the type who made her own bread from scratch, was handy at filleting and smoking salmon, and knew how to make a salad from the local wild plants.

On more than one warm summer day Chuck had espied the couple frolicking au naturel in the cove, reminding him of otters at play. A certain amount of nudity was normal in Spruce Cove. One of the small sheds had been converted by a previous resident into a community bath house. It was a weekly ritual on Wednesday evenings to gather there. Nothing was more invigorating than a session in the tiny sweltering hut, followed by immediate immersion in the cold waters of the bay.

At times the animal perfection of the couple's bodies glistening in the hot steamy space moved Chuck to tears. Tears for his own lost loves and youth. Tears for the impermanence of all that is healthy and fair. Indiscernible silent tears that quickly commingled with his body's other salty diaphoresis in the vapory murk of the communal sauna. At the heart of Chuck's generosity and hospitality was a core of loneliness.

Thomas Wilson—he never referred to himself as Tom—was a slim, clean-cut man of thirty-five. He lived on the other side of the low ridge which separated the old ruins of Spruce Cove village from a small group of houses and cabins on a section of privately owned lots. These lots had been sold to individuals in the sixties and seventies by a Juneau developer. In the early part of the century the acreage had been the site of a fur farm, and before that an old homestead. Most of the lots were owned by people from Ketchikan or Wrangell, who used them only sporadically during the summer months, usually for fishing excursions. For several years Thomas had been the only permanent resident of the area.

Thomas was a solitary and self-reliant man, but when he felt the need for human companionship he was always welcome at Chuck's house, a twenty minute walk over the ridge or along the beach. A few times a year Thomas hitched a ride with one of the local fishermen to Ketchikan or Juneau for supplies and a dose of civilization, which only reinforced his appreciation of his reclusive life in Spruce Cove. Thomas was a bit of a mystery to the others on the peninsula. He rarely talked about his personal life, and deflected inquiries as to the source of his livelihood. He seemed to prefer keeping a certain emotional distance from his neighbors, but he was always enthusiastic when talk turned to literature, politics, the natural history of the area (he had divulged that he had studied biology in college), or virtually any topic but himself. Thomas had hinted of some "investments" that provided him with a modest income, but Chuck suspected he was supported by a family trust fund. In any case he was affable if not forthcoming, and like Bill was willing to lend a hand when needed. This set him apart from the seasonal occupants from over the ridge who seldom made their way over to the weekly sauna or frequent pot-luck gatherings at Chuck Riggs' home.

Thomas Wilson and the Craften couple were in conversation with Darlene and John Treadwell. The Treadwells were on their way south from their first trip up the inside passage on their large motor yacht, *Elixir*. In their early sixties and comfortably retired from John's career as a Boeing executive, John and his wife were an adventurous couple with time on their hands and enough money to take advantage of it. They were discussing the recently published "Passage To Juneau", by the popular travel writer, Jonathan Raban.

"I loved the way he wove in the stuff about captain Vancouver and the history of the inside passage," Darlene opined.

She was a big flabby woman with a double chin, ready smile, and a penchant for wearing huge dangling earrings, which had the effect of drawing the listener's attention to her especially large fleshy ear lobes.

"I agree with my wife for the most part; in fact, I liked the whole first third of the book a lot, but I thought the part about his wife leaving him was a cheap shot," her husband chimed in.

John Treadwell was a portly man with a florid face framed by an extravagant mass of thick graying hair.

"I agree with you there—that was in poor taste, and it made me uncomfortable to read it, but I think he was spot on with the description of how Alaskans talk—their constant swearing. That part was accurate, as well as hilarious. In any case his wife divorced a popular writer—always a dangerous thing to do," Thomas commented.

Judge Daise, who had spoken little since the introductions, had not read the book, and hoped for a better conversational opening. It came when Chuck entered the room holding a pot of coffee in one hand and a pitcher of his famous home brew in the other.

"...anyone getting thirsty?" he asked.

"Thank you—coffee for me please. You have a very nice place here, Mr. Riggs," the judge remarked.

"Well, it ain't the Ritz, but it keeps the rain off my head—and that's a damn good thing today. Please call me Chuck, everyone else does. Have you had any luck with your engine?" he asked, filling the judge's mug.

"No luck at all. It is definitely not the fuel filters or the line, so it appears I will have to get a real mechanic to look at it. I'm hoping to get a ride out of here with someone tomorrow, if weather permits. I would like to get to Wrangell or Petersburg, and catch a plane to Juneau."

"Well that shouldn't be too difficult. I know that at least a couple of the boats here are heading north when this storm lets up; or you could call for a floatplane charter if you don't mind spending the extra money," Chuck suggested.

Sam Thornton and Mike Schwindel were having their own private conversation. They stood a little apart from the seated group, gazing at the harbor through the tall windows while they enjoyed Chuck's dark fragrant beer. From the slightly higher elevation of Chuck's home they were able to see across the cove and over a low ridge, where the furious winds drove foaming seas upon the rocks of the several small barrier islands that guarded the northwestern end of the harbor entrance. There the tops of the taller trees were bent nearly double from the force of the storm, while in the sheltered cove they were all but isolated from the fierceness of the gale. But the rain that fell in waves and torrential sheets rattled the windows of the old house, giving them an indication of what things must be like out in Clarence Strait.

"I'd bet it's blowin' at least forty knots out there right now—maybe more," Sam said, punctuating his declaration with a great gulp of the brew.

"I wouldn't want to be out there today in anything smaller than a tour ship. It looks like we are in for at least one more night of this until the front blows through, according to the last forecast on the weather channel," Mike replied.

Sam looked around the room quickly to make sure none of the guests were near enough to hear, and leaned in closer to Mike, lowering his voice to just above a whisper.

"I'm not too happy that David and judge Daise are both here in Spruce Cove together. I hope David doesn't show up. He might be tempted to confront that fucker Daise, and I'd hate to see him get tangled up in any more legal bullshit. But if he does decide to come up here, I just want you to know I'll back him up if it comes to any kind of a confrontation—I owe him that much," Sam said, crossing his thick arms over his barrel-like chest in finality.

"Understood. We had a little chat earlier about the situation with Chuck. I hope David decides to stay put too, but if he chooses confrontation, I'm with you. But I think David needs more protection from himself than that wily judge needs from him. I've never known David to pick a fight with anyone in all the years I've known him, and I've seen him defuse a couple of potential ones, back when we were a lot younger and spending a hell of a lot more time in bars. I've never seen him loose his cool, even around some pretty aggressive drunks," Mike replied.

After Chuck determined his guests had sufficiently loosened up with his strong brew he recruited Sharon. Together they brought out the food, which they served buffet-fashion, each guest tasking a plate and silverware from the stack and helping themselves to the simple but hearty meal. Baked salmon and steamed mussels from the waters of Clarence Strait, and venison from the forests of the peninsula provided the protein. Potatoes and greens from the gardens of the Craften couple completed the main course. Chuck's flavorful home brew flowed freely, served from a pitcher that was refilled as quickly as it was emptied. This cornucopia was augmented with crackers, potato chips, wine, hard liquor, and other store bought foods contributed by the visiting boaters. The little group gathered around the improvised tables and fell to.

Conrad took the opportunity to tell Chuck of his early morning hiking adventure.

"I saw a mountain lion this morning," he said.

"Now that is something—are you sure? Where did you see it?" Chuck asked.

Conrad described the area, and how he had fortuitously come upon the animal in the midst of its hunt.

"You are not the first one to see a cougar in that area. We've had several sightings in the last few years. The state game biologist in Juneau says they probably come down to the peninsula now and then from inland Canada, where the population is growing. Back about ten years ago a guy shot one up near Wrangell, and just a couple of years ago—I think it was in '98 or '99—one was caught in a trap quite a ways northwest of here on Kupreanof Island," Chuck continued.

"Kupreanof? If my geography is right that means the cat would have to do some swimming in addition to one hell of a long walk; that is, unless there is already a population living on the island," Conrad mused.

"You're right. There are at least two places where the mountain lion would have to swim—Dry Straits and the Wrangell Narrows—and that's after traveling all those miles down the Stikine or Unuk Rivers from the interior of Canada. There is no established population of mountain lions on any of the islands in Southeast according to that biologist."

"Mountain lions, Jaguars, and tigers are three big cats that do swim. Excuse me—I don't mean to butt in, but I couldn't help but overhear someone mention mountain lions—one of my favorite subjects," Thomas Wilson said, joining the conversation.

"Thomas is one of the two people in Spruce Cove who have seen a cougar," Chuck said after introductions were made. "Even though I've lived here longer than anyone, I've never seen one myself."

"That's because you spend all your time fishing and brewing beer," Thomas teased. "You've got to work up a sweat and get off this beach to get a glimpse of a puma."

"...and that's another thing. Why the hell does that cat have so many names, anyway?" Chuck asked.

"Well, if you will pardon my little biology lecture; it is because the mountain lion, cougar, puma, panther, or catamount—whatever you want to call it, has very high vagility—that is, the capacity to migrate or move great distances into diverse environments—a most adaptable animal. In fact, the cougar is second only to humans in distribution of land animals in the Americas. There are populations of mountain lions from Patagonia to the Yukon, and it's not uncommon for males especially to wander long distances. They come down this way I'm sure to prey on the Sitka white tail deer—the same meat we've been enjoying. Can you blame them! Of course Chuck didn't have to jump onto the back of the deer and break its neck to supply us with venison. On the other hand, I wouldn't put it past him. I saw him dive into the bay one time after a king salmon," Thomas declared.

"I didn't dive, I fell, and anyway that was at least a sixty pounder—worth diving for if I could have brought it in."

"That was indeed one of the very few fish that has ever escaped your clutches, Chuck," Thomas said, "but it seems to gain weight with every telling."

Mike and Sam, their plates piled high with food, continued their private conversation between bites. They watched a hooded figure hurrying up the boardwalk towards the house.

"It looks like David decided to join the party after all. He sure chose the wrong time to make a run for it. He'll be soaked by the time he gets here," Sam said, pointing with his venison-laden fork towards the rain-drenched man.

"I'm a little surprised to see him. He seemed pretty ambivalent. I thought maybe he might reconsider," Mike replied.

"I don't think anyone has told the judge just who it was that saved his sorry ass last night," Sam said.

"It won't be too comfortable for David here," Mike replied.

"I'm betting it's Daise who's going to be the uncomfortable one," Sam countered.

Mike waited in vain for Sam to explain his terse reply, but the big native continued his meal without elaborating.

David entered, soaking wet and clutching a bottle of Irish whiskey.

"Did I miss lunch yet?" he asked.

"Grab yourself a plate and sit down, David, you're just in time!" Chuck replied a little too loudly, trying to cover up his trepidation with bravado. He took David's dripping coat and pointed to an empty chair.

After filling his plate, David sat, making no sign that he had noticed the presence of either the judge or Conrad in the room.

Conrad too ignored David's entrance, and had anyway struck up a conversation with the Spencers, a father and son team on their first Alaska adventure who had also been driven into the cove by the ferocious weather system. Bob was still hale in his nineties. His son, Jim, was finally making good on a vacation promise decades old. They had chartered their small power boat in Bellingham, and were determined to explore the Inside Passage all the way to Skagway.

Some time later, when the guests had finished their meals, Chuck suggested a game of poker. The game was soon underway, with a rotating cast of players. Chuck furnished the cards and chips. The chips cost a penny or nickel each. The guests who were not playing cards got acquainted with each other while they talked, drank, and looked out over the postcard perfect bay from the comfort of Chuck's homey living room. The poker game continued as the afternoon wore on into evening. Large amounts of Chuck's strong brew were consumed, as well as the harder stuff some of the guests had brought to the gathering. The party got noisier as the guest's blood alcohol percentage increased. There were no teetotalers in the group, though Daise slowly sipped his beer, and could perhaps lay claim to being the most sober person in the room. The rain stopped for a time, but dark clouds gathering to the south promised more before the storm spent itself.

CHAPTER 12

The Wager

Card players quit and others took their place. Finally six people remained; Sam Thornton, Thomas Wilson, judge Henry Daise, Darlene Treadwell, her husband John, and David. By far the biggest piles of chips were in front of the judge and John Treadwell. The cards were dealt again. Sam and the Treadwells took three cards each. Judge Daise and Thomas Wilson took two.

"I'll be fine with one card," David said.

"Shit! I've got no luck today," Sam said throwing his cards down. "That's it for me. I need another beer anyway," he said getting up.

"Everyone else in?" Thomas asked.

"Damn right!," John said moving a chip onto the pile.

"I can't let my husband win or he'll rub it in the rest of the trip," Darlene said. "I see yours and raise you," she went on, shoving four more chips at the pile.

"Whoa, big spender!" Thomas exclaimed.

"Now this is getting interesting." The judge looked at his cards, and added five more chips.

"Time to separate the men—and women, from

the boys," David said. He put all his remaining poker chips on the pile in the center.

"I think I'll cut my losses after all," Darlene exclaimed, turning her cards over.

"Too rich for me," her husband agreed.

"Likewise," Thomas Wilson echoed.

"I think you're bluffing," the judge said, matching David's gambit, and adding another stack to the large pile.

"Maybe I am and maybe I'm not, but I'm out of chips," David replied.

"You'll have to buy some from Sam or John," Chuck said. He had been uncomfortable ever since David arrived—had in fact hoped fervently that he would not show up. Chuck had introduced David to all the others as a group, referring to him as 'his friend David.' He had carefully avoided saying anything about Daise's rescue the previous night or David's involvement in the incident.

"The chips don't matter," David said. "I have got a more interesting wager to make anyway—one that won't require any chips or money."

"Hey now, this is just a friendly game. I'll take some of my chips back and call you," the judge said diplomatically. Something about the man's agitated playing style bothered him, and he was not happy to see the game down to just the two of them. The man seemed somehow familiar, but he could not place him. On the other hand Daise was a competitive card player, and he had a good hand.

"I don't think so, Henry, or do you prefer Hank? It is against the rules even in a friendly card game to take back a bet. You of all people should know about rules."

"Well I have had enough of this at any rate." Daise said, rising.

He was a fit man in his late fifties. A self-made man from a working class family who had put his army benefits to good use in law school. Henry Daise had moved to Alaska in the nineteen seventies, taking a job with the district attorney's office in Anchorage where he had risen quickly to become a prominent state prosecutor. He had been appointed a superior court judge a few years later. He was used to having the last word.

"But you haven't heard my wager yet. You might find it interesting," David insisted.

By now they had attracted the attention of all in the room, and it was to the entire gathering that David addressed his next remarks.

"First of all I would like to introduce myself and Mr. Daise—I mean really introduce both myself and Henry here, to all of you. My name is David Stuckrath. Standing across from me is judge Henry Daise. Those of you in this room who live in Alaska might be familiar with those names from a recent court case involving my late son, Marshall. You probably also remember how my son died, in a fight with another prisoner, after being sentenced to serve time in the penitentiary by this man."

"That was a terrible tragedy. Your son was a fine

boy who did not deserve such a fate," the judge countered.

"There are some who would say he did not deserve to have been in your court in the first place, let alone in that prison, and there may be those who would say I should have let you drift onto the rocks last night —but these are things that have already occurred, and we can't change the past, now can we?"

David struggled to control his emotions and voice. His face was preternaturally pale.

"I can understand some of what you feel. I have children of my own," Daise responded.

"And what would you have done if the same had happened to one of your children? Would you have locked up your own son for a trace of cocaine? Locked him up in a prison with murderers and rapists!"

David's self-restraint began to crack. His fists clenched and face contorted with the effort to control his anger.

"I don't think this is the place or time to discuss my personal feelings, or your son's unfortunate case. I am a duly appointed judge, and I serve the state of Alaska and her citizens. My judgements are constrained by the law in any case. I am truly sorry for your son, but you must understand we live under the rule of law. This is not a personal matter between you and I, Mr. Stuckrath. I am in your debt for saving my boat and possibly my life last night. I wish there was something I could do or say to repay that debt, or to lesson your grief, but I don't think this is the time. I would be glad to meet with you privately whenever you wish."

"I wish it now! This is the time and the place! By god you will hear me out! You owe me that much!"

The judge moved to leave the room, but was blocked by Sam Thornton, who had edged gradually closer during the exchange. He tried to slip past, but Sam moved in front of him again.

"I will see you in court if you don't get out of my way this instant!" the judge roared, his face flushing.

"Oh, I'm sure you will. You might not remember, but you sent me up Lime River for a spell a few years back. But I don't mind that. You might even say a good percentage of my friends are pretty familiar with that place," Sam said smiling dangerously.

Sam was one part Norwegian and three parts Tlingit native, and had the muscular barrel-like shape common to many men of that latter race strikingly combined with Nordic features. His blue eyes contrasted strangely with his dark hair and skin. Sam's face was scared and weathered from years of exposure to the harsh chilly winds of the fjords where he set his gill nets. His big square hands had dislodged the teeth of more than one rival, and his high cheek bones had deflected the rare blows of the scrappers who occasionally managed to land one or two before inevitably yielding to Sam's superior force and stamina. He sealed off exit from the room far more effectively than any door could.

"As long as I'm here I want you all to hold on a minute," Sam continued, almost casually. "My friend David here would like to speak, and I say nobody is going to leave this room until he has said his piece."

The big man crossed his arms on his chest and took up a position blocking passage into the kitchen, and to the only door opening to the outside from Chuck's house.

"Now see here! You've got no right to keep us here! This is none of our business. We are strangers and guests here. Is this the way you Alaskans show your hospitality?" John Treadwell exclaimed.

He had been heading towards the door behind Daise with his wife in tow when Sam blocked the way.

"Come on Sam," Chuck added. "This is my home and I should have the last word."

"That's up to David," was all Sam said, shifting his weight and setting his jaw.

"Thank you, Sam," David replied, and he turned to address everyone in the room.

"I would like you all to stay for a while longer, if you don't mind, or even if you do. Chuck, I realize this is poor form on my part at the very least, but as I have recently learned much of what happens in life is not fair or polite, and the world does not seem to care very much about our opinions anyway. As I said earlier, I would like to make a little wager with the judge. He apparently thinks I'm bluffing, and I am out of chips. I think most of you would agree Mr. Daise owes me something for my efforts on his behalf last night. So I am insisting as payment for that debt that he indulge me."

David paused briefly catch his breath and settle

his nerves.

"Here are the terms of the wager: If my hand wins we conduct our own little trial of the judge for his responsibility in the death of my son, with all of you here as the jury. If Henry's hand wins we call it even, and I will leave this room immediately. If you think about it, you will see this is a much better deal than my son was given."

"This is absurd and illegal!" declared the judge. "It will not bring back your son and you will only end up in jail yourself!"

"I really must insist. It is my house," Chuck said approaching David.

"Sit the fuck down Chuck! The rest of you too! Get comfortable, because something tells me I have got a winning hand for once, and I'm going to play it now!" David's hands shook with emotion.

"Well I'm not going to put up with this another minute! Come on Darlene," John Treadwell said.

He attempted to slide past the big native. Sam moved in front of him with arms still crossed. John, a big man in his own right, and with the confidence of long years as a supervisor of other men was not used to being challenged. He attempted to shove Sam out of the way. Sam was immobile. John's anger finally got the better of his judgement. He threw a punch that would have felled a smaller man. Sam caught his fist in mid air. Almost gently he forced Treadwell down, while simultaneously, in a single fluid motion, Sam stepped into Treadwell's armpit with his size thirteen boot as the older man hit the floor. John screamed in pain. Sam jerked him back up just as quickly and gave him a shove back into the room.

"You big bully!" John's wife exclaimed, shaking her fist at Sam.

"Sit down, please! You might even find this entertaining! What were you all going to do anyway—go back to your boats and doze away the evening? Like I said before—Henry, let's see if I really am bluffing. How about some more of that great home brew, Chuck?" David continued, relaxing some now that Sam appeared to have things under control.

Meanwhile Conrad Slocum and Mike Schwindel had interrupted an animated conversation on methods of rigging traditional boats to observe the action. Neither of them moved or spoke to assist the judge, or to interfere in any way with the proceedings. Sharon Craften put down the plates she had been clearing from the tables, and moved close to her husband on the pew with the two Spencers. They too elected to keep their silence, partly from curiosity, and partly out of fear.

"I refuse to take part in these absurd and illegal proceedings," Daise said, giving up his effort to exit the house. "You may be able to keep me here by force, but you cannot make me participate."

"What are you so worried about, Henry? We haven't even had a look at the cards yet. Could it be you were the one bluffing? Mike, could you do us a favor and turn over the judge's cards? Maybe he doesn't have a winning hand after all."

"Okay, but I hope this doesn't make me an accessory or something," he said, trying to strike a lighter tone.

The judge had a full house.

"Not bad, I guess you weren't bluffing," David said. "Well, neither am I."

He exposed his cards one by one, four threes, and the king of spades.

"Karma and willpower," Sharon Craften whispered to her husband. She was fascinated with the tarot.

CHAPTER 13

An Unusual Trial

"I did not accept your wager, therefore your winning hand is meaningless," Daise stated flatly, crossing his arms defiantly.

"Well, that is true in some strict sense I suppose, but I should think you would feel justified enough in your actions to defend your decisions, especially if those decisions might be a matter of life and death," David replied.

"Regardless, you are the one judge in Alaska who has made such a big deal of jury duty. As I recall, just recently you subpoenaed every single person who had excused themselves from jury duty in your court. You fined a good percentage of the ones whose excuses you did not think adequate. Personal responsibility is what you are always harping on."

"And I stand by that," Daise answered. "It's every citizen's duty."

"You have also said any person convicted in your court of any amount of illegal drugs will spend time in jail. You say, that because it is illegal, they must accept the consequences of their actions. You see I have made it a point to learn a little bit about the person whom I hold at least partially responsible for the death of my son."

"I have not changed my mind on that, either," Daise retorted, even more defiantly.

"I say it is time for you take some personal responsibility for your actions as well. Consider this to be my opening statement: I accuse you, judge Henry Daise, of irresponsible and unethical behavior—for considering the law to be more important than the person—legal technicalities more important than justice; specifically in the case of the State of Alaska versus Marshall Stuckrath! Will you speak in your defense or shall we get one of these citizens here to defend you? Is there anyone in this room who will rise to defend the accused?"

"I will speak for myself then, if you insist on going through with this charade. Let's get it over with." The judge sat back down, glaring at David.

"Don't be in too much of a hurry. None of us are going anywhere in this storm, and I see there is plenty of booze left still. I think we have the makings of a pretty fair jury of peers right here. I'm sorry to dispense with traditional jury selection, but as the good judge has previously pointed out, all citizens must perform their civic duty. Therefore none of you will be excused. In the case of my son, Marshall, there was no jury trial due to agreements between the prosecuting and defense attorneys based on plea bargaining, and saving all parties money and time. There will be no such bargains struck here today. All of you may vote as jurors, and any of you may question myself or Mr. Daise at any time. For that matter I will allow any discussion. Unlike the judge, I am interested in what you feel is ethical and just as citizens, not just the letter of the law. After all, both the law and state should serve the citizens, not vice versa."

The others in the room, seeing David's determination aptly enforced by Sam Thornton's muscle, took up their previous places.

"So you appoint yourself as judge and prosecutor. That hardly seems either legal or just," Daise sneered.

"Nevertheless, I will accept the decision of these jurors," David replied. "You see, I am not the least bit interested in the legality of this trial. I am interested in finding out if these people, some who know me and some who are strangers, feel that justice was served in my son's case and if not, how much personal responsibility you should take for his death," David replied.

"Our first question then, is whether or not Marshall's punishment suited his crime. First, for the benefit of those who are not familiar with the case, would someone like to describe his infraction, arrest, and trial?"

"I think I can sum it up pretty well," Mike volunteered. "I would like to designate myself as witness for the prosecution—um—I guess in this case that would be David here," he went on, warming to the occasion.

"You can go ahead and dispense with the legal

jargon, Mike, just tell these people what happened."

Mike looked slightly disappointed, but told the room what he knew from the newspaper reports and his talks with David and others; how Marshall was caught with a small amount of cocaine; how he was accused of a felony which was plea-bargained to a misdemeanor, then convicted and sentenced to do time in Lime River Correction Center, the state penitentiary in Juneau.

Thomas Wilson stood and raised his hand.

"The court recognizes juror Wilson," David spoke, and took a swig from his mug of ale.

"Uh... thank you. Was this his first offense?" Thomas asked.

"Go ahead and answer him, Mike," David directed.

"Yes, he had never been in any trouble with the law previously. He was a straight A student in high school, and a state champion wrestler. I knew the boy well and can speak to his character. He was a fine young man and had every prospect of developing into a good citizen," Mike replied.

"All this was taken into account when his charges were reduced to a misdemeanor. A repeat offender would have been charged and tried for a felony," Daise interjected.

"But what if the lawyers had not come to an agreement? Would he then have been tried for the felony?" Thomas Wilson insisted.

"That depends. The state generally goes for the maximum possible charge in order to have some maneuvering room before the case goes to trial, and to some degree it depends on how aggressively the district attorney chooses to prosecute the case," Daise replied.

"Ah, but you are being disingenuous. After my son was murdered I took it upon myself to do a little research into how drug possession cases were being handled in Alaska. The fact of the matter is that both in the case of my son and in similar cases the state does not reduce charges if the defense goes for a jury trial and chooses to plead not guilty. I don't know if this is policy, but it is the norm. We were told by our lawyer that the D.A. would not reduce charges unless we cooperated; that is, pleaded guilty and waived our right to a jury trial. In fact, the majority of drug defendants accept the plea bargain offers. But when they refuse they generally do get tried under their original charge, even if it is their first offense."

David pulled a small spiral notebook from his shirt pocket. From many years of practice David was as comfortable in front of a classroom as Daise was in the courtroom. Just as he would have for one of his history classes, David had spent some time preparing before joining Chuck's gathering. Now that he was speaking to an attentive room with his notes in hand, David's hands ceased shaking and his thoughts ordered themselves.

"I have here a list of cases tried by judge Daise over the past several years where a first time offender was tried, convicted, and sent to prison for possession of a scheduled drug. Some of these cases were young women. The Lime River facility was not even designed to hold women—they don't have enough space, so they just throw all the women together in one room for most activities. Hardened violent felons with the misdemeanor cases. I also have a list of similar cases where the defendants were found not guilty. The only ones found not guilty chose a jury trial. They had at least some chance that a jury might have some mercy or sense of justice. The people that went to jail chose to forgo a jury. So right away you can see having the money to mount a good defense plays heavily into the results. Justice indeed!"

"My question to the jury is this: Do you think it is fair to send any convicted first time drug possession offender to prison; and by prison I mean any lock down facility, but especially a facility where they are mixed in with violent offenders and habitual criminals? I would like to hear some comments or questions from the jury before we hear more from Daise," David continued.

"What a farce!" Daise exclaimed.

"Is it a farce to want to know what citizens think of your treatment of their children? Because in many cases these are young people, often just out of high school, or college aged—with their future before them. I say the laws themselves are the farce, but that is beside the point. There are any number of laws on the books that are not enforced, or used only to trip up criminals until more serious charges can be pinned on them. It is a judgement call when a cop arrests someone for possessing a drug. It is another judgement call when a prosecutor decides to pursue the case, and still another when a judge decides to throw the defendant into a penitentiary! In any case you are out of order. I ask you to refrain from any more comments until the jury members have spoken, otherwise I shall hold you in contempt of court!"

"You have no right!" Daise began.

At this David stepped up to the judge and grabbed his collar forcefully, twisting it hard and pulling the man towards him. The judge grabbed at his wrist trying to shake free, but David seemed possessed with an uncanny strength.

"I have the same right here as you do in your court! The right of superior force! If someone disrupts your court you have the bailiff haul them out, and you fine or jail them for contempt. Ultimately, you rule by force of arms! Power enforced by the state. Well, it is the same here. For the moment I rule in this room by force—by force of Sam's ample "arms" and by the force of my superior moral position! You will keep your mouth shut while the others speak or I will have the bailiff here (he motioned towards Sam) shut it for you! Do you understand?!" He let go the judge roughly, and Daise sat down abruptly, visibly shaken.

"Is there any one here who does not think I have the moral and ethical right—damn the legal right—to this trial? Did I not rescue Mr. Daise from almost certain death just last night? My son was killed as a result of his bad judgement only months ago. I ask you now: who in this room will stand by my right to proceed and who is against me?"

It had taken a huge effort of will not to smash his fist into the face of the judge. The feeling that he could actually assault another man was a novel experience for David, but there was no time to marvel at it.

John Treadwell was the first to speak. He was still agitated from his confrontation with Sam. A history of thirty years as an executive had not prepared him to take orders from other men. He had been born into a wealthy family with three generations before him of successful entrepreneurs. His contact with the rougher elements of society had been limited to three weeks of rowdiness in Amsterdam during one summer break early in his ivy league college career.

"I can understand your feelings Mr. Stuckrath. My wife and I raised three children of our own. I agree with you that your sons's imprisonment seems overly harsh, but you are going about this in the wrong way. The thing to do is to work through the system to get the laws changed. That is the best thing you can do to honor the memory of your son. What is all this going to accomplish, except to get you into trouble too?"

"Thank you sir. I appreciate your point of view, and when the time is right, I may take your advice. Anyone else?" David asked looking around the room.

"Fuck working within the system," Bill Craften said, rising from his seat. "The system itself is corrupt. The prison lobby is one of the best funded lobbies in the country. It's just business as usual. Big contractors build the jails, then they lobby the politicians to pass laws to fill them up so thousands of prison employees and their families depend on that income as jailers and maintenance people. The United States has the largest percentage of its people behind bars in the world, and a big percentage of them are there on drug charges, and haven't hurt anyone except maybe themselves. Most of those people are poor and black or brown. Meanwhile rapists, robbers, and violent criminals get short or suspended sentences. Grandparents have had their property taken away by the courts because of their grandkids getting busted in their homes with pot. It's no different than prohibition—and look how well that worked!"

"Well I think you are absolutely nuts," the younger Spencer spoke next.

He was an awkward looking man in is mid forties. His face seemed patched together like some dadaist sculpture—reminiscent of a Mr. Potato Head on which had been pasted an incongruous set of features—mouth too small for the nose, which jutted out at a sharp angle over a wisp of a mustache, and a large cleft chin that would only have worked on a more robust visage. He was bald except for a ring of graying hair around the back of his head and a small tuft precisely on the top of his otherwise shiny scalp.

"You're taking the law into your own hands here. You can't force someone to stay against their will and expect to get away with it! The law is the law! If you didn't like the judgement against your son why didn't you appeal? We have a legal system that isn't perfect, but it does work most of the time from what I have seen. You may still have options in civil court even now.

I don't need to hear another word to tell you I'll be voting for judge Daise, if vote I must in this ridiculous game you are forcing us to play!"

"I appreciate your candor," David replied.

"I want to say I totally disagree with my son on this," the elder Spencer said, standing slowly with the aid of his cane.

His face was deeply creased and all that remained on his age-spotted head were a few forlorn hairs like stubble from a harvested field. His shoulders were stooped and his voice weak and raspy, but his eyes were still clear and bright. Even at his great age he used glasses only for reading.

"A couple of days ago I turned ninety-two, so you see I've been around a little. I just want to say that if my son was ever injured or killed by anyone, I wouldn't stop at anything to punish 'em, unless it was an accident. Sometimes the only sane reaction to a wrong is vengeance. Otherwise it's just gonna eat away at you forever. As for your son's sentence—I think that was more of a crime than what he was arrested for. Well, that's about all I have to say, I guess." He sat back down carefully.

The younger Spencer looked at his father in amazement, wondering how well he really knew him, after all.

Chuck Riggs spoke next.

"I see my house has been commandeered whether I like it or not. I gotta say I don't much like the way you and Sam here—and even Mike, seem to be runnin' the show. I think you're asking too much from our friendship David, even though you know I sympathize with your loss. If the time comes that this affair goes to a real court I am going to be sad to have to be a witness against you. I don't want to see anything violent go down here. I saw enough of that during the war."

"Chuck, I've always had a great deal of respect for you, but in this case I do not give a fuck whether you testify against me some day or not, and I don't give a god damn what you think of my behavior here. So far I have not hurt anyone and I don't intend to. Sam is just as likely to thump me if I get carried away as he is anyone else. I'm not asking your opinion as a friend, but as a fellow citizen. You are avoiding the question, dammit!"

"Okay, okay, David. How would you like it if someone did this in your home? You wanna know what I think about your son? I think it's a crying shame. In the war lots of us, especially the pilots, used pep pills to stay alert. We drank booze we mixed up in fifty-five gallon drums when we couldn't get anything else—whatever we could do to get high and get our minds off the daily grind and the thought that we might be the next casualty. I think it is a crime your boy went to jail for doing something nearly all of us older folks have done—just like I think it's damn stupid the drinking age is twenty-one and a kid of eighteen can go fight for his country and die or get maimed, and not even go to a bar legally to have a drink. In other words, I think your son was treated unfairly pretty much all the way by the laws, but I also think judge Daise was doing his job properly, and that he can't be held in any way responsible for the laws he has sworn to enforce, or your son's death."

"Thank you Chuck—and I am truly sorry to have abused your hospitality, but there is a much bigger issue here—certainly greater than proper etiquette. Just who then do you think does bear responsibility for my son's death? Grant Tadlock only? The man who actually used the knife? Does anyone else have comments before judge Daise has his say? I want to remind you that you are deciding on whether or not Marshall's punishment was appropriate for his crime, regardless of the legal issues," David elaborated.

"You can't seriously expect judges and prosecutors to be held responsible for what happens in prisons. That is preposterous!" Jim Spencer insisted.

"May I say something?" Sharon Craften asked.

"Of course. This court would like to hear from every one of you," David answered.

"I can't believe what your family has been through. Your wife must be devastated. I wonder why she isn't here with you, or you with her. Someday I hope to have a child of my own, and..." She turned to her husband, who smiled and nodded at her. "I think I would run away if it happened to my child. I would take my child and just run—anywhere—someplace more civilized!"

She sat down abruptly. David felt a sudden rush of guilt and regret at Sharon's words, recalling Karen's wish to take Marshall to Canada. With an effort he continued.

"Thank you Sharon. Marshall was not the only casualty in our family. My marriage died that day too."

No one else spoke.

"All right then. Judge Daise, it's your turn," David said after a long pause.

"Thank you so much," the judge said contemptuously.

"I see some of you think you know better than the experts what does or does not work in the fight against drugs, and make no mistake about it—we are in an all-out war against drugs! It is my job as a judge to sentence those who are brought to trial and convicted through due process. It is true that I believe the only really effective deterrent to drug use and distribution is imprisonment. For that opinion I offer no apology. In the specific case of your son and in the general case of first time offenders I feel it is even more important, as there is some chance they may not re-offend if the sentence is stern enough. If a child runs out into the street do we stand on the corner and lecture him on the dangers of traffic? No! We run quickly out and grab the child, and perhaps administer a whack or two on the behind so that he will remember. We cannot afford to be lax in our fight against this social evil which continues to spread. I am proud of my previous record as a prosecutor, and equally proud of my record as a judge in this fight."

"You mean to tell the jurors gathered here you

think Marshall's sentence was totally appropriate?" David asked.

"For the record, these people held here under duress are in no sense jurors," the judge replied. "But yes, under the circumstances I believe his arrest, trial, and sentence were proper. His death was unfortunate, tragic, and unusual. It has been investigated, and the man responsible was convicted."

"That is partly true. The man who knifed my son, a habitual felon, was only convicted of illegally having a knife in jail. He served just ninety days for murdering my son!"

"Grant Tadlock did have a jury trial, and the jury determined it was self defense. Witnesses said your son attacked the man," Daise countered.

"Even if I believed that—which I don't for a minute—what in the hell was a young man with no criminal history doing locked up with men like that?"

"It is true that other jurisdictions have more facilities that make it easier to separate the violent from non-violent offenders. It is unfortunate Juneau and much of Alaska don't, but Im stuck with the system that we have."

"But you still don't get it, do you? In your capacity as judge that too should be taken into consideration! As a judge you are entrusted with just that responsibility—that is the fair, legal, and just imposition of sentencing. You have forgotten the part about 'fair and just,' and you only consider the legality and your own personal moral stance against drug use. You and your kind totally ignore the larger ramifications of what you do!" David exclaimed.

Thomas Wilson stood again.

"There is another part of this I haven't heard anyone talk about. Daise here thinks by throwing young offenders and casual drug users into the jaws of the legal system he can frighten them into becoming good law-abiding citizens. I don't think that is what actually happens. Most young people make friends and hang out with others in their peer group. If they are forced to spend long months in penitentiaries, drug treatment centers, and half-way houses they end up by making friends with and absorbing some of the values of more hardened criminals and addicts. Young people are especially impressionable, and their more cautious friends may avoid them after they become 'ex-cons,' while the people they meet who have less respect for the law will naturally be more accepting. So you are actually helping some young people learn more criminal behavior by locking them up for activities that huge percentages of adults have experimented and come to terms with, or discarded entirely. Statistics and common sense show most people who try drugs of any kind eventually give them up, or at least regulate their use so that they are able to function as otherwise productive and law-abiding citizens. This is true even of alcohol—the most addictive and damaging of all the drugs."

"That was quite a speech. What are you—some kind of expert?" the judge snapped.

"You don't have to be an expert. It's just common sense—something you appear to be short on!" Wilson retorted.

Conrad Slocum observed the proceedings closely, but said nothing. He understood and sympathized with David's anguish and his need to expose the hypocrisy of Daise and the system he served. His friend David had spent much of his adult life as a teacher in the public school system. Even in his grief and despair he still believed in the potential for people to learn from their mistakes, if only they could be made to see them. Conrad supposed David even now thought that some good might come of his son's death if only enough light could be shed on the event. Conrad had no such illusions. He knew the drug war for what it was; essentially an entrenched witch hunt that was so fully institutionalized it would probably take something akin to a revolution to change the laws significantly. As was the case before alcohol prohibition was repealed, the fact that millions of Americans still defied the drug laws just resulted in ever greater numbers of people going to prison, rather than a change in the laws.

When he left Seattle Conrad had no doubt as to how he would deal with the man who had killed Marshall, but he had not been sure about the judge, although he, like David believed him to be at least partially responsible for the boy's death. He began to realize as he watched the mock trial, that Daise's arrogant self-righteous attitude and complicity with the corrupt system from his position of power had ultimately led to

Marshall being placed into unnecessary danger. Conrad had made use of his intelligence gathering skills and the Agency data bases in researching Daise's past before he had cast off from the Seattle dock. He knew Daise had powerful friends in both state and federal government offices. He had a history of association with conservative politicians, although he was careful not to join any popular right wing organizations, knowing that would compromise his position as a supposedly impartial adjudicator. Daise had not been afraid to stand up to corporate pressure during the hearings after the Valdez oil spill. The man certainly had principles, and genuinely believed in his crusade against drug use.

Conrad had sailed north to Alaska with only one purpose; to determine who was responsible for Marshall's death and take his revenge. But he found himself still undecided about the judge. In spite of his arrogance there was no doubt the judge was an honest man—a man who stood by the law and his moral convictions—but also a man who could be inflexible and opaque where things might not be so clear cut. For the time being he resolved to observe and withhold judgement, at least until he knew the man better.

"Does anyone else have any comments or questions?" David asked, after Thomas Wilson had spoken.

The group was silent. Judge Daise seethed quietly at his seat.

"Okay, then, if no one has anything else to say it is time to hear the jury's verdict. All you have to do is write guilty or not guilty on a scrap of paper, and put it in this bowl," David said, holding aloft one of Chuck's serving bowls which had been emptied of its cracker contents.

"If you vote Henry Daise guilty you may also suggest an appropriate punishment. If you vote not guilty you may want to suggest a reasonable compensation based on what the judge had to endure this evening. Of course, you do not have to vote, but if you don't, you have no right to complain about the final verdict."

One by one they deposited torn up squares of notebook paper in the bowl. Only Conrad and Chuck abstained.

"Since you didn't vote, perhaps you could read the verdicts?" David asked Conrad.

Conrad read each slip in turn, and placed the guilty and not guilty verdicts in separate piles. Three of the guilty verdicts had suggested punishments. Two suggested removal from the bench, and another compensation to the Stuckrath family. One of the not guilty verdicts recommended that David Stuckrath pay the judge compensation and do jail time. The vote was five guilty versus three not guilty.

"It looks like the majority favor my point of view," David said.

"That may be true in this room, but it won't help you when you are on trial in Juneau," Daise said. He was not surprised at the vote.

"Every person in this room can expect a subpoena, and two of you can expect indictments in the very near future," he continued, pointing at David and Sam. "

May I leave now, or am I to be incarcerated here as well?"

"You are free to go," David answered. "I had hoped you might actually get some inkling of the attitudes and opinions of the people you purportedly serve. Maybe in the future you might consider mercy, as a possible alternative in your sentencing decisions. There is no reason to think the folks here are any different than the rest of our citizens."

Daise hurried out of the room without further acknowledging Stuckrath, not even stopping to zip his coat before he stepped out into the rainy darkness.

"I am truly sorry about your son, but it will not keep me from testifying against you if this goes to court. As a teacher I should think you would know better. It will serve you and your bully friend here right to spend some time in prison yourselves," John Treadwell lectured David as he put on his coat.

"John, it's not necessary—can we just get back to the boat?" Darlene tugged on her husband's arm as if she intended to drag him bodily out of the house.

"I must tell you this has been a most interesting and educational evening, Mr. Riggs," old Bob Spencer told Chuck. "I know it may not have been what you intended, but you have been a most gracious host, and this has been the highlight of my trip to Alaska so far."

"Well, it was definitely more excitement than

I'm used to, but thank you. Please feel free to drop by again tomorrow anytime," Chuck replied, shaking the older man's hand.

"Dad, I'm sure Mr. Riggs has had enough company and excitement for one night. We should be going."

The younger Spencer proffered his father's coat insistently.

"Now it has got to the point that I'm taking orders from my son. How far we fall," the old man protested, but he put on his coat, hesitating once again on his way out to address David.

"I want to shake your hand too before I leave. You are a courageous man. No doubt that vindictive ass of a judge will make it a point to haul you into court. I have seen his kind more than once over the years. Those people are everywhere and in every time. I've had a couple of run-ins with that sort myself, but I've outlasted 'em, and you will too by God! Yes, I think you will too! Don't give up the fight. Don't ever give it up! I'm sorry about your son, but the best way to honor him is to fight people like that judge every way you can."

While his dad spoke the younger Spencer, who had voted in favor of the judge, kept his eyes to the floor, waiting impatiently for his father to finish. Although he loved and enjoyed spending time with him, especially knowing each day could be his father's last, he had learned over the years to avoid certain social and political topics. He had often wondered how they could be so far apart on so many issues, but he respected his father's opinions even while he refused to be swayed by them.

In the bustle and confusion at the end of the gathering Conrad slipped out of the door without saying good bye to any of the guests or the host, and headed back down the muddy trail that led to the wharf where the visiting boats were secured. The trail and dock were saturated and mud-slick. Conrad slid, caught himself, and realized he was a little drunk. He stopped at the *Legal Eagle* and knocked loudly on the fiberglass hull.

"Oh, it's you. I thought maybe the lynch mob had come for me," the judge said after opening the cabin door. "Come on in out of the rain."

"Thanks, but I don't want to track mud into your boat. I just wanted you to know that if the weather is decent, I plan to leave for Wrangell in the morning, and you are welcome aboard if you wish. I'm on my way to Juneau as well, but I will be overnighting in Wrangell. We should be there in plenty of time for you to catch a flight."

"That is a generous offer. I had planned on radioing Thorne Bay tomorrow, but who knows how soon they could pick me up anyway. Thank you. I accept your offer Mr.—I don't think we were introduced, were we?"

The judge extended his hand.

"Conrad Slocum. I expect my crew to call me by my first name, or captain. Mine is the sailboat at the end of the dock," Conrad said, taking the judge's hand.

"Oh yes, a salty looking vessel if ever I saw one. Looks like she could sail the seven seas. What is your home port?"

"I'm up from Seattle. This is my first trip to Alaska," he lied. "It will be nice to have someone aboard with local knowledge. I'm a pretty early riser. How do you feel about casting off at six in the morning?"

"The sooner I get out of this place the better," the judge said. "I'll be ready to go."

"Fine. Then we'll head out with the tide. I suspect it will be a pretty fast passage north, with a good following breeze."

"The sooner I get back to Juneau the better. I wish I had never left," the judge said.

Conrad made his way carefully along the slippery dock and back to his boat. The tide was out, and the exposed beach smelled of rotting fish and kelp. He heard a splashing in the water close by, but could not make out its cause in the darkness. *Probably a spawned-out salmon,* he thought. He paused on the dock before stepping aboard his boat. The storm had finally blown itself out. A light drizzle remained, and glimpses of the stars and moon could now be seen through the gaps in the dispersing clouds. With no artificial lighting to detract from the display the stars seemed preternaturally sharp and bright against their bituminous backdrop. Conrad stood for a moment and took in the spectacle before sliding back the hatch cover and stepping down the companionway ladder into *Tisiphone's* cabin.

CHAPTER 14

Conrad And The Judge

The *Tisiphone*, with its crew of two was making nearly eight knots up Clarence Strait, aided by a favorable wind and tide. A short steep chop remained from the storm, but the heavy cutter hardly noticed the waves as she flew along. To the south the sky had finally cleared. The new frontal system had pushed the band of dark nimbus away to the northern horizon. Not another vessel was in sight the length and breadth of the strait. Barely visible some thirty miles south, the channel widened where the waters of Behm Canal, another deep glacier-cut fjord, joined with Clarence Strait before merging with the Pacific Ocean at Dixon Entrance. Even farther south was Ketchikan, about fifty miles from Spruce Cove—a good day's run. The only other settlements in the area were Thorne Bay, a logging and fishing town of some five hundred souls across the strait on Prince of Wales Island a dozen miles southwest of their position, and even tinier Coffman Cove, also on the opposite side of Clarence Strait, about fifteen miles to northwest. The residents of Spruce Cove sometimes bought fuel and groceries at Thorne Bay, although Ketchikan or

Wrangell with their greater amenities were normally the first choices. The fishing town of Wrangell, which was Conrad Slocum's and the judge's goal was a good day's sail northeast from Spruce Cove, even with favorable conditions.

At the helm Conrad gazed north to the steep cliffs of Zarembo Island in the distance and thought of the Spanish and Russian explorers who had reconnoitered the area even before Vancouver charted it for the British Empire. Not much had changed since those rugged men had first explored the archipelago in the latter half of the eighteenth century. There were few roads, and the population was probably less now than at its peak in the early eighteenth century, before the outbreaks of smallpox, complements of those same explorers, had decimated the native settlements. The modern descendants of the original native inhabitants, like the more recent interlopers, had removed to a handful of towns. Much of the vast area remained unpopulated, including many of the islands and most of the mainland.

The Tlingit and their ancestors had occupied this area for thousands of years, but the first Europeans to explore Clarence Strait and vicinity were the Spanish in a series of voyages originating from San Blas Mexico, starting in the late eighteenth century, although a recent publication by a Canadian researcher suggested Sir Frances Drake might have explored the region as far north as Chatham Strait during his circumnavigation two hundred years earlier.

The Spanish voyages were inspired by the fear

that the Russians and the English were infringing on Spanish territory, which according to the division of the New World by the Catholic church in 1494, they were. Although the Spanish explored the area they had not had the resources to colonize or otherwise exert any control over the territories north of their outposts in California, having by that time overextended themselves in Mexico and South America.

The Russians, who had been well entrenched in the Aleutian Islands and on parts of the Alaskan mainland since the 1740s following the Vitus Bering expeditions, established a colony near present day Sitka in 1784. They were the first westerners to encounter the Tlingit, who unlike the unfortunate Aleut, proved to be more than a match for the fur traders, and forcefully resisted Russian incursions, eventually coming to trading agreements and restrictions which were beneficial to both parties.

The town of Wrangell was founded early in the next century as a Russian fort in an unsuccessful effort to keep the English of Hudson's Bay Company from competing in the lucrative fur trade, but the Russian American company ultimately found it was more profitable to trade than fight with the more efficient English, and the fort changed hands. The local Stikine Tlingit protested, but after the devastating small pox epidemics of 1836 and 1840 there were not many left to complain. By 1849 the sea otters were gone, and the fort was abandoned until the Americans built a post there in 1868, after having purchased "Seward's Folly" from the Russians the year before.

Many of the place names in Southeast Alaska were derived from charts made by the early explorers—tough, able seamen like Valdez, Quadra, Hezeta, and Caamano. In many cases Cook, Vancouver, and later explorers simply adapted the early Spanish charts and kept the names, but just as often they gave their own names to the local features, honoring powerful patrons, government officials, or officers from their own crews. Clarence Strait had originally been called "Canal de Nuestra Señora del Carmen,"or Channel of Our Lady of the Carmel, by captain Jacinto Caamano after his ship of the same name, in which he had explored the area in 1792, noting that it was an area of "very strong currents." Other islands and features in the region were given Spanish names that had also stuck. Revillagigedo Island and Channel to the east; Caamano Point to the south; and Zarembo Island to the north of the Cleveland Penisula were only a few of the examples from the early voyages of the Spanish explorers.

The Russians, Spanish, French, English, and Americans had each added their labels to charts which detailed the myriad of islands and maze of channels and fjords of the area. This polyglot collection reflected the convoluted history and constantly changing alignments of the various peoples who had settled or visited here over the past three centuries. Conrad could not help but notice the charts reflected a certain Western bias. While many Native American names had been retained for smaller geographic features, most of the major islands and fjords detailed on Conrad's charts had English, Spanish, or Russian labels.

The NOAA charts which Conrad relied on for navigation gave him the feeling he was sailing through some sort of limbo where nationality was indeterminate and irrelevant. Conrad could imagine a Tlingit native of the late nineteenth century being bewildered by the changing expectations of the succeeding governments; their regulations, laws, and idiosyncrasies. Why should they respect the rules of the current regime any more than the Russians, English, or Spanish who had come before? Perhaps they bided their time still, knowing that this too would pass. Even now, the general population of Southeast Alaska had declined from its peak in the early twentieth century, and only the native population, after its precipitous fall during the eighteenth and nineteenth centuries, was actually increasing. In such a place, Conrad considered, the only true moral compass might be the individual or tribal conscience.

These reflections were intensified by the moral dilemma presented by the presence of judge Henry Daise aboard. After having listened to the man defend himself the day before there was no doubt in Conrad's mind that the judge was wrong in his approach to interpreting and enforcing the laws concerning non-violent drug offenders, and was partially responsible for Marshall's death. It angered him that such men held power all over the nation—a country that contained some five per cent of the world's population yet held twenty-five per cent of the world's prisoners, according to one estimate he was aware of.

But what to do about the judge, if anything? David had opted for exposing the man's hubris to the handful of people at Spruce Cove, and Conrad hoped his old friend would have the will and means to make his opinions more public, but he doubted that it would have much effect on the lawmakers, courts, or public opinion in Alaska. A reactionary administration had gained control in the state, and the prosecution of drug users was big business here as in the rest of the nation. The one thing Conrad knew was that he did not want David to take any sort of action which would result in more suffering for him or his remaining family. He was aware that a man holding such grief and rage within himself was capable of just about anything, for his and David's loss was much the same. He no longer knew David well enough to predict his actions.

Would he be satisfied with his limited public exposure of Daise at Spruce Cove, or would he press matters even further?

Conrad's original reason for this voyage north was to avenge his son's death, and to that end he had acquired all the information he could about Marshall's killer, Grant Tadlock, and the events leading up to the murder, but the Spruce Cove experience had been unexpected, and he now had a second goal; he must protect David from any retribution the judge might have in mind as retaliation for his humiliation at the Spruce Cove gathering. This trip was his only chance to convince the judge not to take legal action against his friend, and it was the reason he had invited Daise aboard. No matter what, Conrad simply could not let the judge subject David or his family to any more torment. David had already been through enough.

Conrad had found some of the judge's arguments persuasive, but only if he accepted certain assumptions—assumptions based on a false morality and ignorance of or disdain for the scientific research on historical patterns of drug use. When greater damage to an individual, a family, and a community was caused by the laws and punishment for the crime than by the criminal activity itself, the furies—those ancient attendants to true justice, would inevitably be unleashed in some form.

Conrad, though an atheist and skeptic since his youth believed there existed certain balancing forces in the world and society, and that the classical Greeks had come the closest to describing these implacable powers metaphorically in the mythologies of their multiple gods and demigods. If the outcome of his voyage, like Odysseus', be ruled by a combination of the manipulations of the gods and fates in tandem with his own cunning and resourcefulness, then so be it. He could not imagine a better theater or a more appropriate setting. The land and waters too would surely have their part to play in these matters, and any one of the dozens of ice-capped peaks surrounding him might be the northwestern outpost of an Olympian pantheon. Surely the crafty Raven of the native Na-Dene speakers was the local incarnation of the wily Hermes, trickster and mediator between the gods and men.

Conrad was roused from these reflections by the voice of judge Daise.

"That's Burnett Inlet over there. ...used to be a cannery there years ago—now it's a fish hatchery. Our history in a nutshell. The sad fact is the salmon runs have been so reduced even up here that the hatcheries are necessary," Daise said, pointing out the entrance to a narrow fjord off their starboard side.

He had said little so far on the voyage, only commenting on a few of the better fishing areas and the spot near Onslow Island where his engine had failed two days earlier. They were two hours north of Spruce Cove, abreast of the large bay on Etolin Island from which radiated three narrow inlets. Mountains, heavily forested on their lower slopes, rose steeply three thousand feet from the narrow driftwood strewn beaches.

"I don't know why I didn't head to port earlier, way before my engine quit. Fishing wasn't any good anyway. I guess I was just too stubborn to quit without at least one fish in the icebox. What started badly ended badly," Daise continued.

"It could have been a whole lot worse," Conrad replied.

They sat opposite each other in the small cockpit, knees nearly touching. Conrad kept his eyes on the sails and steered a careful course. He was sailing wing on wing, with the huge mainsail out to the starboard and the number two jib to port. The wind was becoming gusty, and Conrad knew he should fasten a preventer—a restraining line, to the massive main boom to protect against a sudden jibe.

"I noticed you and Chuck Riggs were the only two who didn't vote yesterday. I am pretty sure Riggs was undecided, or even on my side of the fence, but I wonder what you thought of all that?"

This was the first mention Daise had made of the events at Chuck's house the day before, and his sudden segue caught Conrad off guard.

"Being a stranger, I didn't feel like I knew enough about things to take a position," Conrad answered, noncommittally.

"Well, I'm just very glad to get out of Spruce Cove," the judge said, shaking his head. "I was beginning to wonder if I was going to make it out of there in one piece."

"It does seem like a couple of those people are not too happy with you."

He had no wish to reveal his impressions or opinions, which in any case were still not fully formed, to the judge, but he wanted to find out if the man still intended to go after David when he returned to Juneau.

"It goes with the job. I get threats sometimes from people who don't like my decisions, but I have to admit I have never felt in any real danger before this. You would think Stuckrath would have learned something from the loss of his son, but perhaps the father was the source of the son's disdain for the law."

"Do you think so? I got the impression he was

just a very distraught father at the end of his rope. My understanding is that he was a respected high school teacher. Does he have a criminal record?"

Conrad was used to dissembling. It was an essential skill in his line of work. Even so, he fought to hold back the wave of emotion. The sea itself seemed to sense his mood. They passed through a line of dirty foam mixed with flotsam which marked the meeting of two opposing currents generated by the changing tide. Conrad felt the increased pressure on the tiller and a sudden loss of momentum as they entered the area of turbulence.

The judge did not seem to notice the change in sea-state, but continued with even more vehemence his diatribe against David Stuckrath.

"It does not matter whether he has ever been in trouble with the law before, or if he is well-respected. Just because he has experienced the tragedy of losing his son does not give him the right to break the law. I can understand his distress, but kidnapping is a felony! I imagine he will have a few months to ponder his actions at Lime River himself."

"So you intend to press charges on Stuckrath? Why not just write it off and let the man go his way? I think calling what he did kidnapping is a bit of a stretch. After all, he didn't harm you physically, and I doubt he will ever bother you again. The man may have used poor judgement, and perhaps he was drinking to excess, but he is after all still in mourning for the loss of his only son."

Conrad had reached the limit of his patience with this line of their conversation, and had no desire to hear anything more from the man. It was clear the judge had every intention of following through on his earlier threats. He now realized that judge Daise might be a more pressing problem than Grant Tadlock. At least Tadlock had no designs on the rest of the Stuckrath family, and David himself seemed to regard Marshall's actual murderer as less culpable than the judge and the legal system he served.

"You are missing the point. No one is above the law! What if everyone who lost a court case abducted the trial judge? Chaos! Anarchy! Stuckrath and everyone else who helped him yesterday—especially that damned Sam Thornton—have committed crimes, and I intend to see them all in court!"

"Are you really interested in justice, or just getting even for the injury to your vanity? Or are you so far removed from the reality of human relations that you think every dispute between people must be settled by some legal means?" Conrad shot back.

As he spoke Conrad leaned in closer to the judge. His challenge was intimate and unmistakable.

"So I see it now—you're on their side too!" Daise replied, recoiling.

"I was wondering why you did nothing to help me at Chuck's house. You just watched that whole circus without so much as a comment. I thought when you offered me this ride to Wrangell you might be sympathetic, but I see I was mistaken."

Daise stood up quickly with the idea of going forward to put some distance between himself and Slocum. He regretted accepting the offer of transportation and wished he had chartered a faster boat or float plane to take him to Wrangell. The additional money would have been well spent. Now he was faced with several more unpleasant hours trapped on a thirty-eight foot boat with this obviously hostile stranger.

"Maybe you should just take me across to Thorne Bay and I can charter a floatplane," he said petulantly.

"It's not on my itinerary," Conrad retorted.

The judge, who had been looking intently across the strait trying to pick out the entrance to Thorne Bay, turned quickly to face Conrad, but at that moment there was a great gust of wind, and in the same instant the tiller slipped from Conrad's grip. The heavy main boom, nearly twenty feet of dense old-growth Douglas Fir, swung abruptly across the cockpit, catching the judge on the bridge of his nose, and knocking him overboard into the chill waters of Clarence Strait.

Conrad was busy for some minutes as he turned the boat, coming up into the wind, tacking, and bearing off again, being careful not to lose sight of the man during the maneuvers. In the process his boat described a rough figure eight of the area where Daise had gone in. It was the standard by-the-book maneuver for a boat under sail in a man overboard emergency. Up until Daise's last tirade he had hoped he could persuade—either by force of argument, threat, or any other means at his disposal—the judge to give up his idea of going after David. But the lubberly way Daise had stood up without regard for the dangerous possibility of a jibe, the fortuitous gust of wind at just that moment, and his momentary loss of control of the tiller had conspired together against the man.

Conrad had not consciously let loose of the tiller. Even years later he could never resolve to his satisfaction whether his action had been accidental or intentional. His loss of steering control had been unplanned and involuntary. Some other more primitive part of his brain had sent the electrical impulse to his muscles, causing the spasm which had released the tiller. Now that the deed was done he must either rescue Daise quickly, before hypothermia finished him, and convince the man the jibe had been an accident, or make sure he did not survive to reach the shore of Etolin Island. If he did nothing at all the odds were Daise would succumb quickly in the cold water, but there was always a chance he might make it to the shore, and live to tell his tale.

Stunned but still conscious, and lacking a life jacket, Henry Daise had just enough awareness to thrash out towards the sailboat, which he could make out only intermittently as the frigid waves washed over him in succession. Through the blood and salt water burning his eyes he strained to make out the vessel as it turned, heading back towards him. He felt his legs and arms begin to grow heavy. Desperately, he tried to concentrate on inhaling during the brief instants when his head was not submerged. Daise had spent many years boating and fishing in Alaskan waters. He knew he had but a few minutes of consciousness left at best in this cold sea, and without flotation that narrow window of survival would be even more limited. He must focus on keeping his arms and legs in motion, but the numbness was creeping ever closer to his core.

All his adult life Henry Daise had been a nominal Christian—a Presbyterian who attended services dutifully on Easter and Christmas, had his three children properly baptized, and generally considered himself a true but not fanatical believer. But now he begged with all the passion and intensity he could muster, praying with each exhaled breath to the deity for the strength to keep going. He saw salvation coming for him in the form of the gleaming white hull of the Ingrid cutter—if only he could stay above the water a few more seconds! He saw the name of the boat on the bow as it angled toward him, *Tisiphone*, it read. His mind fixated on the name as he struggled to remain conscious. It was from Greek mythology he recalled, perhaps a god, but which one? And then, in a sudden flash, he remembered. He had time only for an instant of horror as the cutter bore down, pressing him beneath its heavy lead keel.

Conrad dared not remain long in an area frequented by commercial fishermen, tour ships, and pleasure boaters. Still, he had to make certain no trace of the man remained, so he took the time to circle once more before turning north again on his original course. He scanned Clarence Strait, but fortunately there were still no boats visible in any direction. He decided to wait until the turn into Stikine Strait a couple of hours north to call the Coast Guard. They would waste a lot of time searching the waters between Etolin and Zarembo islands, and perhaps the judge's body would never be found. He did not think there was any way they could connect him with any possible motive for killing the judge, and any reasonable story he made up about how the man died would be impossible to disprove with no witnesses. But there were always unexpected risks, as he knew from his many years of work for the Agency.

He could be connected to David if it occurred to any investigator to do a little research. A little digging would show they had been acquainted since the early nineteen seventies, and a search of phone and postal records would certainly confirm the connection, but to any observer it would seem a casual relationship made up of only seasonal letters and occasional phone calls. The only thing that really concerned him was how much the people he worked for actually knew about his relationship to the Stuckraths, and how much cooperation they would give to the Alaskan authorities if he became a suspect. It was always risky to second-guess the actions and motives of the organization which employed him. Agents were frequently tailed on their time off. He had been assigned such duty himself in the past. The department made it their business to know as much as they could about the private lives of their employees, and this information was put to use in various ways to ensure the fealty of the vassal operatives.

There was always the chance they knew of his affair with Karen so many years ago, but he doubted they would suspect he was the father of Marshall. Conrad and Karen had been careful over the years to never so much as allude to that fact in the course of their correspondence. If anyone at the Agency did know of their connection that information was probably buried in some file or computer hard drive. Most likely whoever's job it was to keep tabs on him (Richard Head at the very least) was unaware of the true nature of his relationship to the Stuckrath family. On the other hand he knew his immediate supervisor would probably jump at any chance to discredit him or make his life uncomfortable, and he imagined supervisor Head would thoroughly enjoy watching him squirm under the scrutiny of any local investigation, for whatever reason.

Most importantly, he must not let this incident jeopardize his ultimate aim, dealing with Grant Tadlock. He meant to finish what he had come so far north to do. Although he was now responsible for the death of the judge, he honestly did not know that if given the same circumstances he would react again in the same way, but regardless he did not regret the outcome or his part in it. Conrad circled the area for the last time. There was no sign of judge Henry Daise.

CHAPTER 15

The Catamount

It had been weeks since the young mountain lion had eaten his fill. After being harried out of his original home range by an older and more dominant male the cat had wandered far in search of prey and freedom from molestation. Twice he had hunted successfully, and both times driven from his feast; first by a pack of wolves, and again by an aggressive she-bear with two hungry cubs in tow. Desperation had forced the animal all the way to the end of Cleveland Peninsula. But there too was no respite. Not long after Conrad's serendipitous surveillance of the cougar at its successful hunt, and well before it could finish gorging itself to complete satiation, the unfortunate cat was forced off its prize yet again. An older black boar, having caught the scent of the fresh kill, claimed the carcass for its own. The cat growled and rushed the interloper, but the experienced old bear refused to back down. It was no contest. The much lighter cougar, though quicker, could not risk being caught by a swipe from the lethal paws of the burly bruin.

The catamount retraced his steps the length of

Cleveland Peninsula, heading generally northeast until he once again reached the mouth of a familiar river. It was the same river he had followed down from the interior to the coast. He paced the shore uneasily until at last he made his decision. He could not go back to the place of his birth, and the familiar scents and sights of the river only increased his unease.

He traveled for three more days and nights, sleeping when he felt secure enough, and taking long detours when he encountered signs of human activity or felt threatened by the close presence of bears or dogs. He crossed several thickly forested ranges and swam three stretches of water in a route that trended first north then west—up the rugged mainland shores to Dry Strait, and across Mitkof and Kuprenof islands. Finally, after swimming the few yards of narrow Keku Strait to the even more isolated Kuiu Island, he sensed he had found the territory he had been searching for.

The new place was thick with deer. Their scat and scent were everywhere. But the black bear were here in numbers too. Still, within hours of arriving he made his first kill on the island—a late-born immature animal that he surprised hiding in a thicket. After opening the gut cavity with almost surgical skill, he removed the stomach and intestines and drug them away from the carcass. Those organs were food fit only for scavengers. He began his feed with the heart, liver, and lungs, the most nutritious parts of the animal. Again he was driven off his kill before he could devour the hindquarters, or hide the remains for another feed upon the slightly less desirable parts of the carcass. No matter, he had eaten enough to satisfy his requirements for several days if need be. The organs in the chest cavity contained the most protein and fat and the essential amino acids he needed to maintain his health and lean muscular form. The local bears were less particular in their eating habits, and had no need to rely on deer as did the cougar. Their nutritional needs were largely met by the spawning salmon and abundant berries this time of the year. Even grubs and beach grass were consumed with gusto. The more abbreviated gut of the mountain lion, like most cats, was more specialized.

Gradually, taking his time to get acquainted with his new hunting grounds, the ever more confident cougar worked his way south to the Tebenkof Bay Wilderness, a complex network of inlets, coves, and islets abounding with game. A small pack of wolves roamed the area, as well as several black bear, but there was plenty of prey for all, and he had no difficulty avoiding the other predators, who for their part paid him little heed.

Kuiu Island comprised seven hundred and fifty square miles of wilderness—virgin forest, mountains, and extensive wetlands dissected by dozens of fjords and coves—a lush land larger than Maui or Rhodes. It was a puma paradise but for one thing—the lack of a prospective mate—for he was the only one of his kind on the entire island.

CHAPTER 16

Three Friends

David awakened the morning after the events at Chuck Riggs' house with an aching head and a parched mouth. Coffee—lots of it and strong, would be necessary. He slid the companionway door back, took a deep breath of the crisp morning air, and surveyed the quiet harbor. To his surprise, the *Tisiphone* was gone.

As he fumbled foggy-brained with the coffee implements he reflected morosely on his family's long love/hate relationship with alcohol. On his father's side the tendency was to long periods of moderate consumption punctuated by periodic binges, followed with the inevitable morning regrets and bleak vows to never again—this pattern often lasting an entire lifetime, but never really interfering with work, or resulting in anything too catastrophic. On his mother's side the family history was either toward absolute teetotaling abstinence, or the opposite—lives and relationships sacrificed to Bacchus. He resolved again to moderate his intake in the future, and in coming to that resolution he became aware that for the first time in months he could contemplate the idea of a future. The events of the previous day had accomplished a needed catharsis, and it slowly dawned on him as he nursed his hangover that he might still find purpose and reason to continue.

I am an idiot—old enough to remember when Crayola changed their flesh color to peach, but still too stupid to avoid a hangover. Age and experience do not always confer wisdom, he reflected ruefully, cursing as he spilled coffee grounds onto the small counter and cabin sole.

Still, even in the grips of his metabolic misery he felt uncharacteristically cheerful, and more like his old self than he had in months. This feeling, he recognized, owed itself mostly to the events of the previous day. At the very least his actions at Chuck's house, no matter what the consequences—and he was sure there would be repercussions—had achieved some sort of beneficial expiation, or at least a purging. Whatever the case, and in spite of his throbbing head, David for the first time since his son's death actually looked forward with anticipation to the new day. He was conscious of his new attitude, and marveled at it.

Reflecting further he came to the conclusion that there seemed to be two kinds of human existence; a generally healthful and happy life punctuated with the inevitable episodes of pain and loss, which are part of the human condition; or a life of more-or-less constant suffering with infrequent and fleeting moments of joy. He realized his life had been an example of the former, and that he still had his good health, a daughter, adequate financial resources, and a future much brighter than many in spite of his loss.

David was constitutionally unable to remain forever in the sort of deep pit of despair that had overcome him the last several months, even after experiencing such a devastating event. His period of blackest mourning had finally come to an end.

Contemplating yesterday's events, he thought it odd that after so long without any contact Conrad should choose to leave without a parting conversation, or even a goodbye. His behavior at the gathering the day before had also been peculiar, David reflected. But of course if he was on assignment his duties must have taken him away, he reasoned, and likewise a secret mission would explain his wish to hide their relationship, as he had all but admitted.

Later that morning, when Mike dropped in to see how he fared and David heard from him that judge Daise had left with Conrad, he thought Conrad's conduct even more baffling.

"Your old friend wasn't very supportive at Chuck's yesterday. He buttonholed me before I went to Chuck's place and asked me to pretend we were not acquainted—why I can only imagine," Mike commented.

"Well, I can only tell you he works for one of the government's intelligence gathering departments," David replied. "I'm sure that means he needs to keep a low profile."

"That's pretty vague. You mean the FBI or CIA?" Mike pressed.

"I have no idea. In all the years we have been

acquainted he has never told me. I doubt it is an acronym we have ever heard of. I think I told you we met way back when I was in Peace Corps—right out of college. I have to admit I just cannot understand why he would offer to take Daise north after everything that went down yesterday."

"Maybe Daise has information about, or is somehow connected with whatever it is he is investigating up here, assuming he is some sort of a secret agent," Mike speculated.

"I suppose that makes some sense. I haven't had much contact with Conrad for years anyway. I guess I don't really know him anymore, only the memory of who he was twenty-five years ago."

After Mike left, David spent much of the day organizing his large collection of charts, and planning his route south from Spruce Cove. He joined Sam and Mike aboard Sam's fishing boat for a protein-rich dinner of crab and salmon that evening. Having made up his mind to cut back on his drinking, and in spite of the protests of his friends, he excused himself early and went back to his boat. That night he fell asleep early, with the soothing sounds of Bach playing on his stereo and a dog-eared old 1960's pocket edition paperback of Durrell's "Justine" as his companion.

The following day two crew members from the *Acushnet*, a Coast Guard Cutter stationed in Ketchikan, arrived and informed the little community and visitors of the death of judge Henry Daise. They spent several hours interviewing the residents and visitors. The two men, an officer and younger cadet, said little but took copious notes, barely registering surprise at the novelty of the descriptions of the mock trial of the judge. By an unspoken understanding Mike, Sam, and David did not bring up David's relationship with Conrad Slocum.

Later the same evening the three men gathered together for drinks and a game of cards in David's sailboat. David started the water boiling for coffee, and set out his last bottle of Irish whisky. He inserted a mixed tape of some of his favorite rock and pop songs into the cassette player, turning the volume down low so it did not distract, but provided a pleasant background for their game and conversation.

"I didn't know you were such a cardsharp, David. Maybe I'm outta my league," Sam teased after David's deal.

"Yeah, I'm thinking about heading to Las Vegas. No reason to slave away teaching history anymore," David riposted.

"I'll take three cards," Mike said. "What would you have done if you had not had that winning hand at Chuck's place?"

"Two for me," Sam interjected.

David took three cards and rearranged his hand while he pondered his response.

"You know, I'm really not sure. Maybe I would have just left the party and gone back to my boat. It seemed somehow like chance, or fate, or whatever you want to call it had to make the ultimate decision. Most of my life seems out of my control these days. I used to think I was in charge, but not anymore. I don't know if I could have mustered up the courage to have confronted Daise without that four of a kind."

"I had your back no matter what," Sam said.

"Yes, and I'll always be grateful to you for that."

"You've got to roll me," the backing vocals insisted as the refrain of The Rolling Stones', "Tumbling Dice," faded away while they finished their first hand.

Mike gathered up the cards. It was his turn to deal.

The opening riffs of "Don't Fear The Reaper" drifted out of the small bulkhead-mounted speakers.

"Well, that son-of-a-bitch is dead now regardless—rest his soul," Sam said, as Mike dealt out the next hand.

"Do you think it was really an accident?" Mike asked, carefully arranging his cards. He clenched his pipe between his teeth as he spoke, and a thin curl of smoke wafted upwards a short distance before it dissipated in a stray air current.

David studied his hand and put two cards down before responding.

"I've been thinking about that too. Like I said before—it's been many years since I spent any amount of time with Conrad. Even back in the seventies when we were thrown together in Kabul he was always a bit of a mystery. I think he is capable of it, but I don't think of him as a very close friend anymore, and I doubt he sees me that way—so what reason would he have to kill him?

—I mean, even assuming he would kill to avenge a friend's injury? As far as I know Conrad had not even met the judge before, so I can't imagine why he would want to harm him."

David thought back to a particular night many years earlier in Kabul. He remembered vividly how Conrad had immediately chased after a young radical Islamist who had attacked an unveiled Afghan woman in their company. He recalled that when he had later questioned Conrad about the outcome, his friend had been evasive, only saying that the situation was in hand, and that there was nothing to worry about. He decided to keep this incident to himself. For some reason that he could not quite define, it made him uneasy to talk about Conrad Slocum, even in the company of two of his closest confidants.

"Maybe old Daise's luck just finally ran out. The near thing out on Clarence Strait before you rescued him. The cards at Chuck's house. And his final boat ride. Bad things come in threes they say," Sam commented. "Two cards again for me, if you don't mind."

"Or maybe he had it coming. What did the the Greeks call it—hubris? The man was an arrogant bastard, may he rest in peace," Mike replied, forming an exaggerated cross with his free hand.

"Well, as Mr. Eastwood so eloquently put it; "we've all got it coming,"" David countered.

"I think around here the Tlingit spirits or even the old Nordic gods hold sway, not the Greeks. Maybe Njörđr or the Kooshtakaa had something to do with it,"

Sam suggested.

"Poor Sam—your mythology is so confused—comes from having such a mongrel background I suppose. How many people can say their relations include Tlingit, Norwegian, Aleut, Russian, and Hawaiian ancestors. I suppose next you will suggest that Pele had something to do with Daise's misfortunes."

Mike was one of the few people close enough to Sam who could get away with such a taunt. He had known Sam nearly as long as he had been acquainted with David. He had crewed for several seasons on Sam's fishing boat, remodeled Sam's old Petersburg house, and posted bail for him on two occasions.

"Actually, you're the one that has your mythology wrong. It would be Nāmaka, sister of Pele. Pele rules over volcanos and lightning, Nāmaka is the sea goddess," Sam retorted. "And as for mongrels—at least I'm not the offspring of a series of whisky-addled Irishmen and their rum-swilling British slaver cousins."

"You have me there Sam. It's true my ancestors were mostly a bunch of reprobates, and I guess the apple does not fall far from the tree. I suppose we will all be comfortable together in one of Dante's lower circles or the pagan equivalent when the time comes. Reminds me, I could use another shot of that whiskey. ... and I will have the last word with this hand!"

Mike slapped his cards down on the little galley table. He had a full house to Sam's pair and David's three of a kind.

"Read 'em and weep gentlemen," he pronounced, and swept up the small pile of change.

The men played, talked, and drank until well past midnight before Mike and Sam went back to their respective boats. David had limited himself to nursing three watered whiskeys the entire night. For only the second time in many weeks he went to bed sober. But even at the late hour he did not fall immediately to sleep. His feelings about the death of Daise were ambivalent. On the one hand, he mused, there was at least a chance the empty judge's chair might now be filled with an adjudicator of more humane temperament. More immediately, he and Sam Thornton were no longer likely to be called on to defend their actions at Chuck Riggs' house. Chuck would rather forget it ever happened, and he doubted the Treadwells, who were on vacation and not Alaskan residents, would go to the trouble to bring suit.

On the other hand, the catharsis he had experienced from the holding his own sort of tribunal had given David a new sense of direction, or at least a budding feeling of purpose. He had accepted and even looked forward to the idea of courtroom confrontation with the judge, and had begun to form a plan of action; a plan that would have garnered the greatest possible public exposure for the case, and would have given him and others a chance to air their arguments against the drug war in the most public of forums. Now this was not to be. He would have to find another strategy to bring attention to the ways the drug inquisition was damaging families and society.

He fell asleep finally as the faint outlines of a new plan began to form in his mind, and the low soothing sounds of Boz Scaggs' "I'll Be Long Gone" issued from the cabin speakers.

CHAPTER 17

David Sails South

The next morning Mike Schwindel woke to the sounds of sputtering exhaust from David's boat. He dressed quickly and stepped out onto the dew covered deck of the *Black Hawk*. David was in the cockpit of *Lethe*, obviously making ready to leave the dock.

"Where are you off to so early?" Mike queried.

"South," was David's curt answer.

"Without so much as a goodbye or a fare-thee-well to an old comrade?"

"It seems I have worn out my welcome in Spruce Cove, and I'm done with Alaska. The forecast looks decent. Good time for me to go. I'll give you a call when I land somewhere. I promise to stay in touch." David continued to make preparations to leave as he spoke, removing the mainsail cover and attaching the main halyard.

"Did you forget the Coast Guard told us to stay put until the troopers can send someone down to get statements from everyone?"

"I have had just about enough of the Alaskan legal system. The troopers can go fuck themselves. Besides, I only make five or six knots. They can easily catch me if they want to. Let them work a little for their pay. Anyway, I'm obviously not the first one to leave." David indicated the vacant space the Treadwell's boat, *Elixir*, had occupied.

"Well, at least let me help you cast off."

Mike pushed *Lethe* away from the mossy wharf and tossed the bow and stern lines to David. He waved a final farewell, and watched as the boat motored slowly out of the little cove. The top few feet of the mast remained visible for a few minutes over the low entrance spit, then vanished entirely behind the thickly wooded ridge that protected the inlet from the open waters of Clarence Strait. Mike lingered for some minutes on the dock, smoking his pipe and gazing at the narrow harbor entrance. Only when the small wavelets created by *Lethe's* parting wake had ceased to lap against the dock, and his pipe load of tobacco had turned to cold ash, did he finally turn away and re-board his own boat.

The day was exceptional, and although David sailed into a brisk southerly breeze he was able to make good headway towards his day's goal of Ketchikan by making long alternating tacks, first southwest towards Prince of Wales Island, and then southeast back in the direction of Revillagigedo Island and the mainland. He was sure if the wind held that his fourth tack would put him on a heading to bring him into Ketchikan well before the dinner hour.

Lethe bounded through the three foot chop

making a steady five to six knots under reefed main and working jib, with the occasional larger frothy wave breaking against the bow and sending a cold spray of salt water over the deck. Secure and dry in the cockpit, David listened to the VHF radio and watched for traffic and flotsam in the strait. There was plenty of the latter, as stumps, branches, and even whole trees still cluttered the waters from the previous days of stormy weather. Just barely visible in the distance he could make out another sailboat running straight into the weather under power, all sails furled. With his binoculars he had earlier discerned the boat was the Treadwell's yacht, *Elixir*. They would be in Ketchikan hours earlier than David, but would miss the extraordinary day of sailing. He wondered why such people bought sailboats, when they spent most of their time motoring anyway.

As he settled into the comfortable rhythm of the sail south David reflected on his emerging plan. He had not decided exactly on his ultimate destination. He pondered his options. Seattle and Tacoma were both too large for his tastes, so it would have to be one of the smaller coastal towns of Washington, but populous enough to find the resources he would need, and it was important to him that there were decent sailing destinations close by. He was familiar with Bellingham, Port Townsend, and Anacortes. Any of those would do for his purposes, but Bellingham was the logical first stop. That city would be his goal then.

He was in no hurry, though. This was his first opportunity to explore the Canadian section of the Inside Passage, and he still had two or three weeks of decent weather left if he was lucky. He intended to use every bit of that time. Now that his senses were open and receptive again, David hungered to experience this scenic, wild, and nearly unpopulated region—the part of southern British Columbia between Prince Rupert and the northern end of Vancouver Island—an area even less populated than Southeast Alaska. His only regret was that his family, especially Marshall, could not be along to share the experience with him.

CHAPTER 18

Juneau Again

Karen Stuckrath had only a vague idea where David was. Her daughter at least she knew had moved south to Washington state, having broken up with her erstwhile boyfriend. The summer, not unusually for Juneau had been wet and gloomy, with the infrequent sunny days inevitably followed by periods of overcast or rainy weather. Her dysphoria had deepened with each passing week. She put the house up for sale and accepted the first offer. It wasn't a bad price, but probably not what she could have expected had she been more engaged in the process. The sales contract had given her thirty days to move. The first garage sale was scheduled a few days hence, and she had not even begun to sift through her broken family's belongings. At least her daughter had volunteered to fly back to Juneau to help with the packing and sorting. She looked forward to her arrival, even though she knew the process would be painful. She could not imagine how they would decide which of Marshall's things to keep and which to part with. Karen had a vague idea of heading south to Oregon or Washington where she had both family and friends, but beyond that she still had no real plans.

As she read the news of the judge's death in the local paper, with the name of the boat he had fallen from and its owner, she realized Conrad must now be in Juneau. She knew where to find him. She was well acquainted with the marina. He would most likely be docked at the moorage reserved for transient boats.

The unexpected news of the judge's death and Conrad's presumed presence roused her from her now habitual lassitude. The face Karen apprehended in the mirror as she prepared to leave her house had noticeably aged of late. Her skin was still winter-pale, and she noticed lines that surely were not there even a few months earlier. She did the best she could with her cosmetic compounds, but she was not very satisfied at the results. She dressed for the weather, knowing she could expect a wet hike through the harbor.

Karen scarcely noticed the fishing boats or the glances of the men at work on them as she walked resolutely down the dock, where she had no trouble picking out Conrad's distinctive sailboat from the few others at the transient moorage area. He helped her down the steep companionway steps. They embraced for some time. Nearly a decade had passed since the last time she had seen Conrad—the time they had taken Marshall to the museum in Seattle. Although the old infatuation had vanished, there was if anything a tighter bond between them. They both felt it, and were neither of them surprised or uncomfortable with their feelings. As they disengaged Karen clutched his arms and stared intently into Conrad's eyes.

"You killed him, didn't you!" she exclaimed.

Conrad held her gaze, but said nothing.

"I know you did it, and I'm glad! As soon as I heard the news I knew, and I am as guilty of it as you are, because I have wished and hoped for his and Tadlock's deaths every day since Marshall was murdered. You are lucky to be able to do something, while I only sit and cry and watch my life fall apart!"

"You know you should not be here, Karen. Someone might see you and make the connection between us, and my work is still not finished here, as you must also realize."

"Oh, I won't stay long, and I won't be back again—but how could I stay away knowing you were here? And besides, I have some useful information for you."

"Useful—how?" Conrad replied, intrigued.

Karen sat down abruptly at the drop-leaf mahogany table which dominated the main cabin. She felt lightheaded and slightly out of breath.

"I know where he lives, and I know where he works."

"Who?" Conrad replied, but of course he knew the answer.

"Grant Tadlock. I know you are here to kill him, and I want—no I need—to help you. You don't know how many times I have wanted to do it myself—how many times I have driven down his street with David's gun on the seat next to me. There was one time when I even got up the courage to point it at him as he walked out of his house—but I just could not do it! I can't do it, but I know you can and will, and I'll help you in any way you want—only I just can't pull the trigger! I only wish I could somehow!" She placed her hands over her face and her elbows on the table, and began to sob softly and resignedly.

Conrad seated himself across from Karen. He reached over the table and caressed her arm gently until she had regained her composure.

"Nor should you be the one, Karen. You still have a daughter and David to think of—and what good would it do them or anyone else if you were imprisoned?" (The irony of this argument, which judge Daise had used against David's actions at Chuck's house, did not escape him.) "Tell me what you know about Tadlock, and let me take the responsibility for whatever ensues," he insisted.

Knowing she wanted and needed to feel useful, Conrad did not reveal to Karen that through his previous research on the Agency's computers he had weeks earlier discovered Tadlock's current home address. But to his surprise and pleasure Karen did have other information about Tadlock's habits that Conrad was not aware of. As she had followed Tadlock on her grim but unconsummated mission she had discovered that he regularly frequented a certain bar in Juneau, the "Moby Dick," where she had observed the man coming and going through an alley entrance. This was crucial new information, and Conrad decided immediately he must investigate further.

"Listen Karen. I don't want you to follow him anymore. He is a very dangerous character. What if he had noticed you tailing him?"

"Then maybe I might have had the courage to use the gun. I never followed him without it, and David taught me years ago when we first moved to Alaska how to shoot, and how to hit what I shot at."

"I spoke with David. A couple of days ago in Spruce Cove," Conrad said.

"How does he seem?" Karen replied, her eyes again welling with tears.

"Well enough, considering. He had a confrontation with judge Daise the day before the judge died. I have the feeling it was just the thing he needed. We spoke only briefly before I left, and I think he seems better now, somehow."

"Did he say what his plans were? Does he even have any plans?" Karen wanted to know.

"Like I said—our conversation was short, but I was there when he put judge Daise on the spot. David got one of his friends to help him and held a sort of kangaroo court. He put Daise himself on trial in front of a small group of people for his responsibility in Marshall's death. That was something to see, and I'm really glad that storm forced me into Spruce Cove at just the right time to witness it. He was really tenacious—like I've never seen him before. You would have been amazed. He was fearless, and had Daise on the defensive."

"So he's still in Alaska, then?"

"I doubt it. David is headed south, but beyond that I have no idea what he will do. He seems okay though. I mean, somehow he seems to be recovering from his grief. Judge Daise had designs to bring charges against him, but of course that is no longer something he has to worry about."

"All the years we've been together—I can't even imagine him doing something like that. It makes me feel better to think he might be healing. I've been worried about him—out there on the water week after week all alone. ...and what about you Conrad? What about me? Will we ever heal?"

Conrad took a moment to answer her. Before his time in Spruce Cove he had given little thought to what his life might be after he dealt with Tadlock, but since the death of the judge, he, much like David, had entertained the idea of wiping the slate clean and perhaps starting a new sort of existence. But such a fresh start would be far more difficult for him than for David. Wherever he went and whatever he did, he would always be tethered in some way to the Agency, and if they were to connect him with the deaths of the judge and Grant Tadlock (for he was more determined than ever now to pay the man in kind for the death of his son), that leash would become a noose.

"My way ahead is clear for now. After that I don't know. Life goes on until it ends I suppose—for all of us, no matter how badly wounded. I can't say I have given the future very much thought lately."

This last statement at least was not true, but as

close as he was to Karen (for though he had often dated during the past decade, she was the only woman with whom he had ever been remotely candid), he was unwilling to reveal to her or anyone else his plans after his undertaking in Alaska was accomplished. In fact he had given much thought to that future, down to the smallest details, but Conrad's life was such that dissimulation and deception were the rule, even with friends and lovers. He deflected her question with one of his own.

"What will you do now that your house is sold?"

"Well, first I have to get our stuff out of there. That is a much bigger job than I thought it would be, so I'll be pretty busy the next few days. After that, who knows. I suppose I'll head south too. Cindy will never live here again, so there is nothing left for me in Juneau. Besides, I never really liked it here before all this, and now I can't stand it at all."

The two of them were silent for a long moment, then Karen stood and embraced Conrad once again. At the top of the companionway ladder she hesitated.

"Be careful Conrad. I could not stand to lose you, too!"

"Yes, yes Karen. You take care of yourself and let me worry about Tadlock and myself—and one more thing... Don't give up on David."

He watched her walk through the dismal drizzle. Her hooded head was inclined, her body, draped in its long dark raincoat hunched into the weather—a somber and bowed figure against a slate background. It was a scene that would have looked the same filmed in black and white or color. The clouds had descended right to the ground, and the cinereous surrounds of the marina seemed devoid of all vitality and life, save for the glaucous shades of the omnipresent gulls circling vulture-like above.

He glimpsed a bleak presage of Karen as a prematurely aged woman, alone with her tragic memories. The manifestation nearly unnerved him, for his image of Karen had always been that of the spirited and beguiling girl of decades past. Conrad shivered involuntarily, though he was not the least bit cold, and only finally turned away when she had disappeared into the mist far down the dock.

From the marina parking lot, sitting in a rented car, agent Jack Dolon also observed Karen Stuckrath as she returned from her visit with Conrad Slocum. He snapped several more close-ups using a powerful telephoto lens to add to the ones he had taken earlier as she had stepped onto Conrad's boat. He was sure his boss, Richard Head, would be pleased with his initiative and the photographs.

CHAPTER 19

A Suspicious Trooper

Ray Standers navigated the Alaska Department of Fish and Game boat carefully past the crenelated coastline of Etolin Island. He probably knew the network of fjords and islands in this part of Southeast Alaska better than any man alive. Even when he was not on duty he spent most of his free time subsistence fishing or hunting. In his early fifties, Ray had black hair just beginning to gray at the temples, the fit physique and the weather-worn features of a life lived outdoors. He had the stamina to endure long hours in the elements—an essential requirement for his job. Unafraid to try a new challenge, Ray had recently taken up snowboarding in order to spend more time with his teenage son. Ray had a degree in biology and was respected throughout Southeast Alaska by both the commercial fisherman and environmentalists for his efforts in protecting the wild salmon fisheries. Ray also had a reputation for fairness and bluntness that endeared him to both the working men and the native tribal members of the region, but occasionally caused him problems with his superiors and the politicians in Juneau.

A local fisherman had brought up the partially crab-consumed remains of a man subsequently identified as judge Henry Daise. He had been reported to the Coast Guard as a man overboard by the captain of the sailing vessel *Tisiphone* the day before. According to the skipper, the judge must have fallen into the water and drowned while he had briefly gone into the cabin. The captain, Mr. Slocum, had returned to the cockpit to find the judge had vanished. He had circled back, but Daise, who was not wearing flotation, could not be found. The Coast Guard had immediately sent out a helicopter and rescue boat and searched the area until nightfall, but it was left to the fisherman to discover the remains the following day.

All these facts were detailed in the copy of the report Ray had been given. The cause of death was being tentatively written off as an accidental drowning, but in the meantime he had been asked by the Alaska State Troopers in Juneau to check the area for any other evidence, and to interview anyone in Spruce Cove, where the judge had spent his last night before the accident.

"There are a couple of things that bother me about this," the state trooper in charge of the investigation, sergeant Joe Tenax, told Ray.

Tenax was technically an Alaska Wildlife Trooper (AWT). His division of the state police, unique to Alaska, was responsible for a wide variety of duties, including those commonly associated with that of game wardens, marine patrol, and wildlife conservation enforcement. They also performed many of the same duties as the regular troopers, including arrests for crimes not related to wildlife, and regular traffic violations. Locally they were called the "Brown Shirts," as their uniforms differed from the regular troopers in being brown instead of blue. The Fish and Game and Wildlife Troopers departments often worked closely together, since the AWT had taken over the responsibilities of the game wardens in the mid nineteen seventies.

Ray had worked on many cases with Joe in the past. They got on well, and had gone on several hunting and fishing expeditions together over the years. Joe was a big man, a good two hundred fifty pounds, and six feet four inches tall. He had been a linebacker in high school with great college prospects until a knee injury had ended over soon his nascent football career.

"In the first place, Mr. Slocum, the owner of the sailboat said the main boom was swinging when he returned to the deck and realized Daise was gone. He surmised it might have knocked the judge overboard. Now I don't know a hell of a lot about sailing, but I do know about the danger of a heavy boom flying around on a downwind course, so why the hell would he have left a stranger at the helm without tying that boom off first in those conditions? Secondly, Daise was found miles south of where he reportedly fell in, and unless I'm a total idiot at reading nautical charts and weather reports, both the tide and wind should have moved the body north, if anything."

"My guess was Daise was just taking a piss and

fell or was knocked overboard," Ray responded. He was aware the greatest percentage of men falling from boats were found with their pants unzipped.

"He was pretty banged up from bouncing around in Clarence Strait, and the crabs had a good feast, but as you will see in the report his pants were definitely on and zipped, though he was missing one tennis shoe," sergeant Tenax responded.

"Does this Mr. Slocum have any reason to dislike the judge—any motive? Did he know Daise?"

"Not that I know of, but there are at least two other people who were with Daise the night before who might have reason—your buddy Sam Thornton, and David Stuckrath. You might remember Stuckrath's the guy whose son was killed earlier this year in a prison fight, and Daise is the judge who sent his kid up to Lime River."

"I don't really know Stuckrath well, although I have met him. I guess everyone has heard about his son, Marshall. ...a very sad story. My son knew him from high school—said he was a great snowboarder, as well as runner and wrestler. So young—what a fucking waste," Ray said, shaking his head.

"Well, it's common knowledge Sam had reason enough to dislike the judge," the trooper continued.

The topic of Marshall Stuckrath's death was an uncomfortable one for trooper Tenax. He had differed vehemently with Daise on incarceration for simple drug possession, and he had directed his officers not to make arrests for small amounts of marijuana possession, which had infuriated the judge.

"Yeah, but Sam is no dummy. He has a reputation as a brawler, but I can't believe he would kill Daise or anyone else. I have known Sam for a helluva long time, and I know of a few fights he has finished, but I can't think of even one he started. Besides, he wasn't on that sailboat when judge Daise fell off, was he?"

"Nope, but maybe somehow he or Stuckrath put this Slocum guy up to it. I know, it sounds pretty farfetched, and I admit I'm grasping at straws, but something about this just does not sit right with me. The Coast Guard did get statements from the folks at Spruce Cove. According to their report Stuckrath was there with Daise, Thornton, Slocum, and a few other people. They were all waiting out that storm. Apparently some sort of altercation occurred at Chuck Riggs' house between Stuckrath and Daise. A sort of mock trial of the judge was held, but the Coasties that did the interviews didn't dig too deep."

"So you want me to follow up with a bigger shovel, right?" Ray replied.

"That's right. I've been in law enforcement for nearly thirty years, and I've learned that if things don't smell so good there is usually a dead fish or a skunk in the neighborhood. I've got a corpse and at least two guys who were with him the day before he died who might have motive. I don't know of any connection between the people who were there in the cove and this guy Slocum, but I'd like to be sure. According to his statement, which one of my officers got shortly after he arrived in Juneau, he volunteered to give Daise a lift to Wrangell when the judge's engine wouldn't start. Everything I have on this so far is in this file," Joe said, handing a thin folder over to Ray.

"So that's all you need? You just want me to go interview everyone? Are they all still in Spruce Cove?"

"I've given the order for everyone to stay put, at least until you can talk to them, and I have asked the captain, Mr. Slocum, to remain where he is at the harbor here in Juneau. I thought you might want to speak to him too, even though he has already given us his statement. Otherwise, anything else you might think of that could bear on the case. I admit I've only got my hunch to go on, but it's a strong enough hunch that I can't seem to let it go. I can't spare a trooper at the moment, and even if I could you know way more about that stretch of water than any of my officers do."

"I don't know how much help I can be, but sure, I'll check things out. Anything you can add that isn't in this file?"

"There is one other thing. Technically I am not supposed to reveal this information, but we go back a ways, and I have confidence in your judgement and discretion." Sergeant Tenax tapped his pen nervously on the worn desk and leaned forward conspiratorially in the old oak office chair.

"This whole investigation is complicated by the fact that Mr. Slocum happens to be up here on an assignment to help with an ongoing drug investigation. He is apparently employed by some government intelligence agency, but my boss will not or cannot tell me which one, although I have my suspicions. When I tried to retrieve information on him through our computers, messages popped up saying that all information concerning him was classified, so I called Anchorage. They at least told me the reason he is up here, but they would or could not give me any more information. When I got a little pushy on the phone I was told to back off in no uncertain terms, and that any investigation of the judge's death would be handled by the Anchorage office. Of course you know me well enough to know I'm not one to be browbeaten. Besides, I'm close enough to retirement that I don't give a god-damn about any of their bureaucratic bullshit."

"It's no secret there wasn't much love lost between you and Daise either," Ray said.

"Yes, he never forgave me for agreeing with most of the rest of the troopers over the marijuana issue. He maintained it was our job to actively investigate those cases. I tried to tell him we just did not have the manpower to bust every pimply-faced teenager and pony-tailed hippie with a joint in Alaska. Hell, we're stretched way too thin anyway—biggest state in the union with the worst weather and fewest roads—but I don't have to tell you that... Henry—damn him and rest his soul!—would never budge on the drug issue. Why, if he had his way I guess half of the state would be in jail. He tried to get me fired when I refused to cooperate with AKNET on a pot case a few years back, so I guess I should consider myself a suspect too."

"You and a good part of Southeast if that was reason enough to kill," Ray replied. "There are a lot of people around here who will call it karma."

"Well, you're right about that. He was not well-liked in his district by some folks, although he always got a lot of support from the administration and the state bar. The D.A. doesn't think there is enough evidence of foul play to justify the expense of a full investigation. He was ready to write it off as an unfortunate accident, but I convinced him to give me a little time to look into things. The autopsy found nothing suspicious. There was bruising on Daise's forehead and he had a broken nose, but that was consistent with Slocum's speculation that he might have been smacked by the main boom."

"I'd better get going then, while I've still got plenty of daylight." Ray stood to leave.

He could not refuse Tenax, but it was bad timing. This was the busiest part of the year for Fish & Game, and Ray hoped this additional chore would not take up too much additional time and energy.

"I can keep Slocum in Juneau a few more days as a person of interest—or at least until the investigation, such as it is, is over. I thought since you were heading out to Thorne Bay anyway this week, you could detour over to the other side of the strait and sniff around a little in the area where they found Daise on your way to Spruce Cove. I can't get away from Juneau myself right now—too much god-damned paperwork to catch up on.

I'll keep trying to see what else I can scrounge up on Slocum, but I doubt it will be much," the trooper elaborated.

CHAPTER 20

Ray Wanders

Ray Standers always relished any time away from his desk and out in the field, although he did not like the idea of being an errand boy for the troopers, even though he liked sergeant Tenax. But it would be a break from the normal routine and give him an excuse to drop into Spruce Cove, where he always enjoyed visiting his old acquaintance, Chuck Riggs. He did not expect to find out anything more about Daise's fate. Most probably he had just fallen off the boat like the owner said. It was an all too common occurrence in these waters. On the other hand, if there had been foul play it was not likely any convincing evidence would be forthcoming either. With the only witnesses likely to be gulls, eagles, or sea lions a man could certainly get away with murder in these parts. There were plenty of unsolved cause of death cases on the books. Much of the time the bodies were never found. The fjords were deep, the currents strong, and there were lots of scavengers in the sea and on land.

Ray booked a flight on a small charter plane to Wrangell, where he picked up a Fish and Game boat.

From there it was less than three hours of motoring down Stikine Strait to Steamer bay. The Forest Service maintained a small A-frame cabin there. He planned to begin his reconnaissance of the western shore of Etolin Island starting from that location. The body had been found several miles farther south, near Lincoln Rock, but he hoped to have lunch in the more protected waters of the bay and perhaps interview anyone who might be renting the cabin there.

A good part of Etolin was designated wilderness area, and the rest of the island was almost equally undeveloped. The 2000 census had counted fifteen people on the roughly two hundred thousand acre island, and Ray was pretty sure that count was exaggerated. He probably knew most everyone on the island. They were mostly trappers, an archeologist or two employed by the Forest Service, and employees of the geoduck farms farther south at Cannery Point. Most of the denizens were seasonal workers, and he doubted more than three or four souls actually spent winters on the island. There were no towns at all, though the archeology research had so far revealed several thousands of years of habitation by Native Americans in the past, and evidence of at least one large prehistoric village.

Stikine Strait was another of the numerous deep glacier-carved fjords that criss-crossed all of Southeast Alaska and the northern coast of British Columbia. It extended in a southwesterly direction from the extensive mud flats at the mouth of the Stikine River for some thirty miles until it merged with the waters of

Clarence Strait. For most of its length it washed the shores of Etolin Island to the south and Zarembo to the north. Because it was protected from the prevailing winds by the two land masses, the seas here were generally calmer than in Clarence Strait.

The sun cast its rays through scattered popcorn clouds and a light breeze barely ruffled the seas. The temperature was in the mid sixties—not bad for late August. Two bald eagles circled high above him, their abrasive screeching calls contrasting strongly with their otherwise noble demeanor. Ray knew the eagles for what they were—glorified vultures who scrapped with the much craftier ravens and crows over the guts of rotting salmon carcasses—but he appreciated the birds at a more profound level than the average awe-stricken tourist because of his understanding of their essential place in the ecology of the land.

The birds continued to circle above him as he turned the boat into Steamer Bay and set the anchor. A faint curl of smoke drifted up from the metal flue of the forest service cabin some yards back behind the highest tide line at the edge of the forest. A man on the shore who had been observing Ray's arrival walked quickly back to the little shelter. Ray winched the inflatable Zodiac down from its davits. The well-maintained outboard engine started on the second pull, and he was at the beach in minutes. It took him a few more minutes to drag the inflatable up onto the shore beyond the lapping waves, and tie it off to one of the convenient sea-smoothed logs the tides had deposited on the shore in orderly parallel rows. The door of the cabin opened immediately to his knock, and a grizzled man with a cigarette dangling from his lips and a slip of paper in his hand confronted him.

"Oh it's you. What d'you want. I ain't done nothin' wrong. I paid the cabin rental, and I've got the receipt here to prove it," the man said, waving the paper in front of the biologist's face.

Ray knew the man well. Craig Martes was a long-time hunting guide with a notorious reputation as a poacher and fencer of illegal animal parts. He was a man who had richly earned his well-deserved status as one of the most prolific violators of both state and federal Fish and Game ordinances. He and Ray had crossed paths on many occasions, and had developed a certain mutual respect for one another. The crafty Craig knew the Fish and Game officers were spread thinly, and that budget restraints made it impossible for them to monitor all of his actions, but he had learned caution several years earlier when Ray had helped organize a sting that had finally netted the wily Martes and several other violators. That infraction had cost Craig a three day stint in jail, the loss of his favorite hunting rifle, and a hefty fine for hunting moose out of season.

"I am sure you are a hundred per cent on the level as always, Craig, but I wonder why you made such a bee-line to the house when you saw me? I don't suppose you would mind me having a look around the place —especially that shack out back, eh?" Ray said, enjoying the other man's discomfort.

Ray was not totally unsympathetic to Craig Martes' plight. It was in many ways a difficult way of life he had chosen, and the man had amassed decades of experience in tracking, trapping, hunting, and exploring in the wilds of Southeast Alaska. A hundred or even fifty years ago most of his activities would have been perfectly acceptable, even praiseworthy, but times had changed and civilization had at last caught up with him even in this remote corner of the world. Regardless of Craig's disdain for legal niceties Ray could not think of many other men who would be more reliable company if it ever came down to a survival situation in the wilderness.

"Let's see your search warrant! I know my rights!" the man declared.

"Now come on Craig. You know as well as I do I don't need a warrant to search Tongass National Forest property, but I'll give you a break this time, even though I would be willing to bet my next paycheck that you are hiding something in that old shed. I want to ask you a few questions, and I promise that I will leave you in peace if you don't try to bullshit me too much."

Back in the nineteen eighties a small herd of elk had been successfully transplanted to Etolin Island. The herd had prospered and even enlarged their range to neighboring Zarembo Island, a swim of a mile and more across Stikine Strait. Ray suspected Martes was here for the elk, although he probably would not pass up one of the brown bear or wolves that also roamed the rugged island.

"Well, that seems okay—when you put it that way. I guess you might as well come on in," he said, after briefly considering Ray's offer.

"Like I said. I got nothing to hide anyways. I was just headin' back to the house to heat us up some coffee. I was thinkin' you might need a little pick-me-up after your voyage."

Craig was a small, wiry, goat-like man somewhat past middle age who still retained a thick shock of unruly jet-black hair. His grizzled beard had not been shaved in several weeks, and his stained and smeared plaid wool shirt looked as though it had not been washed for an even longer time.

"Where'd you run from—Wrangell or Petersburg?" Craig continued, feigning nonchalance.

Ray followed him into the small kitchen of the two room cabin, where he was surprised to see there actually was a kettle of water heating on the rusty propane range, and a Melita coffee filter and carafe freshly prepared. Craig carefully poured the hot water through the filter as Ray quickly scanned the twenty by twenty cabin's interior. If Craig was up to something illegal there was no obvious evidence of it on display in the confines of the small shelter. Ray accepted the coffee and thanked Craig for his hospitality, before getting down to his real reason for the visit.

"How long have you been here in Steamer Bay?" Ray asked.

"Well, countin' today—I guess six days. I might stay on a few more too. I don't have to tell you how good the fishing is this time of year."

Ray doubted that Craig was doing much fishing. It was far more likely he was running an illegal trap line, or hanging an elk or bear carcass out in the shed. Or perhaps he had chosen the place as a convenient rendezvous for the start of one of his notorious guided hunting trips, with mostly wealthy out-of-state clients who cared little for seasonal restrictions or bag limits.

"I was just wondering how much boat traffic you've noticed over the last several days. Have any other boats anchored in here, or have you noticed any unusual boat traffic? I mean besides the usual fishing boats and tour ships," Ray asked.

"I did notice a sailboat a few days ago. I'm thinking it was probably on Wednesday," Craig answered, after giving the question some thought.

"I was quite a ways up above Streets Lake on Steamer Knoll. It's a pretty good view from there—must have been close to fifteen hundred feet up—and I seen a sailboat I never noticed before around these parts. It was headin' north. I had my binoculars on me and I scoped him out pretty good—a nice lookin' boat with an awful lot of sail up. I guess it was just another one of those yachties a headin' up the Inside Passage. Kind'a late in the year, though. That's probably why I remember it so well."

The hill he referred to afforded a spectacular view of the complex topography of the surrounding islands and fjords, including the area where Daise's remains had been found.

"Now Craig, I am not going to ask you what you were up to over at Streets Lake. I'm sure you were just out hiking for the good of your health, or perhaps gathering fiddle-head ferns for your salad—but did you happen to get the name of that sailboat?"

"No, I couldn't make out the name, but I do remember it was moving' along pretty fast for a sailboat, and I saw two guys back in the stern."

"Two men, eh—you're sure? Can you remember exactly where the boat was when you saw it, and where it was when you quit watching it?"

"Well, I'm not so sure—my memory seems a little bit cloudy sometimes. I guess maybe I'm gettin' a little long in the tooth as they say. I don't rightly recall just where that boat was when I quit watchin' it," Craig answered with a sly grin.

"Craig, have you ever heard of something called a mnemonic trigger," Ray responded, smiling in spite of himself.

"...don't rightly recall," he repeated, grinning even more widely.

"It is a little prompt that helps a person recollect something that might really be in his memory, but he might have a hard time remembering, okay?" Ray continued, playing along.

"Now I have got a feeling you do rightly recall quite a bit about that boat, but you just need a little motivation to help you remember the details—something to trigger all those blocked memories. How about this; you tell me every little thing you can about that boat with those big sails, and then I will just head out of here after I've had my coffee without taking a look in that outbuilding, and without calling up anyone from Fish and Game in Wrangell to check on you for the next week or so. Does that help jog your memory some?"

"You know, that does seem to be clearin' away the cobwebs quite a bit," the canny old guide answered.

Ray took a small pad from a pocket and began taking notes as Martes continued.

"Now that I think about it—seems like I watched that boat sail from down around Lincoln Rock clear up past Mariposa—maybe a little farther even—and there was something funny I remember about the way he was steerin' too. When I first spotted him he was headin' north, maybe a little north of Point Stanhope. When I checked again a little while later I expected he'd be even farther north, but there he was a goin' back south. I thought at the time that was a little bit odd, so I watched him a while longer. He circled clear around pretty close to shore, and then headed on back north again."

"Do I understand you correctly? You mean the boat turned completely around and sailed back south, then turned again, all before he went up Stikine Strait?"

"Yeah, I guess I was a little surprised because I was goin' back to the cabin so's I could be there if he came in. You know—he might need some help or something, and you never know about strangers these days... But then he turned back the other way, made a kind of a figure eight, and sailed back up Clarence. I lost sight of him when I went back down into the valley. Later that day—after I got back to the cabin, I seen a Coast Guard boat out in the strait, and they had a helicopter out flyin' around too. ...looked like they were running search patterns between here and Zarembo."

"Did you happen to see how many men were on the sailboat during all that maneuvering?" Ray queried.

"That's another thing—now that you bring it up —that also seemed a little funny to me at the time. I could swear there had been two guys on the back end of the boat, but when he was turning the boat around I only seen one person on deck. I thought that was a little strange because I know a little bit about sailboats, and it seems like when you are making a turn like that is when you need the help on deck—what with all the ropes and sails and all—so I was a little surprised that only one guy was handlin' the boat. Not only that—I could see he was looking through his binoculars and the sails were flappin' around pretty good until he came 'round again."

"Now think carefully. Did you happen to see anything fall in the water, or anything floating in the water, or did anything lead you to think something was not right on the boat—other than the odd maneuvering you observed?"

Craig Martes hesitated briefly and answered: "I didn't see anyone or anything fall in the water, and I didn't see anything at all floating in the water that I can recall. I gather someone must have drowned out there, right?"

"Yeah, that's it," Ray said, putting his notepad away. "The troopers are pretty sure it was an accident and so am I, but they want me to help them tie up a few loose ends. I appreciate you telling me what you know Craig, and if you happen to remember anything else be sure to let trooper Tenax or me know—might save you some trouble someday, you never can tell. Thanks for the coffee. I'd better be getting along before it gets any later. I've still got to get down to Spruce Cove."

"Well I'm sorry you can't stay longer Ray. I'm sure I could rustle up a pretty nice dinner for us."

"I bet you could at that," Ray said as he turned to go. "I imagine I am missing quite a feast."

"Say hello to old Chuck for me," Craig called as Ray continued down the beach to his waiting inflatable.

Once outside the harbor Ray followed closely the southwestern coastline of Etolin Island. He cruised slowly and cautiously as near to the shore as he dared. The rock-strewn edge of the island was littered with partially submerged boulders waiting to snag the unwary mariner.

About three miles south, when he had traveled about half the distance to where the judge's body had been found near Lincoln Rock, he saw something unusual tangled up in a patch of kelp and driftwood. Ray had been picking his way gingerly through the jumble of reefs, kelp beds, and half awash boulders labeled on the chart as the "Steamer Rocks." Using his boathook he managed to fish the item out of the slimy mass. It was a canvas boat shoe; a right foot, size ten, sodden and and much abraded, but the Lands End tag was still legible. The find seemed a little unusual to Ray as most Alaskan fisherman and boaters favored the high rubber or neoprene boots known locally as "Ketchikan sneakers." He checked his copy of the trooper's report. Sure enough, under the description of the clothing Daise had been wearing at the time his body was found, was a notation that only the left shoe, a size ten Lands End canvas boat shoe, had been present.

Ray resumed his slow reconnaissance of the shore line and pondered his fortuitous find. It was obviously Daise's shoe. Taking into account Slocum's version of what had happened, poacher Craig Martes' description of the odd maneuvers of the sailboat that same day, and the location of the missing shoe, he had the uneasy feeling there was something wrong with Conrad Slocum's story.

In the first place Slocum had reported his position to the Coast Guard as "...just west of Steamer Bay at the entrance of Stikine Strait," seven or eight miles north of Lincoln Rock and three miles or so north of the missing shoe. At the time of the call and subsequent search the moderate southerly wind and tide would have moved any floating object north, so the Coast Guard had concentrated their search in the immediate area and to the north up to Steamer Point and Mulver Island, and along the south shores of Zarembo Island, near the position Slocum had reported as the site of the accident. They had not searched the area south of Point Harrington where the body was actually found two days later, and where Ray now found himself wondering whether he was really investigating an accidental drowning, or perhaps something else altogether.

Was trooper Tenax's hunch correct? And if so, what was Slocum's motive?

Ray let his mind wander as he continued slowly down the coast. His intuition told him there had to be a connection between David Stuckrath and Conrad Slocum—a very close connection, but what could it be? Although he was now closer to Spruce Cove than Wrangell he decided it was more important to get back to the town to research that question than to go on to the harbor, where he would only be duplicating the Coast Guard's previous investigation. He had plenty of time before dark to make it back to Wrangell. There he would be able to use the trooper's computers and resources.

The return voyage to Wrangell was tiring. He bucked a steep chop most of the trip which made for a bumpy and wet ride, but after a hamburger and some strong coffee at one of the dock-side restaurants he felt alert enough for his task. Checking high school enrollment records turned up nothing useful; likewise college archives. David Stuckrath had been raised and gone to school in Oregon, and Slocum had spent his youth in Seattle. He could find no connection through military service enlistment records. He began to suspect his intuition had been wrong, and there was no connection after all.

Four hours later he was frazzled and ready to give up. His bleary eyes needed a break from focusing so long on the computer display. Looking away, Ray scanned the austere trooper office. His aching eyes roamed about the room and then back to the computer station. On the desk where he sat were the usual array of family pictures, a recent a bowling trophy, a framed service award, and something else that immediately drew his attention. A framed certificate of service from the Peace Corps. The trooper at whose desk he sat had served many years earlier as a Peace Corps Volunteer in Ethiopia.

Ray remembered his son had been especially excited during the high school's annual Career Week over a presentation given by his history teacher, David Stuckrath. The boy had been fascinated by Stuckrath's description of his Peace Corps experiences in Kabul, Afghanistan.

On a hunch he turned back to the computer and began searching Peace Corps related sites for the names of volunteers stationed in Afghanistan in the 1970s. His intuition proved correct. Stuckrath had served there in 1973 and 1974, and Slocum had been employed for a time during the same years by Peace Corps as a part-time language instructor. They had to have been very well acquainted, perhaps even friends! Friendship bonds likely strengthened by being young Americans together in such an exotic environment. Their presence together in Spruce Cove could not have been coincidence, Ray reasoned. He had no doubt he had found the link between the two men. He wondered if it was possible that they had colluded somehow in the judge's death, or could Slocum have killed Daise on his own, without Stuckrath's knowledge, but motivated by friendship? It was certainly a long shot, but worth investigating, as sergeant Tenax had suspected.

By the time Ray got back to his motel room it was after midnight. Although he was exhausted from the the hours of physical and mental exertion he was unable to fall asleep immediately. He considered his findings:

*A shoe in an unexpected location: Circumstantial evidence at best.

*Craig Martes' observations of Slocum's sailboat maneuvers: The statements of a convicted poacher and black marketeer with a reputation for duplicity.

*A possible connection between Slocum and Stuckrath more than twenty-five years old.

Would this evidence be strong enough to convince a jury to convict a man of murder? Ray had served as a juror himself a time or two, and he knew he would never vote a man guilty on such dubious findings alone. Should he continue the investigation, which would take up valuable time on what could turn out to be a wild goose chase? He wondered if it was all just coincidence. Perhaps he was just wasting his time.

Ultimately Ray decided it would be best to interview Mr. Slocum himself, in light of what he had learned. But first he would head down to Spruce Cove in the morning and interview those who had been at Chuck's house the day before Daise's demise, as he had promised the sergeant.

As Ray drifted off to sleep he pondered what to

do with the new information. He decided he would wait until after both interviews before reporting back to trooper Tenax.

CHAPTER 21

Ray Wonders

The next day Ray Standers arrived in Spruce cove. Mike Schwindel and Ray had been acquainted for over two decades. The two had met during the frenzied Alyeska pipeline years when they had worked in Valdez, the pipeline terminus, and had both, like so many other suddenly flush laborers, been caught up in the fee-wheeling booze and cocaine fueled state-wide party that had overtaken Alaska in the mid nineteen seventies. Ray, after ripping through several thousands of dollars on parties and a wild European adventure had in the end saved enough of his pipeline earnings to finish college and make the down payment on a home. Mike had likewise managed to stop just short of snorting up his good fortune, using his remaining Alyeska income to buy and restore his beloved sailboat, and investing enough to allow him to just get by on interest from those investments with the occasional odd-job cash infusion.

Though their dispositions and interests had led them down very different paths, Ray to family and government employment, and Mike to a life as a waterborne bachelor nomad they had remained friends and kept in sporadic contact.

Ray wanted to interview David Stuckrath first, and was disappointed and irritated to find he had left the harbor in spite of explicit instructions to remain there by the trooper's office. Discovering no one aboard *Black Hawk* Ray moved on to the next boat, *Bad Attitude*, which had moved from its previous anchorage in the cove to the spot *Lethe* had vacated. He was pleased to find both Mike and Sam were on board.

Ray had hoped the presence of Mike Schwindel in the harbor would make his chore less awkward. He was aware that Mike was close to David Stuckrath and reasoned that Mike's friendship with Stuckrath might make that interview less invasive and uncomfortable for Stuckrath, with whom he was barely acquainted, and only through his son, who had been one of David's history students.

With Stuckrath and the Treadwells no longer in the cove Ray could only interview the remaining people who had witnessed the mock trial. He had no desire to chase after the other three down Clarence Strait. Besides, they now had more than a twenty-four hour head start and could very well be in Canadian waters. Ray had never liked the enforcement part of his duties. He was already chafing under the assignment he had grudgingly accepted from sergeant Tenax. He hoped Mike or Sam might have useful information, and if not, so be it. He was ill-suited to the role of inquisitor anyway.

"What brings you to Spruce Cove, Ray? Are you

counting fish or looking for poachers?" Mike asked after a few minutes of small talk.

"You might call it a fishing expedition of sorts. The troopers have got me on their leash for a few days. They're hoping to find out just exactly what happened at Chuck's house during the storm, among other things. I was told a few people here apparently held some sort of trial of judge Daise, and kept him at Chuck's place against his will. I'm hoping you guys can fill me in on the details."

"Well, maybe something interesting did happen Ray, but why should the troopers give a shit about our little kangaroo court? The Coast Guard has already been here and gotten the whole story, and now that Daise is dead I doubt anyone will prosecute David or anybody else, unless that couple from Seattle wants to press charges on Sam," Mike responded.

Although Mike had a history with Ray Standers, his loyalty to David was stronger. The many hours he had spent with the Stuckrath family during the finishing of their boat had deepened the friendship which had already existed between them. Mike was a loner who had no children or relations in Alaska, and whose two brief marriages had failed. The Stuckraths were the closest thing he had to family. He had every reason to hold back if he sensed the least threat to David.

"It's not about that at all. Nobody has come forward as far as I know to make any sort of charges regarding what ever it was that went on at Chuck's place. The problem is sergeant Tenax is not convinced Daise's death was an accident, and he wants me to nose around here and see if I can dredge up any information about the events that took place either here, or between Spruce Cove and where the judge was found that might point to a motive for murder."

"Oh for Christ's sake! Does Tenax really think Slocum killed the judge?" Mike exclaimed. "What nonsense!"

"He doesn't have any evidence, and he can't find a motive, but he thinks it is pretty odd that an obviously seasoned sailor would be so careless as to let a passenger fall overboard, and there are some things that don't add up about the way the incident was reported. So here I am." Ray spread his arms out palms up in a gesture of resignation.

"Well I will give you a motive," Sam interjected. "Mr. Slocum, being an intelligent and reasonable man figured Daise for the arrogant prick he was, and did us and all of Southeast Alaska a favor by letting the miserable motherfucker drown after he was careless enough to fall overboard."

"Look guys, I don't enjoy this part of my job, and I would rather be tagging fish any day than playing shoeshine boy for trooper Tenax, so I will level with you and tell you I know Slocum and Stuckrath are acquainted—more than just acquainted. In fact, I am pretty damned sure they have been friends for years. I'm no shamus, but I do know how to use a computer, and it turns out they go back to the seventies—and god-damnit!—I think you and Sam already knew that, and that you also know a hell-of-a-lot more than what you told the Coast Guard about this whole affair!"

"So what if we do," Sam replied insolently. "Like I said before—fuck Daise anyway. He's where he belongs and good riddance—rest his lousy soul."

"Now hang on Sam," Mike said. "Ray's just trying to do his job—or at least trying to do trooper Tenax's job. We've got no reason to be offensive, or to hold back what we do know about things. After all, we had nothing to do with the judge's untimely demise, and I don't think the fact that Conrad and David are acquainted proves Daise was murdered."

"Does Tenax know about their connection, Ray?" Mike asked.

"I haven't talked to him since I discovered it last night," Ray answered.

Ray could see no reason to hide this fact from these men, and his curiosity was piqued by Mike's question.

"Maybe you shouldn't tell him," Mike said, and drew so deeply on his ever-present pipe that his already thin face seemed about to collapse into itself.

"Mike is right. No reason to waste any more time or effort on such a wild goose chase," Sam added, affecting a slightly more amenable attitude.

"What do you mean?" the biologist responded.

"Prosecuting Slocum won't bring Daise back. The sea meant to claim him and it did. It doesn't really matter if he was pushed or fell—the sea took him! It wanted him, and David was the only person who could keep the judge out of Davy Jones' Locker, and not even him for long. Who knows, maybe the Kooshtakaa pulled him in," Sam suggested, referring to the Tlingit equivalent of the bogeyman—a shape-shifting otter-man from Tlingit mythology that sometimes lured boaters to their deaths.

"Anyway, the score is evened up now, and I don't blame David for leaving all this behind."

"Not quite evened. Daise put David's son in jail, but there is still the guy that actually knifed him," Mike said. "That son-of-a-bitch is still alive and well, last I heard."

"You mean Grant Tadlock? I know that slimy bastard. Hangs out at the Moby Dick a lot—not that that makes him bad. He fishes off *Deep Runner*, if you could call what he does fishing. ...not exactly a high-liner. It's a pretty sleazy operation. That shit-bag once asked me if I needed any crew. Hell, I wouldn't even use him for crab bait—that would be disrespectful—I mean to the crabs of course," Sam interjected.

"Why the hell do you hate that guy so much anyway?" Mike asked.

"That fucker has been dealing animal parts for years—and I know he's been smuggling out Tlingit and Haida artifacts too. Tadlock would whore his own mother for a hundred bucks. Hell, he'd probably sell her for twenty!"

Ray did not comment on this. His office knew something of Tadlock's involvement in the illegal animal parts trade, and in fact had been observing him for some time, hoping to apprehend the buyers as well as Tadlock and his partner, Jim Lothar, when the time was right. The irony of their conversation did not escape him. It was judge Daise who had authorized the search warrants and wire taps that had given them their first good intelligence about Lothar and Tadlock's operation. Ray wondered if Sam's opinion of the judge would change if he knew these facts. With such a small population Southeast Alaska made for strange bedfellows. Although Sam hated the judge, he too had been a strong advocate for the protection of endangered wildlife and native artifacts.

"I still don't understand why you guys didn't tell me right away that you both knew about Slocum's connection with Stuckrath? Are you sure there isn't anything else you might want to say about that?" Ray asked.

"All I know is just what you found out. They go back to the seventies, when they met in Afghanistan. I don't think they are very close. Frankly, I didn't think that connection was worth mentioning. The whole time they were here in Spruce Cove I don't think they spent more than a few minutes together," Mike replied, aware that his answer was evasive and would be perceived as such by Ray Standers.

"Slocum came to the party, but I didn't see him say one word to David, and he didn't take sides as far as I could see. He just watched everything and kept his mouth shut," Sam added.

"There does not seem to be much of a motive there, Sherlock," Mike continued. "David was surprised, and I think a little bit hurt that Slocum didn't even stop and say good-bye to him before leaving with Daise. I think he resented the fact that Slocum would do the judge a favor. David didn't say much to me about it, but I know he was miffed. They may have been pretty close many years ago, but not anymore. And Sam's right too. Slocum didn't even support David during our little tribunal of Daise. I talked to the man a bit at the party, but just about boats, fishing, and other such small talk—that and the mountain lion he saw up on the trail."

Mike had no intention of revealing to Ray his awareness that Conrad Slocum was some sort of an intelligence agent, and his conjecture that Slocum and the judge might have been working together on a case. Ironically, Ray had promised sergeant Tenax he would not divulge the same knowledge.

This was as much information and insight as the two men were able or willing to give Ray. David was headed south and intended to leave Alaska for good Mike supposed, and if he wanted to interview him Ray would have to follow. The interviews with Chuck Riggs, Thomas Wilson, and the Craften couple were even less fruitful. Ray had pretty well made up his mind the whole thing was a waste of time, but he felt he needed to at least question Stuckrath or Slocum before he could report back to trooper Tenax that he had faithfully discharged his assignment. He was annoyed that both Stuckrath and the Treadwells had left Spruce Cove in spite of the instructions they had been given. (From the State Troopers, by way of Chuck's radio. There was no phone service in the cove, and reliable cell phone coverage had not yet reached this part of Southeast Alaska.)

Ray deliberated:

Should I try to find Stuckrath in Ketchikan or farther south before he leaves Alaskan jurisdiction, if he has not already done so? On the other hand, Mike brought up a very good point. If Slocum really had killed Daise because of his supposed friendship with Stuckrath, then logically his next target must be Grant Tadlock. In that case it would be better for me to get back to Juneau as soon as possible and check out Slocum's story for myself, or at least inform Tenax of the possibility that Slocum might go after Marshall Stuckrath's killer.

After mulling over his options, Ray decided it best to head back to Juneau. He was curious about this supposed agent, Conrad Slocum, and it seemed the quickest way to acquit himself of his responsibilities to trooper Tenax.

He wished he could have interviewed Stuckrath, if only because the man sounded interesting, and he had only a passing familiarity with him based on a couple of brief encounters at parent-teacher conferences. The very idea of holding a trial of a judge under such circumstances intrigued him. Still, he felt very strongly that the poor man had suffered enough over the death of his son and should be left alone. After all, no one had been harmed by his actions as far as he could tell.

Ray came to the conclusion there was no more to be learned in Spruce Cove or by further investigation in the area. Nothing he heard on his trip had been compelling. Craig Martes' story of Slocum's unusual boat maneuvers could have just described the maneuvers that any captain of a boat might make while searching for a man overboard. Although Martes had stated that one man had disappeared from the deck, he had unfortunately not observed the critical moment—the instant when the judge had actually gone into the water. The only real mystery, it seemed to Ray, was the apparent delay between the judge's accident and captain Slocum's report to the Coast Guard. Perhaps an interview with Slocum could clear that up.

The fish and game officer still believed the judge's death was probably accidental, but considering the connection between Stuckrath and Slocum it did seem odd that Slocum had apparently been only an observer during the mock trial and afterwards had offered transportation on his boat to his friend's enemy. Ray wondered if perhaps some disagreement had occurred between the two supposed friends. If so, perhaps an interview with Slocum might reveal that as well. On the other hand; assuming that David knew his old friend Conrad Slocum was some sort of an intelligence agent, perhaps that could explain their odd behavior. Ray Standers left Spruce Cove with more questions than answers, and the feeling that he was no closer to the truth than he had been before his investigations.

CHAPTER 22

Ray And Conrad

Ray left his pickup in the Juneau harbor parking lot and and walked down to the entrance gate. He took his time, observing the yachts and fishing boats in the basin, mentally appraising their relative merits and condition as he passed. With his retirement date getting closer Ray's dream was to start his own fishing charter business after leaving his state job. He evaluated the boats as he walked, looking for suitable examples of the type he hoped to own someday. There was a hint of fall, which came so early this far north, in the air. Fog hung over the foul oily slate-gray waters of the inner harbor.

Ray was well-known to the commercial fisherman here. Several of them greeted him as he walked past their boats. Preparing for the next salmon fishing opening, they dissected their deck equipment and dismantled their diesels in order to make sure they were in top shape to take advantage of the two or three day chance they would have to net all the fish they could before the Fish and Game department closed the limited gill-net season. Somewhat incongruously, a woman in a long dark dress coat hurried by, lightly brushing

Ray's shoulder as she passed, heading in the opposite direction.

As he made his way through the rectangular grid of docks, enjoying the sounds and smells of the harbor, the bustle of activity surrounding the fishing boats, and even the hoarse calls of the hovering seagulls, Ray realized how little he really cared about sergeant Tenax's investigation, judge Daise, or even whether or not the man was murdered. He resented so much the role he was expected to play in the investigation that he resolved to be done with the whole thing once he completed his interview with Slocum.

I did not become a biologist and expert on local salmon migration to waste my time as an errand boy for Joe Tenax, he thought.

A strand of stubborn independence and a natural distrust of authority had persisted and even strengthened as Ray had aged. He loved most the part of his job that got him outdoors and into the ecosystem of the salmon; the remote bays and estuaries, the rivers and streams where the salmon returned year after year to spawn, and the days and hours spent alone in the magnificence of the wild back country. He begrudged more and more the time he was obliged to spend in the office, and the necessary tasks of enforcing the ever more complex regulations.

My attitude gets worse every year. It really is time for me to retire, he reflected as he walked on.

Ray had no problem finding the T*isiphone.* There was no other boat like it in that section of the harbor. It was primarily a marina full of gill-netters, trollers, skiffs, and other work boats. The cutter stood out with her busy complement of spars and lines, her lack of fishing gear, graceful sheer, and low deck house. She was docked near the end of the transient berth, directly across from the seaplane float. He knocked sharply on the cabin of the boat without stepping aboard, as custom and manners dictated. The hatch slid open and the head and shoulders of the owner emerged.

"Can I help you?" Conrad asked.

Ray Standers' first impression was of a self-assured man with a slight edge of irritation and cockiness. He had the feeling he had interrupted Slocum at something. In fact, only moments earlier Karen Stuckrath had left, and Conrad was still somewhat disconcerted from her short, but emotionally taxing visit.

"I'm with Fish and Game..." he started.

"I can see that from your badge and uniform. You can bet I have not been fishing in this filthy harbor," Conrad replied.

Both men laughed, relieving the tension some.

"No, I'm not here to check your fishing license. My name is Ray Standers. I would like to ask you a couple of questions about judge Daise's death, if you don't mind."

"Well if I must, but I don't know that I can add anything to what I have already reported. But it's not very polite of me to keep you standing out on the dock. Come on aboard. Care for some coffee or tea?" Conrad asked as Ray descended the steep companionway ladder.

"Whatever you're having is fine with me, but don't go to any trouble. I only need a few minutes of your time."

"Coffee it is then. Sugar? Cream?—I've got some canned milk at least."

"Black is just fine."

Although Ray tried to sound casual he felt the burden of his errand. The evening before he had spoken to trooper Tenax by phone about his finding of the soggy shoe and its curious location, but had not discussed his conversation with guide/poacher Martes, or his discovery that Slocum and Stuckrath had served together in the Peace Corps. He felt he needed to speak to Conrad Slocum face to face before committing himself or the troopers to a more extensive investigation. He knew it was ultimately his decision whether or not the man became a suspect in the Daise drowning, and that responsibility weighed heavily on him.

"I have got plenty of time. I'm on vacation," Conrad said, which was partly true. Most of his day was open, but the evening's hours were carefully choreographed, and he hoped to sail away on tomorrow morning's tide.

"Nice place you got here," Ray said, scanning the comfortable cabin, with its exacting joinery, spartan but attractive appointments, and efficient use of space. The interior of yellow cedar and Douglas fir had mellowed to a muted oiled glow. A glimmer of dim light from eight bronze portlights, whose aged patina contributed to the harmonious and agreeable effect was complimented by the orange flame of a kerosine lamp hanging from a ceiling beam.

"You've got more books on board than a lot of Alaskan villages have in their libraries."

Ray held the steaming cup. He warmed his hands with it while he continued inspecting the interior. He noticed that a great deal of time and attention had gone into utilizing the available space for the dozens of books that seemed to occupy every nook and cranny of the cabin. One shelf contained titles on history, philosophy, biographies of scientists and intellectuals, and classical Greek and Roman works; another seemed to be devoted to seagoing authors, with Conrad, Melville, and O'Brian well represented. Still another nook—this one adjacent the navigation station—was taken up with books on seamanship, maintenance, rope work, and storm survival techniques.

"I find I have a lot of time for reading when I'm out on the water," Conrad replied, taking his own quick measure of the officer. "But I don't imagine you are here to check out a book."

What Ray could not know from his quick but attentive survey of the cabin, was just how thoroughly and painstakingly the craft had been stocked. Hidden in various lockers, the bilges, and virtually every available cranny were enough stores for a long voyage. Conrad had been busy since he had arrived in Juneau. He had topped off his fuel and water tanks, restocked his food and spare parts inventories, and generally rearranged the boat interior so that he could survive weeks, even months away from any town or port facilities.

"Of course you are right. I can see you are a man who likes to cut to the chase, so I won't waste any more your time. I have been asked by the troopers to look into the drowning of Daise, and I just got back from a trip to Spruce Cove," Ray continued. "There are a couple of things I don't understand that maybe you can clear up for me."

"As I said, the troopers already have my statement. I really don't have anything to add to it."

"Of course, but I just wanted to clarify a few details about the incident so we can wrap up the investigation. I must say that in spite of our efforts we have not been able to find out too much about you Mr. Slocum. Apparently the work you do, and even the exact division of the government you work for is classified."

"I don't understand how my employment has anything to do with your investigation of the judge's death."

"It doesn't directly, but I was thinking that because you and I both work for the government you might have some sympathy for my position, and appreciation for the need to be accurate and thorough in these types of investigations. By the way—you are not by chance related to the famous world voyaging Slocum, are you?"

"Not that I know of." (Conrad did know, but was not in the habit of revealing his genealogy to strangers.)

"But of course I have read his writings, like most sailors. It seems to me that you are still beating around the bush. Do you think I know something about the judge's death that I have not already disclosed?"

Unlike Conrad, Ray was not used to dissembling, but he at least knew enough not to lay all his cards on the table at the beginning of the play. He wanted to draw Conrad out as much as possible, and he wanted to see if Conrad would acknowledge his relationship with David Stuckrath without prompting.

"I didn't say that, but there are some things that don't add up. For instance; I interviewed a witness on Etolin Island who observed your boat maneuvering near the area where the body was found, and some other evidence I have seems to contradict or at least question the details of your report. Now, being the obviously good mariner that you seem to be, you must know that the currents and tide were moving north at the time you reported Daise overboard. That doesn't seem to compute. I figure Daise fell off your boat quite a few miles south—maybe around Point Stanhope or Three Way Passage, then drifted north to Lincoln Rock where his body was found. But you reported man overboard to the Coast Guard off Mariposa Rock—miles north, and I'd guess a couple hours later."

"I'm sure you have enough experience on the water up here to know currents can do some pretty strange things, and I know you realize that sometimes countercurrents can flow at lower depths. Why bother to tell me this? If I am really a suspect, why not haul me in and get on with it," Conrad replied, carefully controlling his irritation.

He was not particularly disconcerted by the the improbable coincidence that someone apparently had observed him from the wild and remote slopes of Etolin Island. In his experience this sort of unexpected complication seemed to always accompany even the most straightforward of actions. Even if someone had witnessed the actual instant Daise went over, the fact was Conrad had not laid a hand on the man. Even the best of binoculars would not have been strong enough to convey the exact series of events to their user. He felt confident he was not in immediate danger, or they would have sent a trooper with backup. Regardless, he knew the Agency would most likely protect him from arrest—at least until he completed their assignment.

"In a nutshell—I can't find a motive. Why would you want to get rid of Daise, assuming that was your intention?"

Ray was taking his time in his typically deliberate fashion. Intuitively he knew that Slocum had not been entirely honest in his report of the accident, but he also sensed he was not the sort of man to be goaded or cowed into revealing more than he wished. Still, Ray kept on doggedly, hoping to find a chink in the man's armor.

"There is no evidence you knew Daise; nobody in Spruce Cove witnessed any sort of interaction between you and the judge, and no jury is going to convict without proof of motivation. Besides, I am afraid that unless there really is good cause to hold you as a witness or suspect we are liable to get a message from your boss—whoever that is—to lay off."

"It doesn't look like you have much of a case against me, does it, so why persist in this investigation? ...seems to me your time and effort could be put to better uses."

"Maybe you're right. I can't see much reason to dig into this any further myself, but the trooper who is in charge of the case can sometimes be pretty stubborn when he gets an idea in his head. I suspect that if I bring up my own research results and misgivings he may decide to launch a more thorough investigation, and you might be here quite a while."

"Do I understand you correctly? Are you giving me information about the case the troopers don't yet have? Now it is my turn to wonder about motive. Are you hoping for some sort of confession, or is this your crude attempt at blackmail?"

Conrad had spoken quietly and deliberately, all the while never changing his relaxed and affable demeanor, but Ray sensed a feral menace behind his friendly facade, and for the first time it occurred to him that it might be possible this man had in fact killed the judge, for whatever mysterious motivations.

Ray was reminded of an incident during one winter research excursion when he had found himself inside a mountain cave, and the opening was unexpectedly blocked by a brown bear who was not at all pleased that another animal had found its seasonal den. Aware of a certain danger, he continued more cautiously with his interview.

"But I don't think you killed the judge—at least intentionally. I just wonder why you took so long to report it, and why you seem to be so little moved by his death, considering you took on the responsibility of getting the man to Wrangell."

It was tempting to reveal his knowledge of Slocum's relationship to Stuckrath, but Ray was still loath to play his last card.

Conrad decided feigning cooperation might get rid of the man sooner. He had no wish to further complicate his situation. He knew he could probably get both the Fish and Game officer and the troopers to leave him alone with one call to the Agency, but it was a call he did not want to make, as that would put him uncomfortably in their debt. He still had the one task which had brought him to Juneau yet to accomplish, and he did not want any more attention, either from the locals or his employer.

"Who says I'm not upset? Do you think just because my eyes are not brimming with tears his death has not affected me? As you must know from the report, I was in the cabin when he fell overboard. I don't know when it happened for sure. It could have been farther south I suppose. However it happened, I do feel badly about it. (This was no lie, Conrad did not like killing, although he had killed before and had every intention of doing so again.) I've never lost a passenger or crew until now, and I do feel some responsibility for the man's fate. In retrospect I should have at least insisted he wear flotation."

"It's still hard for me to believe it took you two hours to notice the judge was gone. I have the impression you are a more conscientious sailor than that," Ray said, laconically.

Abruptly it occurred to him that the Stuckrath connection was probably a red herring, unrelated to the judge's fate, and that the whole investigation was pointless. He knew from his earlier interviews and reading of the Coast Guard testimony from Spruce Cove that Conrad had not participated in the mock trial of the judge, and had certainly shown no animosity towards Henry Daise. Besides, if Conrad was really a friend of David's he was probably satisfied with the outcome of the events at Chuck's house, which seemed to have favored Stuckrath. From his reading of what transpired in Spruce Cove it appeared that David Stuckrath had only wanted to humiliate Daise and make his point about the harmful effects of the drug war, and had accomplished his goals. Even if he and Slocum were the closest of friends, there still did not seem to be adequate motivation in Ray's judgement for Slocum to kill the judge.

Of course in coming to this conclusion, Ray, whose only experience with criminal law was related to Fish and Game department regulations enforcement, not murder, failed to consider seriously the possibility that Conrad might have wanted to protect David from possible future prosecution. But more importantly, Ray, like trooper Tenax, had no idea that Marshall Stuckrath was Conrad's biological son.

Conrad smiled at Ray's comment. In spite of his earlier irritation at the interruption he found himself enjoying the exchange with the man, appreciating his tenacity and obvious powers of observation. He imagined in other circumstances they might well become friends, but he could not afford to let his guard down so close to his goal.

"Well, I guess I'm not quite the sailor you take me for. You give me far too much credit. I'm so used to sailing solo I just got lazy with another man on board who obviously knew the area and volunteered to take a watch. He seemed to be an experienced and competent boater, with more knowledge of the local conditions and geography than myself. In any case the wind vane was steering, and all he had to do was keep an eye out for logs in the water or call me if the wind changed direction. As I stated in my report, I went down to rest and fell asleep in my bunk. When I went back on deck he was just gone. As I suggested in my statement, I figured he probably had to take a piss and fell off. I guess it just wasn't judge Daise's week—if you'll excuse the rude wordplay."

Ray chuckled in spite of himself.

"Then why didn't you say anything about falling asleep in your report to the Coast Guard?" Ray countered.

"Didn't I? I must have still been upset and forgot to mention it," Conrad replied.

In reality, Conrad knew that the truly innocent

never tell exactly the same story, and only the guilty rely on perfect repetition. He was pretty sure the officer was astute enough to know that too.

"You know how it is when you doze off. I don't have any idea how long I slept, or if I really slept at all. I just know he was not on deck when I came up. I searched for him until it was nearly dark—until the Coast Guard advised me to continue on to Wrangell. After the troopers took my statement there they gave me permission to go to Juneau—so here I am."

"For some reason I have a hard time imaging you being rattled by much of anything, Mr. Slocum," Ray responded. "I would like to believe your story, but I admit I'm still not totally satisfied. On the other hand, I have no real reason to give to sergeant Tenax to continue his investigation—at least anything that would hold up in court, as we both realize. People die out here every year on the water. Some of the bodies never turn up again, and many of the ones that are found are in such bad condition that it's impossible for the coroner to tell how they died. Much of the time there are no witnesses, as in this case."

"The sea does keep its secrets," Conrad agreed.

"I have to admit some of this still mystifies me, but I learned long ago from my biology professors to accept some degree of uncertainty. The judge certainly had his share of enemies up here, but you don't seem to have any reason to be one of those. Maybe it was just his karma, as some say. I'll be moving along. I don't imagine the troopers or the district attorney will want to follow up, but in any case that's not my concern. I need to get back to my regular duties. This is my busiest time of year. If you do remember any more details I hope you will give me a call." Ray handed Conrad his card.

"Of course I will," Conrad replied.

"There is one thing that interests me even more than Daise's unfortunate end," Ray said, rising to leave. "I heard you saw a cougar in the forest above Spruce Cove. That is remarkable, and I'd love to hear about it."

"Yes, I'm told it is about as rare as a glimpse of Bigfoot in these parts," Conrad replied.

Ray listened raptly as Conrad told him the details of his experience.

"One thing I have learned over the years is that the best photographers and observers of wildlife, like good hunters often seem to have a certain uncanny ability to be in the right place at the right time, along with the other obvious requirements of their work—tenacity, patience, and endurance. You seem to be one of that rare group."

"I doubt it. I think I was just lucky."

But of course Conrad was convinced his sighting of the mountain lion was more than mere chance.

"Perhaps, but it still puts you in very select company. I've been roaming these fjords and forests for over twenty years and I like to think I'm a pretty fair outdoorsman, but I've never seen a cougar in the wild. Hopefully I'll find the time to get down there and follow up once the salmon runs are over."

"Well, now it really is time for me to be going. I suppose you've heard judge Daise's funeral is today," Ray continued.

"No, I haven't had a chance to read the paper. What time?"

"It's at one. Are you planning on going?" Ray asked.

"I plan to now. It might look bad if I didn't make an appearance, eh?"

"It might at that," Ray smiled at Conrad's remark.

"I have enjoyed meeting you. I wish it could have been under more pleasant circumstances," Conrad said, meaning it, and extending his hand.

They shook hands. Ray turned to climb the companionway ladder. He noticed a small scrap of paper taped to the bulkhead over the galley counter. It read:

"If faced with a choice between my country and my friends, I would hope I would have the courage to choose my friends" __E.M. Forster

"Is that your view?" Ray asked, pointing to the note.

"Absolutely," Conrad replied without hesitation, "...and you?"

Once again Ray chose to conceal his awareness of Conrad's connection to David Stuckrath, though it seemed to be the perfect opportunity to reveal the results of his research. Later that evening as he wrote out his notes on the interview, he would wonder why he had been so reticent to divulge what he knew of that perhaps crucial connection.

"I think it would be a terrible choice to have to make, but I would have to agree with you. That is assuming the friend had not done something terribly criminal or immoral."

"Ah, but sometimes it is the law that is criminal and the crime is committed by the state against the individual," Conrad replied.

"We all have to live with our decisions in any case. Enjoy your stay in Juneau. Give me a call if you want to get some bait wet. I am quite a bit better at finding fish than playing detective," Ray said as he climbed out of Conrad's boat.

"Perhaps it is just a matter of timing and the right bait in either case."

"Could be, but I think my tastes and talents run more to the finned than two legged species," Ray responded, fastening the snaps on his rain parka against the chill drizzle which had resumed while they parleyed.

Conrad watched officer Standers walk down the dock and up the ramp to the parking lot. He knew he would have to attend Daise's funeral. Now that it was known he was in Juneau, it would seem odd to those investigating the judge's death if he did not appear, and in spite of what the Fish and Game officer had said he doubted the local authorities were completely through with him. He was also curious to see who would be there, and it was an opportunity to learn more about the man whose life had ended so abruptly and violently in the cold seas of Clarence Strait.

CHAPTER 23

A Funeral

In expectation of a large turnout a convention room in a downtown hotel had been booked for the Henry Daise memorial services. Members of the state legislature, the governor, several prominent attorneys and judges, and Daise's immediate family, his wife and three adult children, were seated close by the flower-bedecked stage near the cumbrous coffin. Conrad sat through the service in a folding chair on the bare hardwood floor with the rest of the audience. The funeral services were mercifully short considering Daise's stature in Juneau, and in the state of Alaska. After the eulogies were finished an hour was allowed before the funeral procession was scheduled to begin. The crowd dispersed, many of them moving to the back of the room where a pictorial of his life was displayed, featuring newspaper articles, photographs, testimonials from friends and members of the legal and law enforcement communities, and a family tableaux.

Conrad examined the photos, noting especially a series showing Daise and his children over a thirty year time span. There were two athletic-looking sons, and an attractive daughter. One of the photographs showed the judge and his teen-aged daughter happily posing with a large king salmon on his boat, the *Legal Eagle*.

As he was about to leave he noticed the girl from the photo, now grown into a woman, somber yet elegant in her black weeds, approaching him. She caught his gaze, and it was too late to exit with grace.

"Hey, I recognize you—from the news article. Aren't you the owner of the sailboat my dad fell from?" She extended a hand.

"Yes, I'm afraid I am. It seems your father was very well known, and quite respected here."

He took her hand. He apprehended a pretty, even striking woman in her mid-thirties, a bit over average height, exaggerated somewhat by her black heels, with a confident bearing born of a privileged pedigree. Her gaze was direct and self-assured, with a hint of challenge.

"...but not necessarily well liked. I'm Linda—Linda Daise."

She held his hand slightly longer than felt comfortable to him, as though she hoped to ascertain something directly from the contact.

"I am not so sure that half of the people here aren't celebrating his demise, or are at least relieved he is gone—but you could hardly have an opinion one way or the other I suppose, as you spent so little time with him."

She finally let go his hand, but continued to hold his gaze.

"They say a man is judged by the quality of his enemies even more than his friends," was Conrad's awkward reply.

He was torn by his conflicting desires both to get away from the uncomfortable situation, and his immediate and visceral attraction to this alluring woman.

"Yes, the quality, and perhaps the quantity too. Well anyway, I wanted to meet the person my dad spent his last hours with, but I don't suppose this is the best place to talk, and there is not much time before the motorcade starts. I should get back to mom and my brothers, but I wonder if you might have time later today to meet somewhere?"

Her manner was insistent and a touch conspiratorial, and there was a something else—unmistakable signals that his attraction to her was reciprocated. There was no diplomatic way to excuse himself in any event, so he agreed to meet her at a downtown eatery that afternoon. A local newspaper reporter, who had been hovering throughout their conversation, cut short their congé and Conrad took advantage of the opportunity to slip away.

They met in a restaurant and coffee shop located in a renovated warehouse perched on old piers on the Juneau waterfront. The structure had started its days as a shipping depot, but had been recently remodeled into a small shopping mall. Their restaurant, essentially a pizza place with the addition of an espresso machine and ice cream offerings, was nestled among a motley collection of souvenir and gift shops and a popular pub.

It would be two hours more before the start of the dinner rush, and they had the restaurant mostly to themselves.

The service was slow in coming and saccadic—a characteristic of Southeast Alaskan culture that more than one visitor had noted. Today the lack of attention by the pouting young waitress (who made two telephone calls in the first few minutes after they were seated) did not perturb Conrad. He found he was enjoying his time with Linda Daise, even though he felt an inevitable uneasiness.

"You are probably wondering why I wanted so much to meet with you," Linda said after they were seated.

"Well, I often have that effect on women," Conrad teased.

"Pretty sure of yourself aren't you?" She laughed, but blushed slightly.

"I only meant they often want to talk to me. Perhaps they see me as priest confessor, the kindly uncle type, or maybe I'm just a good listener."

"Ah, and are they then enticed to sit on your knee and whisper their confessions?"

"I suppose a few have found that comforting, but somehow I don't get the feeling that you are the easily enticed type."

"You are correct, but don't underestimate yourself. In fact I didn't invite you here for an afternoon flirtation, though I confess it might not be such a bad way to spend my time. But unfortunately I'm flying out tomorrow morning and I'm sorry I can barely afford to steal even this time away from the family."

"I doubt that you regret it as much as I do," Conrad replied, surprised that he actually meant it.

The waitress arrived with their coffees and muffins, and set them down abruptly, sloshing their drinks into the saucers. Without asking her customers if they needed anything else, she returned immediately to another telephone conversation.

"Well," Linda sighed, "I suppose I am looking for some closure as much as anything. My relationship with Dad has been complicated, and not all that pleasant for the last few years. I feel terrible that the last time I saw him we ended on a bad note. We had strong philosophical and political differences, and we both foolishly let those opinions affect our personal relationship."

Conrad saw the tears well up in her eyes. After a short pause to collect herself Linda continued.

"After my divorce I went back to college, got my degree, and passed the bar exam. I started here in Juneau with a local firm specializing in defending DUI and drug cases, mostly. I had no axe to grind at first. I had a pretty substantial outstanding college loan to pay off, and I needed the work, but I soon found myself at odds with dad over how the law treats those types of cases. I told him his personal opinions were impairing his ability to be fair and balanced in the courtroom. We even stopped speaking altogether for a few months. A couple of years ago I had a chance to take a position with a firm in Seattle, where I am now. It helped that I was no longer practicing law in the same city and courtroom as my father, but even so our last visit just before he left on his boat trip ended badly, with a pointless disagreement about a minor drug possession case."

"I'm sorry to hear that, but we all have had differences with our parents. I'm sure it didn't affect his feelings for you," Conrad consoled.

"Yes, but our disagreement over this case was worse than any before. He had sentenced a young man —a first time offender—for possession of a small amount of cocaine. The defendant ended up getting killed in prison, and I argued that dad held some responsibility for that, which infuriated him. I had planned to go out fishing with him before our fight, but after that I decided to stay in town with mom and he left without me. Now I can't help but regret that decision. We always had such great times fishing and running around the islands in dad's boat. I know it's not logical, but I feel somehow guilty. Maybe I would have been out on the deck with dad on your boat and seen him in time to have rescued him, or warned him before he fell somehow—or maybe just me being on his boat before that might have changed his route or timing in some way..."

"I doubt you could have saved him, so there is no point in feeling guilty about something you had nothing to do with. Is that why you wanted to talk to me? To hear about his last moments?"

"No, not that so much. I'm actually more curious about what happened in Spruce Cove. I heard that the father of that boy dad sent to jail—the same case we quarreled over—was there, and the people in the cove held some kind of impromptu court and put dad on trial. My quarrel with dad started when I said I wished I could have been that boy's lawyer. Today at the funeral one of the lawyers I know, who practices here in Juneau, told me there is a chance someone may bring legal action against the father of the boy for holding dad and others there against their will while some sort of trial took place. Since you were there, I guess you must know what happened."

"I haven't been subpoenaed, so I don't know about any possible charges against anyone. But yes, I was at Spruce Cove and I know at least one man besides your dad was pretty angry that he was forced to participate. I can't imagine who would bring such a case against Stuckrath, unless it was him. But perhaps I should be careful what I say since I am talking to an attorney, right?"

Linda smiled disarmingly and shook her head.

"Defense lawyer, remember. I'm not a prosecutor. Don't worry, I don't care about the legal aspects of what happened there one way or the other, and in any case I'm no longer practicing law in Alaska—but I am curious about what was said and how dad reacted to it. What very few people know is that dad had very personal reasons for being so adamantly opposed to drug use in any form, and he felt strongly that a prison sentence was the best tool society had to deter people from abusing drugs. These feelings were based more on his own experiences as a young man than any legal arguments."

"You mean he had done drugs himself in his youth?"

"Not himself. Dad did not even drink much, but one of his closest friends died of a heroin overdose. They went to high school together and ended up in the same platoon in Korea, before dad went on to college and law school. His friend got addicted in the army and overdosed just weeks before they were to ship back to the states. Dad never talked about it, but mom told me he was the one who discovered his friend dead in his cot, with a needle still in his arm."

"That explains some of his attitude and inflexibility on the subject I suppose, but other people who have lost friends and family to drugs have certainly come out in favor of more humane alternatives to prison. I watched the whole affair in Spruce Cove without interfering or taking sides myself, but I have to tell you; your father's arguments were not compelling, either emotionally or logically. He totally rejected the possibility that he had any responsibility for the death of (Conrad felt his voice catch)—of that young man. Still, I got the feeling that he was essentially a good and otherwise fair-minded man who somehow had let this one issue cloud his otherwise normally balanced and reasonable judgement."

Linda, thinking of her father's last hours, had not noticed Conrad's uneasiness in speaking about Marshall's incarceration and death.

"...and that was almost exactly my argument with him every time we discussed the issue. Poor father! So he died unhappy and angry?"

Conrad could see her holding back the tears once again and knew it was in his power to dissemble just enough to help alleviate her sadness and regret over having missed her last chance to have enjoyed time with her father. So much of life, it seemed to him, involved just such lost opportunities. It was evident to Conrad how much Linda had suffered from the estrangement, and he realized he wanted desperately to say something to ease her pain. Another part of Conrad's mind calculated that his description of Daise's last moments aboard his boat must be consistent, in light of the fact that at least one official suspected he had some part in the judge's demise. Given Linda Daise's connections to the litigators and law enforcement professionals locally it was certainly probable that someone might tell her he had been and was perhaps still, a "person of interest" in the death of the judge. It was one of those very rare moments when self-interest and altruism coincided. The incongruity and irony of the situation did not escape Conrad, even as he felt himself fall more and more under the spell of this captivating woman.

"No, you are completely wrong about that. After the storm let up in the night that next morning was perfect. The farther away from Spruce Cove we went, the happier he seemed to be. We had a nice strong following breeze. Your dad seemed to have put the events of the previous day completely behind him. He was enjoying the sunshine, the water, and the view of shoreline. He commented some about his close call and rescue when his engine conked out, but in a light-hearted way, and he just seemed pleased to be alive and out on the water on such a morning. He did not seem the least bit bitter or unhappy—in fact just the opposite."

As he spoke these consoling words Conrad could not avoid the memory of their last harsh exchange before Daise went overboard, and the final look of terror on the judge's face the instant before he was crushed beneath the keel of *Tisiphone*. But Conrad's words had the desired effect on Linda. She brightened immediately, and the rest of their meeting was unmarred by any further discussion of the judge's last moments or manner of death.

An hour later, and all too soon for them both, it was time for Linda to leave. She still had to attend to the family duties that would consume the rest of her visit in Juneau. Conrad walked her to her rental car in the parking lot. He too had a busy evening planned.

"Since we both live in Seattle, I hope we do run in to each other again," she said, offering her hand.

"Who knows when I might need a lawyer," Conrad answered, immediately regretting his glib reply.

Her's was no empty parting pleasantry, but an open invitation.

"I was thinking more along the lines of an afternoon of sailing Puget Sound. I am not entirely inexperienced at sea, as you now know."

"I'm surprised you would risk it, considering,"

Conrad replied.

"I am not the least bit worried. I'm sure you will keep an especially close eye on me—considering..."

He watched her drive away—a siren sent too late to lure him away from his grim goal. He held the business card she had given him with the address and phone number of her office in Seattle—a rendezvous he knew he would never realize. Some part of him also apprehended, intuitively and certainly, that because of the circumstances he must forego this rare opportunity to pursue that which he had yet to find, but had always hoped for—a love which was more than ephemeral. He saw clearly that the furies would indeed levy a bitter personal toll in their inexorable pursuit of equilibrium.

For a moment Conrad saw himself clearly and dispassionately as from a distance, and as some future biographer might; a lonely ectopic middle-aged man with an implausible past and a forlorn future.

With an effort he shook off the ache of longing and the sense of possibilities forever lost as he walked through the rain-slick streets and back to his boat in the harbor. He still had much yet to do, and it would require all his faculties and complete commitment to put his plan into motion. His life, though solitary and less rife with future promise, had purpose yet.

CHAPTER 24

The Moby Dick

The Moby Dick was a Juneau drinking establishment with a long and checkered history. Built in the 1890s, it had passed through a half dozen owners and twice as many remodels as it was modified to better serve the clientele and the times. As a bar and brothel it was notorious during the era when Juneau was primarily a mining and cannery town. Then its dank basement had served the segregated coolie population as an opium den. During prohibition the main barroom was changed into a pool and card room, but the basement continued to serve the currently banned substance—in those years Canadian liquor—and the local authorities had mostly looked the other way as long as they got their percentage. After a brief surge in business serving soldiers during the nineteen forties the bar fell upon hard times in the nineteen fifties and sixties, growing progressively more decrepit with each passing year. But before it fell into complete disrepair the Moby Dick was rescued and given a complete face-lift and remodel during the late seventies, when a consortium of new owners, flush with money from pipeline work decided to restore the business to something resembling its former glory. Their timing had been good and business had prospered as tourism grew through the eighties and nineties. But as the Moby Dick entered its second century it started another period of decline. The new owners moved south, relying on a property management company to keep up the maintenance, and a series of lazy or outright dishonest managers had done only the minimum required to keep up the premises.

The nightclub's somewhat louche character was not very harmful to its main tourism business during the day, however. If anything, it helped to create the desired atmosphere, and the pamphlets available on the tour ships and from the tour guides played up and exaggerated the bawdy and lawless history. An assortment of beer mugs, shirts, hats and garters available for purchase at the bar loudly promoted the Moby Dick as the historical center of the red light district. It was just good fun with a taint of naughtiness for the many thousands of tourists who passed through each summer, most of whom were far more likely to gaze at the historical pictures of the ladies of the night on the walls and purchase a Moby Dick shot glass or tee-shirt, than to actually have a drink at the bar. Besides, the cocktails were cheaper or even free back on the tour ships, and the visitors did not want to miss out on the dinner they had paid for as part of their vacation package.

Since the majority of the tourists wandered the downtown streets for only a few hours during the day and were mostly back on board their vessels by the dinner hour, the bar had developed a sort of dual personality. The locals, especially the hard-core drinkers and alcoholics, drank elsewhere during the daytime hours. The overly rustic rubes were actively discouraged from entering the faux wooden swinging doors by the diurnal staff, who knew that too much authenticity could be bad for business. Many locals preferred to mix as little as possible with the tourists and gawkers, so the arrangement worked well. The day shift male staff were required to dress up like late nineteenth century barkeeps with pressed white shirts and black sleeve garters, and the waitress's décolleté dresses encouraged generous tipping, especially from the older male tourists.

But everything changed in the evening. The throngs of tourists threaded their way back down Juneau's claustrophobic streets to their meals, drinks, and gambling on the love boats. The little shops that sold gauche gold nugget jewelry, glacier bear emblazoned sweat shirts, and over-priced smoked salmon in elaborate wooden gift boxes closed down for the evening. The night staff at Moby Dick's made no attempt to costume themselves, preferring typical Northwest casual attire. The theme park-like pretense was dropped altogether.

As the streets disgorged the transients, the regular clientele began to file in; construction trade workers having their beers before dinner; fishermen ready for a few drinks and conversation after a day of working on their boats and gear; a handful of hopeless drunks who had long ago lost their driver's licenses, and were allowed to drink until they could barely stumble out into the night; and a few of the seasonal Anchorage expatriates relaxing after a day of lobbying at the capitol buildings a few blocks away up Juneau's infamously steep and narrow streets.

The busy bartender pegged Conrad as a visiting businessman or independent tourist. He did not have the look of a lobbyist, and at any rate they rarely came to the bar alone. His face was not familiar, but that was not unusual in any club in downtown Juneau, where late summer visitors often as not outnumbered the regulars. Still, the bartender eyed the newcomer closely, as he did any lone male patron. He could not be too careful. The unfamiliar man ordered a Guinness and retired to one of the tables close to the large screen television. The bartender relaxed. Just another visitor watching the Seattle Mariners game, he surmised, and shifted his attention to a potential troublemaker cursing loudly at the other end of the long mahogany bar.

In one way the Moby Dick had not changed at all since its founding. The basement still had its secrets. Tonight's bartender and the club manager, Jim Lothar—a burly and balding man in his early forties—had reason to be cautious as he was also selling cocaine and methamphetamine on the side, working with his partner out of the historically notorious basement. The business was the same as it had been one hundred years earlier—only the strain of contraband had changed.

Grant Tadlock, his business partner, had begun working with him months earlier while Lothar had been employed temporarily as prison guard at the Lime River Penitentiary. Tadlock had been only a few days away from completing his sentence for a burglary charge when he had killed the Stuckrath boy in a prison yard fight. According to the witnesses produced by Tadlock's lawyer—other prison inmates there at the time—Marshall Stuckrath had started the fight and Tadlock had acted in self-defense. It had helped his case that Marshall Stuckrath, bigger, stronger, and an accomplished athlete, had supposedly had Tadlock in a choke hold at the time he was stabbed to death, though not all the witnesses agreed on this point. Grant Tadlock had also argued he only carried the shiv as protection from bullies, being such a small and weak man.

The state had maintained Tadlock had a history of crime including assault, but their case was flawed, and they were only able to produce one witness, who testified Stuckrath had been threatened by Tadlock and other inmates previous to the fight. Unfortunately, the prosecution's witness was a criminal with an unsavory past. In the end it amounted to the testimonies of felons versus felons. The state had to settle for a conviction of Tadlock on the illegal possession of a weapon, and the murder charge was dropped. Tadlock served an additional ninety days at Lime River, another six months at the half way house, and was currently free on probation.

One bit of information that could have badly hurt Tadlock's case was that Moby Dick's bartender, Jim Lothar, had seen Grant threaten Marshall on several occasions during his employment as a part time prison guard at Lime River. Some of the more incorrigible prisoners and ex-cons, including Grant Tadlock, made a practice of hazing the newer prisoners, especially younger men and those with no previous prison experience who might be incarcerated for drinking and driving violations, drug possession, public drunkenness, or other lesser crimes. Much of the time the hazing consisted of verbal teasing, sexual innuendo, or perhaps tripping and other fairly harmless activities. It served to let off steam and relieve the boredom for those on the giving end, and rarely escalated to anything more serious. The guards ignored a lot of this activity, many of them holding to the view that a little of this treatment served as part of the punishment, and worked as an effective deterrent to keep recidivism down among first time offenders.

Marshall had been different though. From the first he refused to take the hazing, and let it be known he would not be bullied. On one occasion Jim had been on guard duty and watched as Tadlock and another prisoner taunted the young man as the inmates were escorted back to their cells after dinner. While a bulky yardbird backed him up, Grant made lewd comments and gestures at Marshall. When Marshall ignored them, he reached out and pinched his cheek. In the blink of an eye Marshall grabbed the smaller man's wrist, twisting his arm up behind him and forcing a cry of pain from Tadlock before Lothar broke them up.

"Aw, he didn't mean nothin' by it. Jest a friendly

little love tap..." Tadlock's felonious friend interposed.

"That'll be enough now. You all know the rules—no physical contact," Jim said, hand on his baton.

"Hey Jim, you know I didn't hurt him none. I was just playin'. Look what he done to my wrist," Tadlock whined, showing a reddened but otherwise uninjured forearm.

"Fuck you, asshole! What did I ever do to you? You've been hassling me ever since I got here!" Marshall yelled.

"All right! I said that's enough! I want you two to stay away from each other. Any more problems from either of you and you'll both go to solitary, understand?" Jim waved his baton, and emphasized his words by striking his left hand as he spoke.

"You'll get yours! Just wait and see... You're gonna be sorry you ever laid a hand on me," Grant threatened, glaring at Marshall as they resumed the walk to their cells.

A few days later Marshall was dead from multiple stab wounds, and Grant Tadlock was in solitary. Jim made it a point to talk to him before his trial.

"It looks like things could go pretty bad for you. I heard a couple of the men are going to testify Marshall attacked you first, but it wouldn't be so good if it got out you had been harassing the boy, or if the court knew you threatened him," Jim said, casually.

"Well, I told them exactly what happened. He attacked me, and I defended myself," Grant said. His thin, pock-marked face looked especially haggard in the harsh glare of the prison cell light.

"Some would say so, and some might say you made the first move," Jim replied. "I guess you don't know your lawyer talked to me yesterday—asked me if I might have anything to say at the trial in your defense. I'm betting he thinks the jury might be more disposed to believe my testimony than that of a bunch of jailbirds."

"What did you tell him?" Grant asked, anxiously.

"I said I would think about it and let him know," Jim replied. "I might have heard the kid threaten you, or it might be the other way around—depends on what's in it for me."

"How's that?"

"I'm gonna come straight to the point. I've heard it around you've got some pretty good connections. In return for my help I'd like a piece of the action. I think we could do pretty well together."

"I'll have to give that some thought," Grant replied slyly.

"Well don't think about it too long," Jim answered, turning to leave. "I told your lawyer I'd let him know tomorrow."

The partnership had worked very well. Jim Lothar's position as manager and bartender at the Moby Dick was the perfect cover. The problems of traffic at odd hours at a private residence that would have aroused the suspicions of neighbors were avoided by using the Moby Dick's basement, with its conveniently discreet alley delivery entrance. Inside was a small elevator which was used to lift the heavy kegs and cases of beer and booze from the storage refrigerators below to the bar above. An intercom on the wall next to the phone connected the bar with the basement. When a special customer came into the bar Jim Lothar buzzed Grant Tadlock on the intercom. Then Lothar would either send the buyer into the alley, where Tadlock let the customer in through the service door, or Lothar himself would go down the elevator on some pretext, leaving one of the waitresses to handle the drink orders. If anyone entered the bar who looked at all like they could be law enforcement they had a pre-arranged signal (Lothar hit the call button three times in succession), and Tadlock quickly left with the contraband. They had experienced a couple of false alarms, but so far nothing had interrupted their profitable alliance.

CHAPTER 25

Conrad Strikes

Conrad Slocum had checked out the Moby Dick earlier in the day before Jim Lothar came on duty, entering with large group of noisy tourists from one of the tour ships. He had listened to the tour guide go through his well embellished spiel on the disreputable history of the bar, and had noticed the service elevator at the end of the short hallway leading to the public bathrooms. Conrad had seen it was possible to surreptitiously observe a reflection of the bar and the people gathered there from one of the several large wall mirrors, while simultaneously watching one of the large screen televisions.

Later that evening, after halibut and chips at a waterfront restaurant he returned to the Moby Dick. Nursing his beer while he feigned watching the game, he kept a close eye on the bartender with side-long glances at the mirror. He could see the man was suspiciously taking his own measure of him as well. Conrad kept his eyes on the televised game, and after a few minutes the bartender appeared to be satisfied that he was just another sports fan relaxing with a drink. After a time Conrad saw the man thumb the intercom. The bartender spoke with his mouth close to the unit, then checked his watch before returning to his regular bartending duties. Conrad waited until he was busy with a customer, left a bill on the table, and slipped out the door into the Juneau night.

A wet cold wind blew up Gastineau Channel and through the gloomy madid streets of the town. A few hardy souls hurried by on the sidewalk, their coats fastened tight against the evening chill. Windshield wipers on a taxi idling in front of the bar slapped out an isochronal rhythm. Conrad walked quickly to the end of the block and turned up a side street, turning again when he reached the corner. A half a block more and he was into the alley that lead past the service door of the Moby Dick. The alley was dark except for a low wattage light fixture above the receiving door. Several large garbage dumpsters were spaced at intervals along the way. Conrad chose one across the alley and a few steps away from the service door, and moved it slightly away from the wall so he could just crouch behind.

He had barely settled himself into position behind the dumpster when a tenebrous figure came down the alleyway from the opposite direction and knocked at the service door. An angular shaft of light split the darkness. A man—presumably a buyer—was quickly let in. This time his wait was longer. Conrad began to feel the cold. His woolen cap and jeans were soaked through, and although his rain coat kept his torso dry enough, he began to shiver from his inability to move from the constricted position. But Conrad was capable of enduring a fair amount of physical distress. He took regular deep breaths and cleared his mind, focusing on the task ahead. Timing would be everything, he knew. His life-long study of the various martial arts would help him of course, but surprise would help even more. Conrad had one absolute rule about combat; when it counts—and he never fought unless it did count —never, ever fight fairly. He took a weighted cestus from his coat pocket, fitted it on his right hand, and adjusted his position as best he could in the cramped confines of his hiding place.

At last the door opened, swinging inward into the stairwell. A man, whom Conrad assumed was the customer, peered cautiously into the alley. Another man, Grant Tadlock, stood behind him on the landing and held the door open. At that instant Conrad sprinted the few feet from the dumpster across the alley and charged straight at the two men. The drug buyer (for so he was) was projected to the edge of the landing where he lost his footing and rolled down the single flight of stairs to the hard concrete floor below, breaking the fall for Conrad, who landed on top of him. But Tadlock had received only a glancing blow. He darted out the doorway and ran from the scene before Conrad could extricate himself. Conrad ignored the drug buyer, leaving him sprawled on the basement floor, and rushed back up the stairs after Tadlock. But by the time he reached the alley there was no sign of the man, and Conrad had no idea in which direction Grant Tadlock had fled.

Knowing it was probably pointless, he nevertheless looked into several neighboring bars and searched the area as best he could in the dark, cursing his bad luck at missing his chance. As he made his way back to the harbor Conrad reflected that at least Tadlock could not possibly have any idea of his identity. He would most likely assume that someone had been out to steal the drugs—probably someone who either the customer or Tadlock and his partner knew. The fact that Tadlock had no idea of who he was still gave Conrad the advantage, and he would not fail a second time, he resolved.

After twenty minutes had passed and he had not received the usual signal from his partner, Jim Lothar told one of the two waitresses on duty to take the bar while he went to the basement supply room. The waitresses knew nothing of Jim and Grant's side venture. He concocted a story about some supplies he had forgotten to put in the cooler.

Lothar stepped cautiously out of the service elevator holding a short-barreled revolver. The basement door was still partially open to the alley, and he could see the room was unoccupied. He mounted the basement stairs with gun at the ready, and quickly scanned the alley in both directions before closing and bolting the door. On the basement receiving desk, where the customer would normally expect to sample the product before completing the transaction lay an open freezer bag of cocaine, a small framed Budweiser mirror, a set of scales, and a partially rolled up twenty dollar bill. Puzzled and worried, Jim put the powder back into the secret safe hidden behind a wall panel in the space under the stairs, before returning to the bar.

Much later, after the bar had closed and he had sent the waitresses home, he was counting the till when the phone rang.

"I've gotta see you as soon as you're done there," the voice said.

It was Tadlock. They were careful never to talk of drugs or specifics on the phone, and had a prearranged meeting site in case of problems or the unexpected.

"I'll be there in half an hour," Jim said, and hung up.

Their rendezvous was in the Juneau harbor on the vessel *Deep Runner*, a fishing boat used by Lothar and Tadlock in their lucrative smuggling business. Ironically, *Deep Runner* was only a short distance away from Slocum's sailboat in Harris Harbor, where even now Conrad slept soundly, recuperating from the evening's activity.

"So what the fuck happened?" Lothar asked, after Charlie Jackson, the third partner in their enterprise and the captain of the *Deep Runner*, let him into the boat's small pilothouse.

"Shit, I was hoping you could tell me! Someone jumped us when I opened the back door."

"You don't have any idea who it was?" Lothar queried.

"I didn't get much of a look at him, and I doubt I

could pick him out if I saw him again. I thought he must be the heat, so I ran like hell. I remember he was pretty tall, and he came pretty damn fast out of nowhere."

"Now dammit Tadlock, you've had enough experience with the law to know those guys don't operate alone. There would have been a half a dozen of them if it was cops," Lothar reasoned.

"Then he must have been after the blow, I guess."

"Well whoever he was, he didn't take the coke. The stuff was still sitting right out there in the open where you left it. He must have been after something else. You got any enemies I should know about?" Jim said, tapping out two cigarettes from a half depleted pack and offering one to Tadlock. Charlie Jackson was a nonsmoker.

"Yeah lots, but all of 'em are either in jail or dead, as far as I know. ...and anyway nobody knows about our partnership," Grant replied, taking the proffered smoke. "What about Bill? What'd he say about it?"

Bill, the buyer that night, was a regular customer.

"There wasn't a fuckin' soul around by the time I got down to the basement, and Bill hasn't called back. I'm guessing it scared the shit out of him, and we won't hear from him again for a while. Damn! Good customer too. We'll have to shut down the Moby Dick operation for awhile. Could be it was a one time thing—somebody trying to make a quick score—or could be we got a problem. Anyway I've got another job for you and Charlie."

"Yeah, what's up now?"

"We've got a pretty big shipment coming in the day after tomorrow. I've got a couple of things going on and I can't get away—and now this mystery to try and figure out. I need you and Charlie to make the pick-up."

Charlie Jackson said nothing. He had been told of the operation earlier by Lothar, and had already prepared the boat for the venture, topping off the fuel tanks and laying in extra provisions for the voyage.

"The Mexicans again?" Tadlock speculated.

"Not the Mexicans. Its the Chinese this time, and a lot more potential profit if we can pull it off. We've got a a big load of ephedrine from Hong Kong to pick up."

"What the fuck?"

"Even more profitable than coke, man—you know—they make meth from it."

"Yeah I know, but that stuff fucks you up. I stay away from it myself—seen too many guys down south out beggin' on the streets with no teeth in their mouths, and no place to sleep but a garbage bag in the alley. Everybody knows speed fuckin' kills."

"Well, that's not our problem. People want that shit, we provide it. If we don't do it, someone else will be sure to step in and reap the profits. Now this deal should set us up nicely for quite a while, if we don't screw it up. I've already lined up a couple of buyers with wads of cash and just chompin' at the bit to take the shit off our hands as soon as we can get it back here

—so no fucking around with selling crumbs out of the basement on this deal. All we have to do is get the stuff to Juneau, and all you got to do is take the boat to the spot I tell you. But you damn well better be on time, 'cause these guys are real paranoid, and they won't wait around. ...and one more thing. Maybe you know the Chinks are paying a pretty penny for animal parts. Check this out."

Lothar took a large duffle bag from under the galley counter, unzipped it, and the gory contents—bear claws, gall bladders, and freshly skinned seal oosiks packaged in plastic zip-lock baggies, spilled out.

"Man, what the hell do they want with all these animal parts?" Tadlock wondered.

"Lots of folks over there believe this shit will cure your ills or get your dick hard. They'll pay big bucks for the stuff, so it just makes this hook-up that much better for our bottom line. Icing on the cake, you might say."

One of the reasons their three-way partnership had worked so well was the natural division of labor between the three men. Lothar handled the business end of their activities, and Tadlock did most of the errand running and smaller face to face transactions. Charlie Jackson was squeamish about some of the more nefarious aspects of the operation. His role was largely restricted to piloting and maintaining the boat for deliveries and pick-ups. Jim Lothar was quick with figures and had even attended a business college for a time—one of the qualifications that had helped him get his position as head bartender and manager of the Moby Dick. His occasional part-time job as a prison guard helped him stay abreast of local law enforcement activities that might interfere with their smuggling business, and provided plenty of connections for selling the contraband.

Lothar, though an unprincipled lawbreaker, was a crook with a prodigious work ethic, and most importantly, he had no criminal record. Grant Tadlock, on the other hand, had never worked a straight job in his life, having commenced his contemptible career of crime as a shoplifter at a tender age, and progressed over the years through an array of more lucrative illicit livelihoods.

"Haven't they heard of viagra?" Tadlock asked, scrutinizing one of the bacula.

The animal parts had been provided by Craig Martes, whom Lothar had met while he served time for poaching in Lime River penitentiary after being busted by sergeant Tenax, partially due to evidence provided by Ray Standers. The lessons learned in business college about diversifying one's portfolio had stuck well with Jim Lothar.

"The fuckin' Chinks are hard to figure. All I know is if this deal comes off the way it should, we'll both have enough cash to spend the whole winter someplace where the rum is cheap, and all we need are a pair of sandals and some swimming trunks, and maybe a bottle or two of sunscreen."

CHAPTER 26

Leaving Juneau

Conrad was up early the next morning. Before having breakfast he went for a brisk walk, stretched, and went through a set of yoga exercises, trying to work out some of the stiffness from his exertions the night before. The weather had changed while he slept. The previous night's cold drizzle had been replaced with a drier but still chilly northerly breeze and overcast skies.

After breakfast on board he reluctantly powered on the cell phone that Carson Septumas and Richard Head from the Agency had both insisted he take along. Cell phones were still a relative novelty here, and service spotty or nonexistent in much of Southeast Alaska, so he had not bothered to even turn on the unit thus far —besides, the Agency's concerns were low on his list of priorities. Not surprisingly he had missed several calls from headquarters. In the latest voice mail from earlier that same morning supervisor Head angrily informed Conrad that he would send Jack Dolon, one of the Agency's operatives, out after him if he did not return the call by noon. Resignedly Conrad hit the call button. There was bad blood between himself and agent Dolon, and he had no desire to encounter or work with him. He could not afford any more complications.

"You are a hard man to get hold of," his supervisor answered, exasperation plainly evident in his voice even though the connection quality was poor.

"Well you know how it is up here. This isn't exactly the I-5 corridor," Conrad responded, equally irritated that he had to deal with this overling, whom he despised.

"I imagine you could have contacted us if you were of a mind to. Regardless, I have got some very important and time sensitive information for you. We have intelligence that the shipment which we discussed in Seattle will arrive in about forty-eight hours. The drop point, we are reasonably sure, will be Egg Harbor on Coronation Island, or nearby. You will observe the rendezvous and photograph it if possible, but in any case you will intercept the local transport boat after the transfer is made and make the arrests."

"By myself? Where's the calvary if I need some backup?"

"AKNET agents are available if you need their assistance, but you should first contact agent Dolon. He has access to a boat, has been briefed, and is expecting your call. I imagine the two of you together can handle the situation. Under no circumstances should you have any contact with the supply ship, which is a documented vessel from Hong Kong, the *Chu Lai*. We have other agents who will be attending to that matter. In fact you should take every precaution to make sure the supply ship does not see you. The name of the local transfer boat is *Deep Runner*, which agent Dolon confirms is a fishing boat in the Juneau Harbor, at least as of yesterday evening. Any additional information you need you can get from Dolon, who unlike you, does answer his phone calls with reasonable consistency."

Richard spoke in his usual officious manner, and it was clear to Conrad that he would have preferred any other agent for this assignment. It galled him that agent Slocum outranked Jack Dolon, his favorite. Ironically, this mutual animosity worked at times to the Agency's advantage. Conrad did not care that Richard Head disliked him, but he would not allow the man to think of him as incapable or incompetent. Unfortunately he would have to put off his personal vendetta with Tadlock for the time being, and get this repellent assignment out of the way first.

After the call ended Conrad got out his charts and gauged the distance to Coronation Island—a rugged, isolated, and thickly forested island located where both Chatham and Sumner Straits merged with the open Pacific. It was an uninhabited and wind ravaged wilderness accessible only by boat, or float plane if the weather was calm enough—often not the case. In 1908 one of Alaska's greatest sea tragedies had occurred in the area when the Star of Bengal, an iron sailing barque crammed with fifty thousand cases of salmon and over one hundred Asian cannery workers had grounded in a storm, killing most of the foreign workers on board.

A few of the more superstitious fisherman

avoided the area, saying the ghosts of the men still haunted the island, luring the unwary, like male versions of the mythical sirens. The most protected anchorage on Coronation Island was Egg Harbor, where a small lead mining operation, the only historical settlement on the island, had been abandoned decades before. Conrad read over the text from the office, which gave a more detailed account of the vessels involved and the suspect's names and descriptions.

It was an astounding stroke of luck, Conrad realized as he read. Jim Lothar, the bartender at the Moby Dick nightclub, and Grant Tadlock's names were both on the list of the probable smugglers that intelligence suspected would meet the foreign vessel at Coronation Island! Both men, along with a fisherman named Charles Jackson, had been the subjects of surveillance by agent Dolon for several months. Lothar was the registered owner of the *Deep Runner*, a typical salmon fishing boat common to the area, and not likely to draw attention anywhere in the archipelago.

Conrad quickly made up his mind to take his own boat, and to hell with agent Dolon. If questioned by his bosses he could justify the decision by pointing out that no criminal operation would suspect a sailboat, but a fast motor launch like the local authorities normally utilized would be a dead giveaway if the smugglers spotted it, and it would be easy for them to track an approaching boat in the open waters surrounding Coronation Island. The smugglers would surely be on the lookout, and would have time to dispose of their contraband

and clear out. Even a helicopter or float plane would be observed in plenty of time for the smugglers to take evasive measures, or at least to get rid of their illicit goods. On the other hand, a slow moving sailboat would most likely be seen by the traffickers as just another tourist or pleasure boater, certainly not as a threat. As for agent Dolon—Conrad had in mind a plan which should keep him occupied while he tracked down Tadlock himself.

Conrad had anticipated a protracted search for Tadlock after having botched his opportunity the night before at the Moby Dick. Now it seemed the fates had given him his second chance. He quickly made ready to leave the harbor. He faced a long voyage to the island through a mostly wild and uninhabited area, with little opportunity for provisioning. Depending on wind, tides, and currents he judged it would take him at least thirty hours to make Coronation Island. Even so he would have to average nearly six knots, which meant he must motor anytime the wind was less than ideal. He hoped to do more than half the run that day. His goal was to make it at least as far as the town of Kake, a small mostly native village at the head of Keku Strait on Kupreanof Island.

Conrad had one more task to accomplish before leaving Harris Harbor. He put on his diving gear and slipped into the murky water of the Juneau harbor. Using a powerful waterproof headlamp he carefully examined his hull until he found what he was looking for. He had no trouble recognizing the device, as he had attached similar instruments himself, though never underwater. It was the sort of electronic locator he had used many times to track other agents or people of interest. It was common knowledge among his colleagues that the Agency probably monitored their employees as often or even more frequently than their enemy targets. He knew it would not be the only way they had of following his movements, but he was fairly sure of the other methods too. He knew the device must have been tracking his sailboat's every move since the night in Seattle when he had observed the diver emerging from the harbor next to his boat. Until now he had not cared that his location was known, but the situation had changed. He hoped to throw the Agency and agent Dolon off his trail for at least the next twenty-four hours, maybe longer if he was lucky.

After carefully removing the tracking device from his own hull, he swam under the dock and attached the unit to the hull of an older wooden fishing boat adjacent to his sailboat, which he knew from a casual conversation with its owner was preparing for a trip south to Wrangell. Conrad was fairly sure no one had gained entry into his boat, but he took the time to disassemble his GPS and VHS radio units, finding no sign that they had been tampered with. Still—erring on the side of caution—he tossed the GPS and his cell phone into the harbor dumpster.

The thought of voyaging without the instruments did not disturb Conrad. He had detailed paper charts for every area he planned to visit, and he was quite proficient at the arts of both dead reckoning and celestial navigation, relying on his competent seamanship abilities and his prized Cassens and Plath sextant. But the VHS radio he needed to monitor the conversations of other boaters, weather forecasts, and as a way of communicating on the water if the need arose.

Conrad eased out of Harris Harbor and out into narrow Gastineau Channel, the thin index finger of Stephens Passage. As he motored out of the harbor, Conrad was not aware that Grant Tadlock and Charlie Jackson slept aboard *Deep Runner* only a short distance away from his own slip. Gradually, behind him to the north, downtown Juneau and the brilliant white form of a visiting cruise ship faded from view. There was a light northerly breeze as he steered *Tisiphone* south into Stephens Passage, but the wind soon freshened. After an hour of motoring he was able to switch off the engine, set sail, and take advantage of the cold, gusty katabatic winds that funneled down from the huge ice fields above treacherous Taku Inlet.

With the combined wind and tide in his favor he made over nine knots as *Tisiphone* raced south past Port Snettisham, another deep branching tributary fjord off Stephens Passage. Once he passed that area of blustery frigid glacial downdrafts a light but steady breeze remained, and Conrad set his topsail, his largest genoa, and adjusted the wind vane to hold the boat on a southerly course down the middle of the channel. The easy northeasterly filled his sails. Yesterday's threatening rainclouds had retreated to the high glacial valleys, and only the faintest wisps of cirrus remained overhead. Conrad dozed in the cockpit under a gentle afternoon sun as he entered the confluence of Stephens Passage and Frederick Sound.

A loud wet crashing noise brought him suddenly to attention. He opened his eyes to see he was in the midst of a group of humpback whales. The tremendous resonant boom that had awakened him was the mighty tail of one of the animals slapping the surface of the water as it sounded, only a hundred yards or so away from his boat. He was apparently sailing a course directly through a browsing pod of a dozen or so of the massive mammals.

Conrad had read that Frederick Sound was a favorite feeding ground for the humpbacks, being ideally located at the convergence of three major fjords and several minor inlets. From the south the waters of Chatham Strait led directly to the open Pacific some sixty miles distant. The colder glacially fed waters of the mainland fjords mixed with the warmer Pacific in the relatively shallower Frederick Sound to create ideal conditions for many species of marine life. Conrad watched in awe as the spouting cetaceans, up to twice as long and three times the weight of his fourteen ton vessel, launched their tremendous bulks out of the water and crashed down again and again, the impact of their bodies reverberating like artillery blasts and displacing foamy fountains of seawater.

The whales migrated each summer from their winter home and breeding grounds in the Hawaiian Islands. They also changed their diet and feeding habits while gathering in Frederick Sound. Normally krill and plankton eaters, they had modified their culinary tastes to take advantage of the large numbers of herring in this area, cooperating together to produce curtains of bubbles which they used to herd the small fish into their huge baleen-filled mouths. It occurred to Conrad that Marshall and David had probably witnessed similar scenes during their fishing and sailing adventures. He felt a twinge of sadness and envy for their time together in such a sublime setting.

After passing through Frederick Sound and the pod of feeding whales Conrad steered closer to the shoreline of Kupreanof Island. He bypassed the entrance to Keku Strait and the Tlingit settlement at Kake and continued south, opting to spend the night in one of the protected anchorages of Saginaw Bay. Just as he made ready to change course into the bay he saw the *Deep Runner*, which he had identified when it had motored past him earlier, sitting at anchor behind Cornwallis Point in Halleck Harbor. Conrad had no desire to spend the night in such close proximity to the smugglers, especially when he could not be absolutely sure that Tadlock might not have gotten a glimpse of his face at the Moby Dick, and might possibly recognize him. More importantly, the location did not seem to Conrad to be well situated for the sort of encounter he had in mind with Tadlock. He sailed on to the next anchorage just a few miles south in Security Bay.

The evening was spectacular. As the sun slowly

set he lay easily at anchor in the calm waters of the bay while a romp of sea otters frolicked between his boat and the nearby shore. A Sitka black-tailed doe and her two nearly grown fawns grazed in the Nootka Reedgrass and salmonberry thickets between the rocky beach and the forest. Overhead an unkindness of ravens—like fighter planes attacking bombers—darted at a pair of soaring bald eagles. The high shrill call of marbled murrelets contrasted with the obscene bawl of the gulls. The air smelled of salt, iodine, and spruce. Alerted by scent or sound indiscernible to Conrad, the deer suddenly fled back into the dense green forest. A large black bear ambled onto the beach and began to graze at exactly the same spot the deer had so recently and wisely vacated.

Oddly, so close to his goal—four miles as the raven flies, and only a low forested ridge away from the snoring Grant Tadlock in Halleck Harbor, Conrad's thoughts were not of his plans for the morrow, his need for vengeance, or of the recent events in Juneau. Somehow it seemed the landscape itself—so much vaster than his mere mortal concerns—had taken hold of him, and as he drifted off to sleep he imagined the great explorers; Bering from Tsarist Russia; Cook and Vancouver of Great Britain; and the canny Spanish captains setting out from ports in Mexico; brave, capable, and acquisitive men who had sailed these waters hundreds of years earlier in search of wealth and the fabled Northwest Passage.

It was the diseases the Spanish and Russian crews carried, not so much the force of arms which ultimately led to the decline of the native population. Although the local tribes suffered from the rifles and cannons of the encroachers, they were wise enough to avoid outright war with the interlopers.

There were also the old stories, passed down by generations of natives, of a far earlier voyage. The persistent legends and tantalizing clues that the great Sir Francis Drake, sailing for the glory of his beloved Queen Elizabeth in the sixteenth century had perhaps reached this archipelago before crossing the Pacific and becoming the second man in history to sail around the world.

Colorful dreamscapes of conquistadors and caravels unreeled in Conrad's slumbering mind as *Tisiphone* tugged gently at her anchor. His tranquil sleep was unperturbed by any plans of pursuit.

CHAPTER 27

Coronation Island

Charlie Jackson had already piloted *Deep Runner* out of the Juneau harbor and some miles down Stephens Passage before Grant Tadlock joined him on deck. At Lothar's insistence both men had spent the night on the boat so they could get an early start. Charlie did not care at all for Tadlock, who was one of the worst crew members he had ever worked with in all his many years on the waters of Southeast Alaska. The man could not steer a straight course to save his soul and knew next to nothing of navigation or seamanship. He could not be trusted to tie a knot that would hold, and if seas were even mildly disturbed he would inevitably be found emptying his stomach over the side. Merely having the man aboard seemed to bring bad luck to any nautical enterprise. He was what sailors called a 'Jonah.' Charlie was happy to let the lubber sleep on long after they left the marina.

At one time Charlie, 'Good Luck Chuck,' had been one of the more successful gill-netters in this part of Southeast Alaska, with his own boat and a coveted limited entry fishing permit—the type of fisherman known locally as a 'high-liner.' He had a knack for sensing where to find the large schools of salmon on their way to the local spawning rivers, and a reputation as a hard worker who kept his boat and gear in top shape and who treated his crew fairly. But a couple of bad seasons and an expensive divorce had left him without boat or permit and deeply in debt. So when his old high school friend, Jim Lothar, had offered him the captain's position on *Deep Runner* he had accepted without hesitation.

Charlie enjoyed fishing more than almost anything else, and he did a fair amount still. Although much of his time and energies were now taken up with excursions to surreptitious rendezvous with unsavory characters his boss was careful to make sure their activities appeared legitimate to any outside observers. Fishermen tended to be discerning by nature, and would be suspicious of anyone who did not take advantage of nearly every permitted salmon fishing opportunity. Their fishing activities were an ideal front for the smuggling business that was Jim Lothar's main concern. Besides providing discreet transportation between the hundreds of sparsely or uninhabited islands of the Tongass National Forest and the even more thinly populated islands and mainland of coastal British Columbia, the legitimate business of fishing provided Jim Lothar and company with a convenient way to launder the cash flow from the illicit sources of income.

Charlie was not happy with the other duties he had been assigned, but at least he was still fishing, even if it was only as cover for their primary business interests. Regardless of its source the money was extremely good, and he hoped that in another year or two he would have his debts paid off and enough saved to buy his own boat and permit once again. Then Grant Tadlock and Jim Lothar could both go to hell. In the meantime all he had to do was keep his mouth shut, do what he was told, and rely on his well-honed seamanship skills. Putting up with Grant Tadlock had so far been the worst part of the work, but at least he had ultimately convinced Lothar to let him pick his own crew for the actual fishing outings. That had made life much more tolerable. But of course this was no fishing trip, and once again he was stuck with the detestable Tadlock.

"Good morning Grant. I hope the engine noise didn't disturb your beauty sleep," Charlie smirked. He could see by the pale hue of Tadlock's face that he was already in the early throes of seasickness.

"Fuck you too. Where the hell are we anyway?" Grant's stomach lurched. He felt the onset of another wave of nausea.

"We're over twenty nautical miles south of Juneau, but we've got hours to go still and it will probably get rougher. You might want to take a seasick pill now, before you start puking all over my nice clean deck."

The *Deep Runner* could make twelve or thirteen knots at full speed in flat water, but she vibrated and used a lot of fuel. Charlie kept the vessel at a more efficient and comfortable nine to ten knots, which meant they could make the north end of Kupreanof Island—roughly the half way point between Juneau and Coronation Island, by early evening.

Lothar had instructed them to stay out of the actual village of Kake and find some isolated anchorage for the night. Charlie was very familiar with Frederick Sound and Chatham Strait. He knew of several anchorages which would serve. He kept his eyes on the water and let the auto-helm steer them down the fjord. There were few boats and no real hazards in this area, other than the occasional floating log and smaller flotsam.

He had passed one other fishing boat going the opposite direction and a sailboat going his way earlier that morning. The fishing boat and its owner he recognized from Wrangell, and something about the sailboat seemed familiar. Moved only by idle curiosity, he eyed the boat through his binoculars. The vessel, *Tisiphone*, had a Washington state registration sticker. Nobody was in the cockpit, but that was no big deal. Like the *Deep Runner*, the sailboat was probably under auto-helm control and the owner most likely getting coffee or something to eat in the galley. He was reminded of his own hunger.

"Hey Grant, why don't you make yourself useful. I could use something to eat and a cup of coffee," Charlie ordered.

"Yeah, okay," Tadlock replied begrudgingly. "I can't understand how you can eat all the time when you're on this boat. It's the last thing I ever feel like doing."

"Nothing gets my appetite up quite like a day on the water," Charlie answered.

Some time later, as he sipped his cooling drink, Charlie remembered seeing the sailboat docked at a slip farther down the pier in the Juneau marina. He dismissed the vessel as a seasonal tourist yacht, probably heading back south again after a summer of exploring Southeast Alaska. Still, it was notable if not entirely exceptional, to see an out of state pleasure boat in this area so late in the summer.

That evening they set anchor in Halleck Harbor, a small bight off Saginaw Bay at the north end of Kuiu Island just south of Keku Strait, which separated Kuiu and Kupreanof Islands. Tadlock, still feeling some of the effects of motion sickness despite taking medication, only picked at his meal. Charlie ate ravenously. After finishing his dinner he took a can of beer from the cooler and went out on the deck, as much to put more distance between himself and the odious Tadlock as to enjoy the sun setting over Frederick Sound and Chatham Strait. He would have rather spent the evening in nearby Kake, where he had several friends among the native fishermen who worked out of that port.

As he took in the expansive views of water and forest the Alaska State Ferry appeared, plying the waters on its route from Kake to Sitka. Shortly afterwards the sails of the yacht he had seen earlier came into view. Its route was closer to the shoreline than the ferry's, and he watched it for some minutes until the boat's masts vanished behind Meade Point, just south of their anchorage.

He found himself wondering why the captain of the sailboat had not put into Kake, or continued on the far more popular course southeasterly down Frederick Sound to Petersburg and Wrangell, the usual route for pleasure boaters heading back to British Columbia or Puget Sound this time of year. Night was coming and either alternative would have been an obvious and safer choice. Judging by the course the boat was sailing, Charlie surmised it was headed for one of the other protected but seldom visited anchorages farther down the coastline of Kuiu Island. He doubted anyone without good local knowledge would continue much farther this time of the evening. Though there was still reasonable visibility on a clear evening this late in the summer until ten o'clock or later, there were several hours of darkness between then and sunrise.

He concluded the boat must be headed on to Sitka, another day's run. This historic city of some nine thousand people on Baranof Island, with its restored Russian Orthodox cathedral was a popular tourist destination, as well as by far the largest town in the region and the second largest city in the entire Alaskan Panhandle.

The following morning, while motoring down Chatham Strait, they once again passed the same sailboat. Although the vessel had obviously gotten a much earlier start they were traveling at nearly double its cruising speed. Their course lay between the rugged western shore of Kuiu Island and the yacht. They were much closer this time, and the cockpit of the sailboat was occupied. The sailor had his back to Charlie, but he could see the captain was focusing binoculars on the shoreline of Baranof Island, several miles distant across the widening Chatham Strait. Apparently sensing that he was being observed, the man lowered his binoculars, turned suddenly, and waved a quick greeting before disappearing into the cabin.

Though he had no real cause to worry about an obvious tourist on an Alaskan sight-seeing voyage Charlie realized the presence of the sailboat had become a source of low level anxiety. The nature of their errand had made him unusually attentive, suspicious, and cautious. Charlie turned his attention once again to the sea in front of him, rationalizing that his paranoia was unfounded. There was certainly no reason to worry about a slow moving sailboat tended by a solitary sailor on an Alaskan cruise. He returned to scanning the waters for hazards, and fine-tuned his course to Coronation Island, still several hours to the south. Outside on the working deck Grant Tadlock retched loudly into their wake, while a group of glaucous-winged gulls wheeled overhead, raucously jeering at his misery.

Late that afternoon they anchored in Egg Harbor, Coronation Island. Fortunately, and not unusually, they were the only boat there. Just beyond the guano encrusted Hazy Islands, less than ten miles out, the captain and the navigator of the Hong Kong flagged vessel *Chu Lai* tracked the *Deep Runner* as it turned into the secluded anchorage. The *Chu Lai* quickly followed, holding position without dropping anchor farther out in the narrow cove. They utilized the Chinese vessel's lifeboat to ferry the tightly sealed containers of valuable powder to the *Deep Runner*. One of the Chinese crew spoke nearly fluent English, and the transfer of the contraband went smoothly. Both parties were anxious to complete the exchange as quickly as possible. The *Chu Lai* dared not risk too much time in U.S. national waters. They seemed especially pleased with the poached animal parts. They presented the Alaskans with a bottle of fine baijiu in parting as a gesture of good will. Charlie and Grant carefully concealed the containers of contraband under fishing gear in *Deep Runner's* hold. The *Chu Lai* left the confines of Egg Harbor well before the *Deep Runner*, making her best speed as soon as she cleared the hazards of the inlet entrance.

The haul was secured. No customs, police, or DEA boats, planes, or helicopters had appeared to disturb the transfer or stowage of the valuable cargo. It seemed only the myriads of birds wheeling and diving around the boat had observed their activities—the puffins, gulls, cormorants, eagles, murrelets and other shore birds which nested by the thousands on Coronation and the Hazy Islands.

Much relieved that things had gone so smoothly, Charlie Jackson started the engine and winched up the anchor. He could not get rid of his cargo or his crew too soon. He planned to run straight back to Juneau without overnighting along the way. Though it would mean motoring the upper end of Stephens Passage to Juneau after dark, Charlie had no qualms. He knew that stretch of water as well as any man, and in his mind an overnight voyage presented far less risk than holding on to the contraband an additional day.

As they cruised back from their successful rendezvous in Egg Harbor Charlie Jackson noticed a change in the normally regular rhythm of the *Deep Runner's* engine. After some minutes it was so obvious that even Tadlock commented.

"That don't sound good, Charlie."

"You got that right. The old diesel doesn't seem very happy. Could be we got some bad fuel, or maybe one of the filters is partially clogged."

"Shit!—what are we goin' to do out here in the middle of nowhere?"

Grant Tadlock was not merely an incompetent and unwilling crew, he had a real horror of drowning at sea. At the age of thirteen his small dingy had capsized in the surf, and he had nearly died when he had been swept out to sea by the strong current. The incident had instilled a fear of the water that had never faded.

"Well, if we can make it that far, there is a nice place to pull in just ahead at Gedney Harbor. I don't know if they are there this year, but some years there is a fish buyer on a scow who hangs out inside, and there is a dock to tie up to. Sometimes you can get fuel and even some supplies."

"That sounds good enough to me. I don't wanna drift around out here in the middle of nowhere," Grant agreed.

"No matter what, I don't want to get caught with a dead engine out in the middle of Chatham Strait, or have to radio the Coast Guard to rescue us with this shit-load of booty in the hold. Worst case scenario, we can tow the boat with the inflatable, but that is a pain in the ass, and it would take forever to get us back to Juneau—I doubt we would make more than three knots or so at best."

In any case, Charlie knew, Grant Tadlock would be incapable of competently handling either craft.

"Our best bet is to pull in and see if I can fix the damn diesel," Charlie explained.

CHAPTER 28

Agent Dolon

Agent Jack Dolon blearily answered his phone after the sixth ring.

"What took you so damn long to get to the phone?"

It was his boss in Seattle, Richard Head.

"Sorry about that. I was out pretty late last night. ...just getting up."

Dolon's rented mobile home was near the Juneau airport. He had spent much of the the night at the airport bar drowning his sorrows in vodka after a visiting Canadian woman, whom he had met several nights earlier at the same club, stood him up for a dinner date.

"Shit, you are getting to be as irresponsible as Slocum—and no doubt it was work that kept you up so late," Richard replied peevishly.

"So what's up? Is Slocum ready to go?" Agent Dolon asked. He had a foul taste in his mouth and his head throbbed.

"What the hell! You mean you haven't heard from him yet? He should have called you yesterday."

"I haven't heard fuck-all from Slocum. When did you talk to him last?"

Dolon was in no shape to go anywhere immediately, and would not be until he at least had coffee, a shower, and pills to dull the ache in his head.

"Well, the son-of-a-bitch has already left, but for some reason he took his own boat so you ought to be able to catch him if you can get your sorry ass out of bed. I don't know what the hell he is up too. He didn't take the most obvious route to Coronation. Maybe he plans to come up on them from the south. He won't answer my phone calls, or else his phone is off. Luckily we can track his boat movements so I can give you his position."

Agent Dolon did not need to ask how they knew Slocum's location. Like Conrad, he too had experience with surreptitious tracking devices.

The vessel the Agency provided had previously been a customs patrol boat stationed near the southern California border, but with a top speed of fifty miles an hour in reasonably tranquil waters it could no longer keep up with the even faster smuggling boats that operated between Mexico and the southern California coast. However, it was a step up in speed and maneuverability over any boat the Juneau troopers had previously owned. It was more than fast enough for their needs even at the slower speeds it was usually limited to in this rugged region.

Jack Dolon, like Conrad Slocum, had grown up around boats, though on the shores of western Florida rather than the Pacific Northwest, and motorboats rather than sailing craft. Although he disliked the cold climate of the region he mostly enjoyed this northern posting, especially when he got paid good money to fly down the fjords at double or triple the speed of the fastest local fishing boats. At his current speed of nearly thirty statute miles an hour, even with his late start, he calculated he would catch Slocum by the time the slower boat made Petersburg. He agreed with his boss that agent Slocum was probably planning on taking the Wrangell Narrows to Sumner Strait. It was a longer route than the more obvious Chatham Strait, but it had the important advantage that Slocum would be hidden from the smugglers sight as he ran down the opposite side of Kuiu Island to the Coronation Island rendezvous.

There was a major problem with their surmises; the boat they were following was not piloted by Conrad Slocum. The vessel, to which Conrad had earlier attached the tracking device, had been recently sold to a Wrangell fisherman, who was transporting it to his home port from Juneau. By the time agent Dolon overtook the surprised new owner of the gill-netter and discovered that Slocum had tricked them, it was early evening.

"I don't understand it. Why the hell would Slocum send us on a wild goose chase?" agent Dolon wondered.

He had docked the agency vessel at the Petersburg boat harbor and called Richard Head's office collect from a phone booth close by. It was obvious to them both they had been duped, but Slocum's motivation was a mystery.

"How the hell would I know what he intends! He has not seen fit to inform this office. That fucker has always been a loose cannon," Head replied, angrily.

"Maybe he just didn't want to share the credit for the bust. He doesn't care much for me anyway—and I don't have to tell you the feeling is mutual," agent Dolon suggested.

"You could be right I suppose. He's never been much of a team player, but I doubt it's that simple. He is up to something, and I don't think it has anything to do with his job. Regardless, the most important thing is salvaging this operation. Let's just forget about Slocum for now. I'll worry about him later. We can assume he will report in after he accomplishes the mission, assuming that is at least part of what he is up to," Head replied.

"What if he fucks it up? After all, he is by himself and there are at least two of those smugglers in a much faster boat. I would bet they are pretty well armed and won't roll over just because some stranger flashes his badge."

"As much as neither of us cares for Slocum or his methods, don't underestimate the man. He is liable to act first and then show his I.D., and he has proven himself on far more dangerous errands than this one. I'm pretty sure he is capable of handling the smugglers even without help if he wants to, but what really bugs me is that I'm not even sure if he is still working this case, or off on some other errand of his own—or maybe both. I haven't been able to contact him, and it seems that is the way he wants it."

"How does Septumas see things?" Dolon asked.

"Oh, Carson agrees with me generally, but he refuses to take Slocum off the case. He's got a soft spot in his heart for him because of his own history in Central Asia. My concern is that Slocum consistently violates chain of command, often refuses to cooperate with fellow agents—as is the case now—and seems to act as though he can interpret Agency assignments anyway he sees fit. He has a terrible record when it comes to cooperating with the DEA, as everyone in the Agency knows, but they are only indirectly involved with this case. They did supply us with some helpful intelligence, but that's about it—the local troopers did most of the work. My hope is that Slocum will not screw things up, but I refuse to put all our eggs in one basket. We need to make sure we intercept *Deep Runner* and her crew one way or the other. So that is where you come in."

"So what the hell can I do? Thanks to this wild goose chase I'm miles away from the action way down here in Petersburg."

"You're right that it's too late for you to try for Coronation, and I'm not going to call in the Coast Guard or Customs while we can still get you into position in Juneau."

Richard Head did not want to admit to agent Dolon that he did not have the authority to take that action, and that he would have to go through his superior, Carson Septumas, to get the okay for any additional resources.

“I think we can safely assume Slocum will make the rendezvous at Egg Harbor in either his own boat, or another vessel which he plans somehow to requisition. Still, it is extremely unprofessional and intolerable that he has left us in the dark as to his movements and strategy. You should head back to Juneau and make sure you are at the harbor to greet them when Slocum and the smugglers arrive, or—if Slocum does not bag them himself—you had better make the bust before they can offload the goods. On the other hand, if agent Slocum is successful maybe you can find out just what in the hell he has been up to and why. If for some reason they do manage to evade him, you will have to make the arrest on your own or with trooper backup, before they can get rid of that contraband.”

“That seems like a reasonable plan. You can count on me,” Dolon replied.

“I sure hope so,” Richard Head responded, and ended the call.

CHAPTER 29

Kuiu Island

After a restful night anchored in Security Bay on the northwest coast of Kuiu island, Conrad spent the next morning running down its wild western coast. The fifteenth largest island in the United States, with a total population of perhaps ten people, the island possessed the densest concentration of black bears in the world.

Certainly few places offered the isolation and privacy that this area did for the business of smuggling. Once again he was leapfrogged by the later starting but faster *Deep Runner*. This time the smugglers were much nearer, and one of the men, apparently the captain, trained his binoculars on Conrad's boat. Conrad kept his back to the other boat and pretended to study the far shoreline. As the fishing boat drew adjacent he waved a quick greeting, making sure his hand passed in front of his face, and descended quickly into the cabin. He was careful to reveal his face for only the briefest of instants. He was reasonably sure that even if by chance Tadlock had gotten a look at him at the Moby Dick—not likely, given the circumstances, he would not be able to identify him in the split second his features were exposed.

This brief encounter was at any rate close enough that Conrad was able to verify that one of the men was indeed Tadlock. The other man steering the boat was certainly not Jim Lothar, whom he assumed must have remained behind in Juneau.

Due to his much slower pace, Conrad was still miles away from Coronation Island when he saw the *Chu Lai* follow *Deep Runner* into Egg harbor, and a short time later steam out of the harbor and away into the open Pacific. Agency intelligence had been correct about the day of the exchange, but not the time. Conrad knew the crew of the *Deep Runner* would not linger once the transaction was finished. He reasoned that since the transfer had occurred so early in the day, it was likely they would motor all afternoon and evening to get back to Juneau as quickly as possible.

His plan had been to anchor in an adjacent cove on Coronation, Alikula Bay, and ambush Tadlock under cover of darkness. He had wrongly assumed the transaction would take place at night. Now, for the third time, Conrad realized his strategy must change. He had no real alternative other than to follow the smugglers back to Juneau. That would certainly complicate things, but there was no help for it. His boat was not fast enough to force a confrontation, and they most certainly would be armed. Surprise was still his best bet.

There was no point in pursuing his present track. Conrad tacked the boat and came around to the upwind reciprocal course. He was off Point Harris, twenty miles from Coronation Island. There were several safe anchorages available to him before dark if he took that option, or he too could continue on to Juneau, which he was reasonably sure was the smuggler's destination, although it would mean running all night at his much slower pace. Studying his chart of the area, he decided Explorer Basin, an area ringed by islands and well protected, but with good sight-lines to Chatham Strait would be perfect for an anchorage, should he chose that option.

Ninety minutes later Conrad was still under sail in the strait, just outside of the basin. Through his binoculars he could make out the now familiar hull of *Deep Runner* several miles behind him. The fishing boat was obviously having engine problems. A thick cloud of smoke trailed the vessel. He saw the boat abruptly change course towards Kuiu Island. A quick look at the chart showed Gedney Harbor, five miles south of his position, as the closest secure anchorage to the stricken boat. He watched until he saw *Deep Runner* disappear behind the headlands of the small island which partially blocked the harbor entrance.

Conrad continued on into Explorer Basin. He dropped his sails and let his boat drift while he studied a more detailed chart of the area. There was a two mile wide isthmus of land that separated the lower reaches of nearby Thetis Bay—one of a number of shallow coves emanating from Explorer Basin—and Gedney Harbor. If he could get there before the smugglers got underway again, and if there were no other boaters nearby to foil his plan, he could possibly hike undetected from Thetis Bay to Gedney Harbor. The entire area was uninhabited and as wild as any place in Alaska, and so far he had seen no other boat traffic in the vicinity.

He started his engine and motored carefully through the eastern gap of Explorer Basin, making a sharp turn to the south into the passage to Thetis Bay. It would take him at least an hour to make the anchorage at the extreme end of the inlet, and he would most likely need yet another hour at minimum to cross the isthmus. He hoped there was no one else in the harbors, and that whatever mechanical troubles the smugglers were having would keep the fishing boat laid up long enough for his purposes.

Charlie Jackson's luck held, though just long enough, and the *Deep Runner*, its engine misfiring and smoking, limped into Gedney Harbor. No fish buyer nor any other boat was present. Theirs was the only boat tied up to the small float that afternoon. The temperature had risen into the high sixties and the sun warmed the surface of the white fiberglass deck. Grant Tadlock lazed in the stern next to the net reel, smoking and slapping at deer flies while Charlie Jackson labored below. After a few minutes he heard Charlie utter a string of expletives.

"What the hell is going on down there?" Grant called down to the captain in the bilge.

"We have got a real fucking problem here. All kinds of shit in the fuel. It's going to take me a while to fix this. I'm going to have to clear out the fuel lines, replace the filters, and shift some clean fuel to the day tank. What a cluster-fuck!" Charlie replied.

"Need a hand?"

"No, you'll just get in the way. There's barely enough room for one man down here. We got a bad batch of diesel last fill-up, I guess. We'll be here a couple hours at least, so best you keep a sharp eye out for visitors. Quite a few folks come up from Sitka or Port Alexander to fish this area, and some of them anchor here or in Tebenkof Bay if they stay the night. I wouldn't be at all surprised if we got some unwelcome company. We don't need anyone nosing around the boat. If anyone shows up you'd best divert their attention somehow."

"What do you want me to do—sing 'em a song—show 'em the sights?"

"Hell, I don't know! Use your fucking imagination! Only keep them away from this boat until I figure out if I can get her running again. If anyone comes around, run over before they can come sniffing' around here—shit!—I've got my hands full here. Do I have to do all the thinking?"

Why do I have to be stuck here with such an idiot, Charlie thought, and returned to disassembling the fuel line.

Grant Tadlock contemplated his instructions. He hoped nobody showed up, as he could not imagine how he could keep visitors away if they chose to tie up to the little dock, which only had room for three or four boats of their size. He was uneasy about their situation, and wanted to get back to Juneau as quickly as possible. Working out of the basement of the Moby Dick had its risks, but at least he would not drown there.

Although Lothar had expressly forbidden them to take any alcohol on this trip, Tadlock and Jackson had at least a mutual love of drink in common, if little else. They were well supplied with beer and Tadlock also knew where the captain had stashed the gift from the *Chu Lai*—in a locker under one of the berths. He took a quart thermos from a bin in the galley and filled it half way up with the clear sorghum liquor. Tadlock found it to his liking—as acceptable as the vodkas he was more familiar with. He drank much of the thermos contents, as well as a can of beer from the case they carried in an ice-filled cooler. After that he felt much better. The sun warmed his skin, and he was content to lounge on the deck while Charlie Jackson continued his repairs below. Only the biting flies and the frequent blasphemies emanating from the cramped engine compartment below deck disturbed his drowsy tranquillity.

After a while Tadlock decided he should check for other boats in Chatham strait. He languidly glassed the entrance of Gedney Harbor and what he could see of waters in the distance beyond the cove. No boats were visible. Relieved for the moment, he turned his attention to the shore. Almost immediately a disturbance in the brush at the edge of the line of evergreen forest caught his eye. He blinked furiously several times and refocused the binoculars. Again he caught a tawny patch of movement in the thick underbrush farther up the shoreline, but it vanished before he could properly bring it into relief. Grant quickly retrieved a rifle from the cradle in the pilot house and chambered a round.

Although they were over one hundred yards distant, both the cougar and the doe that it had been stalking heard the metallic click of the rifle bolt. The doe bounded off through the forest. The frustrated cougar, which had been tensely crouching in a thicket waiting for the perfect moment to attack stood up in frustration, and was once again visible to Tadlock—this time clearly through his rifle scope. In his excitement and drunken exuberance, and without a thought for their situation, Tadlock squeezed the trigger. The report shattered the morning quiet. A murder of crows, cawing loudly, took flight from an ancient spruce snag. The cat, gut shot, fell to the ground writhing and clawing the turf, then tore off through the dense brush.

"I got him! I got him!" Tadlock yelled excitedly.

"Are you a complete imbecile!? What the hell are you shooting at?" Charlie Jackson had emerged from the Stygian depths of the engine compartment at the loud report of the rifle. He was livid. He held a wrench in his hand, and his face and bare arms were smeared with grease and sweat.

"I got him good—I'm sure of it—a fucking mountain lion!"

"You fucking moron! How do you know there isn't a Fish and Game officer on the other side of the ridge, over in Thetis Bay or Explorer Basin, or even closer? Do you even have a hunting license, you dumb fucker? Well, the damage is done, but you can go get the animal yourself or not, I don't give a fuck. I've got to get this engine running before someone discovers us—especially now that you've announced our location to anyone within ten miles of here!"

In spite of his anger Charlie was intrigued, and would have liked to investigate for himself. He was aware that a puma had been killed by a trapper a few years earlier on adjacent Kupreanof Island, so he guessed it might be possible that Tadlock was correct, but even a sighting, let alone a kill of a cougar in Southeast Alaska was so remarkable and so rare as to be semi-mythical—nearly akin to sighting Sasquatch or the Loch Ness monster.

"I don't need your goddamn help. All I want is the parts I can sell anyway, and maybe some claws for a trophy. The bears and ravens can have the rest."

"Well don't take too long out there or you just might have to find your own way back to Juneau. We have to hope nobody heard that shot. When you hear the engine start up you've got fifteen minutes to get back here, or I swear I will leave without you!"

"Thanks for your fucking consideration," Tadlock retorted.

Tadlock stuffed several large plastic garbage bags, a roll of paper towels, his hunting knife, and small saw from the boat's tool kit into a backpack, slung the rifle over his shoulder, and headed down the short floating dock ramp to the rock-strewn shore. Slipping and sliding on the wet stones and beach debris in his haste, he soon found the place where the cat had been hit. There was a fair amount of blood on the ground, and a lot of crushed undergrowth. An obvious trail of blood-smeared bent grass and shrubbery headed away from the place.

It was a nerve-wracking affair following the trail of the wounded animal through the dense alder stand that covered the slope between the spray zone of the shore and the forest edge. He was aware that Kuiu Island supported a large population of black bears, and he did not relish the idea of meeting either a bear or the wounded cougar—if it was still alive—in such close quarters, but the lure of his fantastic luck together with the effects of the alcohol gave him the courage to continue. Even so, the hair on the back of Tadlock's neck stood on end and he shivered involuntarily, though he was warm from his exertions. He advanced slowly, rifle at the ready, listening intently for any sound that would give him a clue as to the location of the injured animal, but he heard nothing.

It must be dead by now—all that blood... Tadlock hoped. He climbed through a dense thicket onto a rocky outcrop devoid of vegetation to orient himself. As he stood catching his breath Tadlock felt a tremendous blow to his thigh. A split second after, as he toppled from the outcrop, he heard the unmistakeable crack of a rifle shot. His own rifle slipped from his grip and slid down the opposite side of the outcrop, landing in the thick bosk below. Tadlock lay on his back on the dark muddy ground, momentarily stunned. His left leg seemed strangely numb. He tried to stand and fell again. A stab of terrible pain gripped his thigh. He looked down to see jagged ends of pale bone jutting from a blood soaked tear in his jeans. The bullet had ripped through the back of his thigh and exploded his femur roughly half way between his hip and knee, before emerging from the front of his leg.

It came to him that he was alone, defenseless, and someone was shooting at him. Desperately he began to drag himself towards the protection of the forest edge some thirty feet distant.

CHAPTER 30

Cat And Mouse

Conrad had been laboriously bushwhacking across a low rise just above the boggy lowland between Thetis Cove and Gedney Harbor when he heard the report of Tadlock's rifle. He thrashed his way furiously upslope to a rocky promontory another sixty feet higher. From this vantage point he could see much of the southern portion of Gedney Harbor, including the floating dock and *Deep Runner*. Through his binoculars he recognized Tadlock. He saw him run from the boat and into the thickets below. The other man in the boat did not follow. He chambered a round into his .308 model 700P Remington. He would not lose his quarry again. When Tadlock stood exposed below him on the rocky outcropping, Conrad took his shot.

When Grant Tadlock fell Conrad plunged downslope into the thick growth, ignoring the branches tearing at him, and forcing his way to the edge of the forest where the going was somewhat easier. There he slowed his pace, cautiously advancing from tree to tree, listening for any sounds from the man. He was sure he had hit him, but unsure of how badly the man had been wounded. Conrad had not seen what Grant Tadlock had been shooting at, but he assumed it was most likely one of the deer or bear that roamed the island in large numbers. Through the scope on his firearm he had seen the rifle fall from Tadlock's hands when his own shot hit its mark, but for all he knew the man might carry a pistol, as many locals did when hunting or hiking in bear country. He circled the outcrop where Tadlock had fallen. The only sign of the man was a smear of blood on the rocks and a trail that led into the dim woods a short distance away.

Close by he heard a low feral growl. Conrad first froze, then carefully eased forward until he was only a few yards from the wounded mountain lion. He had an intuitive feeling it was the same animal he had witnessed on his hike above Spruce Cove. He could see it was mortally wounded. He felt pity for the animal. The cougar moved laboriously, dragging a shattered hind leg the bullet had smashed after tearing through its softer vital organs. It could run no more, and having identified its enemy, the fading but still formidable Felis had turned in its agony and rage to make a last stand.

From where he lay, panting and perspiring with pain and fear Grant Tadlock too heard the menacing snarl of the injured animal. He saw it turn and shuffle toward him. At the same time he saw a man holding a rifle step into the dim clearing behind it.

"For God's sake—shoot it!" Tadlock screamed.

The cat heard Conrad's footsteps and hesitated, balancing on its three good legs and turning its head to look at Conrad, then back again to Tadlock.

"It appears our feline friend cannot make up his mind which one of us to attack," Conrad said. He had another round chambered in his rifle and the safety was off.

Tadlock assumed the stranger had also been shooting at the cougar, but had mistakenly hit him instead.

"I know it was an accident. For Christ's sake it's your trophy! What are you waiting for! Just kill him before he gets one of us—I sure as hell won't report this to anyone—just help me get back to my boat."

Tadlock felt suddenly very faint, and fell back on his elbows.

The cougar slowly turned and advanced to within a few feet of Conrad, then stopped. He could smell its breath and hear its labored breathing. The animal was obviously in great pain, had lost much blood, and was near the end. It seemed to be weighing its options, deciding how best to expend its last remaining vitality. Conrad did not move—did not even bring his rifle up. He sensed he was in no danger. He was convinced the animal somehow knew which man had hurt him, and was only trying to determine whether this additional presence was some kind of new threat.

"Oh, but I was not hunting wild game, I was hunting you," Conrad replied. He stood very still, and spoke just loudly enough for Tadlock to hear his words.

Conrad looked directly into the eyes of the wounded cat. It was a moment he would remember in photographic detail for the rest of his life.

"I'm sorry I did not get to him before he shot you, but he is all yours now. Take him while you still can."

At those words, spoken softly and deliberately, the animal seemed to make up its mind. With surprising speed considering its condition, it turned and fell upon Tadlock. The animal bit down on the man's shoulder and ripped at his body while Tadlock rolled and screamed, trying to keep his backpack between himself and the beast, and fighting desperately to escape the fiend's raking claws and snapping jaws.

When his enemy had finally ceased to struggle the cat backed off a short ways, panting from its grisly labors. The effort seemed to have exhausted it completely. It stood swaying next to its foe, breathing heavily. Tadlock's scalp had been peeled back from his skull on one side, and his arms and torso were lacerated and torn. He struggled to remain conscious. He began to drag himself slowly away, towards the break beyond the forest edge.

"Some say you should play dead if you are attacked by a wild animal, Grant Tadlock. Personally I would not know, but it might be worth a try," Conrad called out. He had not stirred from the edge of the clearing.

"Who are you? How do you know me? Why won't you kill it? God help me!" Tadlock gasped in horror.

"Once again you call out for supernatural help.

No one appears to be listening to you. I don't suppose you thought much of the deity when you were stabbing that young man to death back in Juneau."

"Who am I? Call me Erebus or Yama; call me the Grim Reaper; call me Karma—call me whatever you want. It's time at last for you to pay for the death of the innocent you murdered in prison—Marshall Stuckrath! If this noble animal does not finish the deed, you can count on me to put you out of your misery, but either way, you don't have long to live."

At last Grant Tadlock understood. He remembered the blinding anger he had felt toward the privileged college student who had humiliated him in front of the other prisoners, and the satisfaction he had felt as he had repeatedly plunged the knife into the boy's yielding flesh. He recalled too the long seconds of horror and panic he had experienced when his knife had at last hit home, and the strong youth's hands in one final convulsion had spasmed and then frozen around his neck. It had taken two men to release him from the dying youth's grip.

"You—you were the one—the one in the alley. Are you his father?" Tadlock rasped through mangled lips.

"Yes, but not the father you are thinking of. That father would spare even the likes of you—but I have no such scruples."

Conrad took a step towards the cougar, who seemed on the verge of collapsing. Blood dripped from its muzzle and wounds.

"Now!—finish it!" Conrad insisted.

The cougar, with a last effort of will, threw himself upon Tadlock as the man tried desperately to roll away. This time the animal's jaws opened wide and snapped shut on Tadlock's exposed nape. The curved canines clamped down convulsively in the cat's final death throes, shearing veins and arteries in Tadlock's neck, finishing the task that Marshall had not been able to accomplish. The animal did not open its jaws again, expiring on the spot and collapsing against the body of its nemesis. The two-legged beast beneath the mountain lion shuddered briefly and ceased moving.

Conrad did not linger to savor his success. He made haste to return to *Tisiphone* in Thetis Bay, though his pace was somewhat slowed by the slight limp he had developed. Besides the inevitable scratches and scrapes he had incurred during his passage through the dense undergrowth of the isthmus, he had somehow injured his Achilles tendon, which continued to bother him for some months after—a painful memento of his arduous odyssey.

Charlie Jackson had taken a brief break from his travails with the engine to watch Tadlock chase after the cougar. Angry but powerless to control his irresponsible partner, he went back to the cramped engine compartment to put the fuel system back together. He was bleeding the air from the fuel line, and was nearly ready to try the engine when he heard the second shot.

Charlie was an experienced outdoorsman. He

instantly recognized that the second shot had come from an entirely different rifle. He gauged the shot had originated from a location some distance north of the area where his partner had entered the thickets above the highest tide line. He surmised there must be another hunter, probably shooting at the same animal. It was a dangerous development, but in spite of what he had told Tadlock, he could not just leave without his partner. Perhaps he was mistaken after all and Tadlock had shot the animal a second time. He might be wrong about the second shot being from a different rifle—he doubted it, but he hoped so. Regardless, he had to get Tadlock back to the boat so they could be on their way before they were discovered. As the day wore on it would become more and more likely that some boater might enter the harbor to anchor or tie up to the dock for the night.

Charlie had his own high-powered hunting rifle on board, as well as a shotgun and a .44 magnum revolver. He did not think the rifle would be of much use in the thick brush, so he took the shotgun and the revolver. He moved slowly, stopping frequently to listen for any suspicious sounds, but heard nothing but the noises of his own stealthy movements and the cries of the crows circling above. At the base of the rocky knoll he saw Tadlock's rifle lodged in a tangle of alder branches. The knoll itself was covered in blood, and a trail of gore led to the forest edge. Charlie loosed the strap on his pistol holster, released the safety on the shotgun, and advanced cautiously into the gloom with the shotgun raised.

Grant Tadlock and the mountain lion lay together as they had died. Tadlock was partially curled on his left side in a nearly fetal position, his sightless eyes still open wide and his mouth agape. The cougar was astride him with its teeth sunk deeply into the man's neck. The carpet of spruce needles and moss below them was dark with their combined blood. Charlie searched the perimeter of the clearing and found what he suspected must be there—clear signs that a second person had been present as well. Broken limbs and tracks led away from the spot into the denser growth off to the northwest. Charlie had no intention of following. The mysterious second shooter might be anywhere—perhaps watching his movements even now from the slopes of the adjacent hill. He might be waiting for Charlie to leave so that he could claim the cougar carcass.

Charlie reasoned that whoever this other gunman was, he could not have missed seeing their boat at the floating dock. The obvious course of action for any legitimate hunter would have been to go to the *Deep Runner* to report the event and get help. Whatever the identity of the person, he too must be operating outside the law. Charlie's best guess was that the other hunter, like the late Grant Tadlock was also a poacher, and had decided it best to leave the scene as quickly as possible. Whoever he was, Charlie reasoned, he must have a camp or boat very close by. Charlie had no desire to make his acquaintance.

Charlie hesitated, debating on his best course of action. After several moments he concluded it would not help his cause to bring the body of Grant Tadlock back to Juneau. He needed to get the contraband to Jim Lothar as quickly as possible. Lothar would not be happy, but with no other witnesses he would have to accept Charlie's explanation and judgement. Once the ephedrine was in Lothar's hands he could get back to fishing for the remainder of the season and put this distasteful business behind him. Unless someone reported him in the area he had little to worry about. Any investigation would show that Tadlock had been killed by the cat after having first shot the animal. He would need to come up with an explanation for what he had been doing in Gedney Harbor, and why he had not reported Tadlock's demise if the connection between himself and Tadlock was uncovered by investigators, but maybe that would not come to light. Regardless, he had plenty of time to come up with an alibi if it proved necessary. In the meantime he looked forward to the cash that would be his when Lothar sold the contraband. He also had reason to believe he was due at least a part of Tadlock's cut as well, as a reward for his solo efforts.

Charlie Jackson felt no sorrow over Tadlock's death. The man had been a fool, a thorn in his side and had certainly put the whole enterprise at risk. He doubted the unfortunate man would be missed by many. Even Lothar seemed to have no fondness for him, but only seemed to value the relationship because of Tadlock's willingness to take on many of the more abhorrent duties the nature of their business required. Charlie could think of no suitable epitaph for a man who had died as he had lived—unloved and unloving. A phrase seemed to come to mind, but he could not place it. Perhaps he had heard it in a song.

"*...a man without love is no man at all, but a cold bitter wind passing by...*"

Charlie did his best to erase his own footprints from the scene by dragging a spruce branch behind him as he made his way back to the boat. He was pleased when the engine started promptly, and after warming up for a few minutes, ran smoothly. He untied the dock lines and motored out of the harbor and into the open waters of Chatham Strait. There were no other boats in sight, to his great relief.

CHAPTER 31

Conrad Sails Away

"... how I spurned that turnpike earth!—that common highway all over dented with the marks of slavish heels and hoofs; and turned me to admire the magnanimity of the sea which will permit no records."—Moby Dick, Herman Melville

Conrad felt neither remorse, guilt, elation, nor moral superiority for his actions. Now that he had accomplished his goal, with the aid of his cougar confederate, which seemed to validate his actions all the more, he experienced a serenity which was not exactly contentment and certainly not happiness. His was more a feeling that what had been inevitable had come to pass, and he had properly played his part in the course of things. It was as if he had performed as a supporting actor who had effectively inhabited his role in some greater production. The curtain had fallen, and would ultimately open again to a new act.

The original cresting wave of rage and sorrow over his son's death had passed weeks before, but Conrad was foremost a man of action and it was inevitable that soon thereafter he began to channel all the dark savage potency of his emotions into his vision of vengeance and justice.

Conrad was as capable of introspection as any man, and was well aware that both the law and popular morality would condemn him if he were found out, just as in the judge's death. His ethics however were of a more primordial order, and were heavily influenced by the time he had spent in the tribal areas of Pakistan and Afghanistan during his youth, as well as his long infatuation with classical Greek culture. He did not consider his actions noble so much as necessary. Although he had always rejected religion and the laws of the state as the ultimate sources of morality, Conrad considered himself to be a principled person. He had been favored with not one, but two incredibly rare and extraordinary mountain lion sightings, and his spirit or totem animal had administered the coup de grace to his sworn enemy. The cougar had culled correctly—had unerringly administered a more just verdict than any court of human law.

For the first time in months Conrad felt at peace. A weight had been lifted. The world was in balance again, though his future was potentially perilous. The loss of the never-to-be-realized promise of the young man who had been Marshall Stuckrath, and the possibilities of his future relationship to him (for he had often fantasized about how he might eventually win the youth's trust and friendship once he began to live independently of David and Karen) could never be undone. Still somehow, the gods, fates, energy patterns—or whatever forces shaped the lives of men, harnessed to his will, had been assuaged. Life for him was once again possible, if not the same life he had led before.

Conrad weighed anchor and motored out of the bight in Thetis Bay. It was a dozen miles to the open waters of Chatham Strait. By the time he reached the deeper waters of the strait beyond Tebenkof Bay Charlie Jackson in *Deep Runner* was off Point Sullivan, some fifteen miles north of Conrad's position. It was more than likely its captain had taken note of Conrad's boat, and by now he must be wondering at *Tisiphone's* frequent appearances and odd maneuvers. Regardless, Conrad supposed the man would be pushing on to Juneau with all speed now—putting as much distance between himself and recent events as possible.

He assumed that agent Dolon, the state troopers, or other law enforcement agencies would intercept the boat and its illicit cargo either en route or after it arrived in Juneau. It did not matter to Conrad one way or the other. His failure to perform his duty would make waves he knew, and the Agency would make their displeasure known when they caught up to him. He was sure his next posting would be particularly disagreeable. They would find him eventually—there was no avoiding or escaping them for long—but in the meantime he would enjoy a few weeks, or months if he was careful and lucky, of relative freedom.

As he entered the rougher waters at the south end of Chatham Strait the welcome northwesterly, which had been his constant friend throughout this part of his voyage, freshened. Coronation Island grew steadily larger, and the Hazy Islands, white with guano, floated just beyond. Cape Ommaney, the bane of so many ships—'Cape Ominous'—loomed off his starboard beam. The Cape Decision lighthouse winked its welcoming white flash every five seconds to port. He had made his decision, and the lighthouse seemed to approve—a friendly beacon marking the last western point of Kuiu Island.

Ahead of him lay a vast expanse of empty ocean. On his present course the closest land, the island of Hawaii, was some twenty-five hundred miles distant. No land lay between *Tisiphone* and Japan thousands of leagues to the west, and Seattle was a voyage of nearly a thousand miles south.

Abreast of the cliffs of Coronation Island under wheeling flocks of seabirds, a pod of playful Orcas joined him, spouting and frolicking just off his starboard bow. With any luck the northerly would hold until he passed from the continental shelf into the deeper waters of the open Pacific. There he could count on the help of the cold subarctic and California currents and the predominant westerly winds to push the boat steadily southward. At some point, probably around the latitude of San Francisco, he would pick up the north equatorial current and the northeast trades, which should carry him to his planned landfall of Hilo, Hawaii. From that port the whole of the South Pacific beckoned. He took in the clean salty air and reflected on how good it would be to leave this savage land of ice and snow behind. It seemed to Conrad that the gentle healing zephyrs of the tropics were what he most needed now.

Shortly after arriving in Juneau he had made up his mind to extend his 'vacation' and damn the Agency. He had put off the ultimate voyage—sailing the South Pacific—for too long. Before the year's end he would celebrate his fiftieth birthday—as good a time as any to start an epic cruise. Conrad had put his time to good use in Juneau while waiting for his opportunity to deal with Grant Tadlock. *Tisiphone* was well-stocked with food, water, and all the necessities for this ultimate expedition. Even more significantly, he finally felt free of all obligation and duty to family, friend, or foe.

Once clear of the spectacular sheer cliffs of Helm Point on southern Coronation Island—the last point of land he would see for the next several weeks—Conrad set up the wind vane mechanism to keep *Tisiphone* on her new heading. Stepping below, he filled a pot to boil water for tea and prepared a sandwich of Juneau lunchmeat leftovers. As he began to eat an idea came to him—so insistent and compelling that he interrupted his meal. He found the small plastic container of cinders and ash which were all that remained to him of Marshall Stuckrath. Moving to the foredeck, he paused and thought of the residuum dissolving into the sea, where perhaps someday the very molecules making up those remnants might be recycled into the body of a cetacean, like one of the creatures which still escorted him as he pressed on into the open Pacific. He imagined the cycle; from the dissolved elements to the drifting plankton, and on up the food chain through ever larger nektonic species—perhaps even Alaskan salmon—finally culminating in the majestic Orca.

The concept was cold comfort, but he felt the boy would have approved. An alternate scenario, with the salmon ending up in the stomach of a bruin or human was somehow less aesthetically appealing, but still better than the insufferable idea of the remains gathering dust for years in his apartment, only to be tossed into the garbage after his own demise.

With the whales spouting and splashing around him, and the hematic sun low over the endless ianthine ocean Conrad bid his son farewell, full in the knowledge that he had done all in his power to avenge the boy, and to assuage the awful wrath of the relentless and unforgiving furies.

CHAPTER 32

Fish And Game

The government office Ray Standers oversaw was an unpretentious and drab building, low-slung with a forest green metal roof littered with fir and spruce needles from the surrounding trees. The parking lot, filled with official vehicles, inflatable boats, and drying fishing nets left little room for Ray's scratched and dented pickup. Although he was the supervisor of an office that swelled to over a dozen employees during the summer season, it had never occurred to him to order a specially marked parking place. Like the other workers, he parked where he could.

"Howdy stranger!"

The officer who got up from the desk to greet Ray was a hulking bearded bear of a man. Despite being past his prime he was still imposing, though his uniform these days needed to allow for the extra bulge around his mid section.

"Yeah, I suppose I am getting to be an unfamiliar face around here. How have things been Steve? Did I miss any excitement?"

Steve Howard had been with the department

almost as long as Ray, and the two were on the friendliest of terms. Their wives were also close, and their children had grown up together. When not at work Ray and Steve often fished and hunted together, spending much of their leisure time exploring the vast tracts of the Tongass National Forest.

"How was your trip to Tenakee?" Steve asked.

The hamlet of Tenakee Springs on Chichagof Island, named after the natural mineral hot springs there, was a settlement of around one hundred people. It was unique in having banned all automobiles, except for the fire and fuel oil trucks, and off-road four wheelers. It was a laid-back community of retirees, artists, fisherman, and independent self-reliant characters who found the pace of life too brisk in the more populous towns of Southeast Alaska. Ray had diverted to Tenakee Springs on his way back to Juneau, ostensibly on department business, but that had not stopped him from enjoying the hot springs and having a few drinks with his friends there.

"The place was great as always. Almost like a vacation, and of course there is nothing quite as relaxing as soaking in the bathhouse at the end of the day. I wish my wife liked it more there. That's a place I could retire to," Ray responded.

"Are you still working on that case for the troopers?"

"I hope I'm all done with that now. I can't say I was much help either. Do you guys still want me around here, or am I just in the way—anything need my immediate attention?" Ray looked with vexation at the pile of papers that had accumulated while he had been gone.

"If not, I'd just as soon get back to Tenakee," Ray said, only half-joking. He was not excited about the prospect of getting back to the duties of his office again, and the neglected pile of paperwork cluttering his desk.

Although it was clear Steve would have liked to have heard more about his recent activities, Ray did not feel comfortable discussing them, even with his colleague and friend—especially since he had not been completely transparent with trooper Tenax. In the end Ray had decided not to reveal his knowledge of the connection between Slocum and Stuckrath—partly because he wanted to get back to his regular duties, and partly because he did not think there was enough evidence, even circumstantial, to justify expending any more resources on investigating Conrad Slocum as a suspect in judge Henry Daise's death.

"Well, you might want to take a look at this—just came in from the state troopers office this morning," Steve said, passing a memo to Ray.

Ray studied the paper.

"Shit! Now Tenax wants me to go to Kuiu Island. ...as if I haven't already beat Stephens Passage to a froth the last week. And since when does Fish and Game investigate death scenes for the troopers anyway?"

"Maybe when the death is caused by a wild animal. You haven't even heard the best part. This is one investigation I would love to be on myself," Howard replied.

"What do you mean, a wild animal—a bear?"

"What that memo does not say, is that it looks like the man was killed by a mountain lion."

"Are you kidding? A cougar on Kuiu Island—now that would be something!"

"I'm not making this shit up. I got the lowdown from Tenax himself while you were in Tenakee basking in those hot springs. Apparently he tried to hail you on the radio, but it seems you were not answering—imagine that..." Steve winked, and Ray shrugged his shoulders.

"Yesterday morning a fisherman from Sitka put into Gedney Harbor. He saw a big gathering of seagulls and ravens circling and got curious. He found the remains of a man, and he swears there was a dead cougar on top of him. He also reported there were some other animal tracks around, and that the bodies had been disturbed by scavengers, but it did not look like they had been dead too long," officer Howard continued.

"It was probably just a cinnamon or brown phase bear. It's hard to believe a mountain lion could make it all the way out to Kuiu, let alone survive long there with that dense a bear population," Ray replied.

"Maybe so, but I would bet that fisherman knows the difference between a bear and a big cat, and of course there was that report years ago of a cougar on Kupreanof not so far away—but I guess we will find out soon enough one way or the other. I took the liberty of stocking up the launch for the trip. You are supposed to contact this federal agent named Jack Dolon—someone

I have never heard of, but the troopers insist he goes with you. They wouldn't give me much more information, but I gather he was instrumental in helping them intercept that boatload of contraband that was all over the news reports a couple of days ago. It seems this dead man on Kuiu might have been involved somehow in that affair, according to a confession they got from Charlie Jackson, who apparently ran the boat. It looks like 'Hard Luck Chuck' will be spending some time in the big house."

"That's too bad. That poor fucker never had much success at anything other than catching fish. I like Charlie. He's always been a conscientious fisherman. I tried to warn him to stay away from the likes of Martes and Tadlock, but I guess he must have been pretty desperate for money after his divorce—maybe as desperate for money as that cougar was for meat—and whether it is the human animal or wild, desperation seems like it mostly leads to bad decisions. I would rather face a mountain lion or an angry sow with cubs any day than that woman he married. Well anyway, it looks like I had better get ready for another outing."

"Damn, I would love to go with you Ray, but I'm afraid someone has got to be at that meeting up in Haines tomorrow," officer Howard said. "More bear problems on the Chilkoot, as usual."

"So I heard. Those god-damned tourists and photographers again. I guess it will take one of them getting eaten up there before the state decides to give us another officer to patrol that river full time in the summer. You say some federal agent is supposed to help me out—what was his name again?"

"Dolon—Jack Dolon. Sergeant Tenax says he is some sort of intelligence agent for the feds. Tenax either can't or won't tell me exactly who he works for. Here is his phone number." Howard peeled a yellow sticky note off a metal file cabinet and handed it to Ray.

Ray was pretty sure that Dolon must be associated with the same government bureau that employed agent Slocum. Sergeant Tenax had told him earlier that Slocum was involved in a drug trafficking investigation, and though he had not elaborated, it seemed likely it was the one Charlie Jackson had been arrested in connection with. He wondered why Slocum himself was not going out to Kuiu Island. Perhaps Slocum was still busy with the contraband case in Juneau.

Shortly after his interview with Conrad Slocum Ray had visited sergeant Tenax's office with the intention of handing over judge Daise's tennis shoe and the notes of his investigation. He had been relieved to find officer Tenax was out, and had left the items with a secretary. The typed sheets Ray had prepared for the sergeant did not include either his research on the connection between Slocum and Stuckrath, or his conversation with the poacher Craig Martes.

Ray, like Conrad, had come to the conclusion that the Stuckrath family had suffered enough, and he was unwilling to encourage sergeant Tenax's investigation further, knowing that Stuckrath could be forced to come back to Alaska to testify. Even with all the suggestive information he had gathered he did not think it likely a jury would convict Slocum of the judge's death, so he had chosen to do what he could to discourage any more investigation into the case—or at least not encourage it. Ray was still ambivalent, but he had accepted the fact that he would never be absolutely sure if the judge's death had been an accident or murder.

In the days since his interview with Conrad Ray had been busy with other matters, including his trip to Tenakee Springs, and had spent little time thinking about the circumstances of judge Daise's death, or of his decision to hold back information from trooper Joe Tenax. It was the busiest time of the year for the Fish and Game department, and Ray had lost days of valuable time on sergeant Tenax's errands, which he now must scramble to make up. But at least this latest request by the trooper was more to his taste. Kuiu Island was one of Ray's favorite destinations, and the possibility that a mountain lion had killed a man there was intriguing.

CHAPTER 33

Ray And Jack

Ray Standers was pleased that agent Dolon arrived at the harbor five minutes earlier than the five AM time they had arranged. After brief introductions and stowing their gear the two men set off. Ray found Jack Dolon to be a taciturn presence. He was the type of man who, while not unpleasant, seemed completely comfortable with silence. Ray had the feeling that if he had not initiated conversation the man might not have spoken the entire trip, which took most of the day in the Fish and Game vessel they had requisitioned for the trip.

Jack Dolon was the epitome of the perfect secret agent. Average height and weight; brown eyes and brown neatly trimmed hair; nose average sized; unremarkable mouth and chin—not particularly handsome, but certainly not ugly; no tattoos or obvious scars or disfigurations. The type of man who had the chameleon-like ability to go unnoticed in virtually any social gathering. He had a face you could look at all night and not recall the next day. Appropriately too, agent Dolon was also a skilled master of disguise. In high school and college he had participated in theatre.

Although he had never played a leading or even supporting acting role, he had excelled as a make-up artist, costumer, and props technician. It was here that he had discovered he most enjoyed working behind the scenes. Eventually he had gravitated to criminal justice, serving for a time as a crime scene investigator before being recruited by his college friend, Richard Head, into the Agency.

"That was a pretty impressive amount of contraband you intercepted," Ray offered early in their trip.

"For Alaska I suppose. Nothing like what you see down south," he replied laconically.

"I understand Mr. Slocum was working with you on the case," Ray ventured.

"Sorry, I can't comment on that."

"Sure. I understand," Ray replied.

"Have you been up in Juneau long?" he tried again.

"Not long."

"So what do you think of our town?"

"I've worked in worse places."

"I know what you mean. I worked out in Bethel early in my career. Pretty bleak. Where is the worst place you've ever been stationed?"

"I probably shouldn't say," Dolon replied.

After that brusque exchange Ray gave up the attempt to draw the man out, focusing instead on piloting the boat and enjoying the majestic surroundings. Ray never grew tired of the sight of the dark green mountain flanks rising straight from the depths of the fjords to their glacier scoured heights. His binoculars hung at the ready round his neck, and he periodically raised them to zoom in on anything that piqued his interest. Once he spied a group of goats just above the tree line, and later a brown bear with two cubs grazing on the delta of a stream near the water's edge.

Otherwise the trip down Stephens Passage and Chatham Strait was rapid and uneventful. There was little wind, and seas were unusually flat. After a time Ray found he did not mind the lack of conversation. The agent seemed content to take in the scenery without comment. Ray could appreciate a man who did not feel the need to fill up every moment with unnecessary chatter, and who like himself seemed to enjoy just being out on the water in such a setting.

They arrived in Gedney Harbor late in the afternoon. Within minutes of stepping onto the dock Ray noticed the shell casing wedged between two of the dock's decking boards. Agent Dolon used a pair of tweezers to put the find into a small evidence bag.

"Somebody took a shot from here. Could be our dead man or could have been someone else. I guess we'll find out."

"Thirty-aught-six shell, I see. Probably the most common rifle cartridge size used in these parts. Some of the old World War Two veterans still use M1 Garand rifles and clips for hunting," Ray observed.

Using the directions from the fisherman who had discovered the body, they struck off, following the same faint deer trail Tadlock had used days earlier.

While scrambling up the rocky knoll, Dolon noticed something the fisherman who reported the dead man had not; the rifle which had slid from Tadlock's grasp when Conrad Slocum's bullet had felled him.

"Here's his rifle. Remington model seven hundred, thirty-aught-six. Without ballistics we can't be absolutely sure, but it's pretty reasonable to assume that shell casing was ejected from this rifle," the agent said.

Donning rubber gloves from his pack of investigative supplies, he inspected the rifle closely. He took a large folded evidence bag, and very carefully, (double-checking that safety was engaged) placed the rifle inside. Now that they were engaged in the actual investigation, agent Dolon, who was obviously enthusiastic about this line of work, became more communicative, if not quite loquacious.

"Looks like quite a bit of dried blood on these rocks. It could be this is where he was attacked. He either dropped his rifle or it got swatted out of his hands," Dolon speculated. He carefully took several flakes of the dried blood, placing them in evidence bags.

The bodies of the cougar and the man still lay together on the forest floor. The activities of the scavengers had moved the corpses somewhat from their original configuration, but the two remained mostly as they had fallen, with the cougar's jaws still clamped in rigor mortis on the dead man's neck. The man lay on his side with the cat clutching him from behind. Both the cougar's and the man's eye sockets were picked clean, and the man had lost his lips, tongue, and much of the flesh of his face to the forest scavengers. Both were missing their mid sections, where a bear had obviously enjoyed a succulent meal of their tender and nutritious organs. Tadlock's legs had been separated at the hip joints, and rested grotesquely intertwined in fern fronds several feet away from his torso.

Both Ray and Jack had brought cameras. They took numerous photographs from every angle before proceeding with the unpleasant task of bagging up the remains. The corpses of the man and animal would be taken to the coroner in Juneau. After the coroner examination, the mountain lion carcass would go back to Fish and Game, where Ray and his colleagues would document the exceptional find, and try to determine what they could about the history and place of origin of the cat.

The fisherman had disturbed the site little, other than leaving a few tracks, having immediately gone back to his boat and radioed in his report. He had been too spooked by the find to loiter long at the gruesome scene. Tadlock's wallet was still in the back pocket of his soiled and bloody jeans. Using examination gloves, agent Dolon removed the drivers license.

"Grant S. Tadlock was our unfortunate victim."

"I would say that mountain lion was just as unlucky," Ray observed.

"Now this is interesting," agent Dolon continued as they prepared to bag up the legs.

He pointed to the ragged end of the broken femur jutting through the torn jeans.

"Does that look like the work of a bear to you?" he asked.

"Not at all. No bite marks on the bone or jeans. I wonder how the hell he broke his leg? Maybe that's why the cat got him. Could he have done it climbing or falling on the rocks?" Ray speculated.

Agent Dolon extracted scissors from his kit and carefully cut away the material, now stiff with dried blood, from around the wound. He studied the shattered limb. As a crime scene investigator for a large metropolitan police department, he had observed and analyzed a fair number of traumatic injuries. Although his duties were different now, he had not forgotten those skills.

"See that. There's the entry point. This guy was shot. That's what broke the femur," the agent pronounced, pointing a gloved finger at a small hole in the back side of the gory thigh.

"Good call. You are absolutely right. That is definitely an entry wound," Ray confirmed.

"I've seen quite a few gunshot wounds in my day, and I don't have a single doubt about it. Someone shot Tadlock when he climbed up on that knoll, and that's why he dropped his rifle. It is a reasonable assumption that after Tadlock got hit, he limped or crawled into this clearing, and that is when the cougar got him."

"I don't suppose Tadlock could have accidentally shot himself," Ray suggested, somewhat rhetorically.

"I don't think so. As far as I can tell without

ballistics conformation only one shot was fired from that rifle, and I don't see how he could have shot himself in the back of the leg," agent Dolon replied, unnecessarily. Both men realized the improbability of that scenario.

"The obvious question is who shot him, and was it accidental?" Ray replied.

"Could be there was another hunter and he mistakenly hit Tadlock, or could be someone wanted Tadlock dead," agent Dolon deadpanned, with a shrug.

The two men searched the the small glade for other clues. Ray systematically explored the clearing while the agent sifted through the forest floor detritus around the corpses.

"Somebody came in here this way," Ray said, pointing out the disturbed underbrush and broken twigs in the area directly opposite the corpses at the edge of the forest clearing.

"We should follow that trail," agent Dolon insisted.

Ray had many years of tracking experience, and the signs of Conrad's route were easy for him to discern even days later. They retraced the path to the rise where Conrad had taken his shot. From that vantage point the men could see both Gedney Harbor and Thetis Bay. Though they searched the area they were unable to find the expended shell casing which must have been ejected from the shooter's rifle.

"Either the guy was smart enough to pick up that shell, or we just can't find it," Dolon said, after they had searched the thickets for some time.

"...like looking for a needle in a haystack in this brush," Ray replied.

"Regardless, we know Tadlock was shot purposely. It was no accident. Somebody had a perfectly clear shot from here. There was no way he could have mistaken Tadlock for a cougar from this place, even without a scope."

"My idea is that our shooter was holed up in that bay," Dolon speculated, pointing to the northwest across the isthmus. "He must have bushwhacked his way across and climbed to this rise to shoot Tadlock, which means he planned it. Even though we can't find the shell, it is the perfect spot. After that he went down to finish him off, but the cougar had already taken care of that."

"That's Thetis Bay. Pretty good anchorage. He could have done what you said. It would have been tough going through those lowlands, but doable. It must have been someone who wanted a piece of the drug deal," Ray suggested.

"Maybe. Or somebody just had it in for Tadlock," Dolon countered.

"Charlie Jackson confessed they had detoured to Gedney with engine trouble. He said his partner Tadlock shot a cougar and went to claim it, but when he did not come back Jackson investigated and saw he had been killed by the animal. Jackson didn't say anything about another shooter though," Dolon continued.

"Well it's common knowledge among the local

fishermen that Charlie had no love for Grant Tadlock. As far as I can tell Jim Lothar was Tadlock's only friend in the world. Charlie would never have let Tadlock step foot on any boat he captained if Lothar hadn't made him take him along as crew," Ray explained.

"So I guess you knew about this even before the fisherman found the body, then?" Ray added, irritated that he had not been better informed earlier.

"Well, about the same time. It took a couple of days and some wheeling and dealing between the lawyers before Mr. Jackson finally confessed all the details."

"Even so, It seems he didn't tell you everything," Ray observed. "He had to have heard the shot that hit Tadlock."

"What is just as interesting is the fact that as far as we can tell the ephedrine was all still there when we busted Jackson, although we know Lothar was there to greet Jackson as soon as he arrived in Juneau. Of course our intelligence could have been wrong about the amount of contraband, and I suppose Jackson could have made his own separate deal without Tadlock or Lothar's knowledge."

"Yeah, maybe Charlie double-crossed both Lothar and Tadlock. That would explain why he didn't mention the shooter. He might even have money from that other deal waiting for him when he gets out of the slammer—sort of an insurance policy, I guess."

The men returned to the clearing in the forest and together carried and dragged the bagged remains of

Grant Tadlock and the mountain lion back to the boat.

"We have still got plenty of light. I would like to check out Thetis Bay if you don't mind," agent Dolon said, once they had left Gedney Harbor and were motoring their way north along the coast of Kuiu island.

"Why not. We'll be traveling back to Juneau in the dark anyway unless we decide to spend the night here. We've got plenty of grub for a couple of meals and snacks, and I'm in no hurry to get back to my desk in Juneau," Ray agreed.

"Something else just occurred to me anyway. A couple of Park Service archeologists have been working on a dig in Petrof Bay, just a few miles from Thetis. It might be worth checking in with them. Maybe they heard or saw something," Ray suggested.

As it tuned out the archeologists were nowhere to be seen, but they encountered a pair of kayakers in Explorer Basin.

"Hey guys, got a minute to chat?" Ray asked as they pulled even with the paddlers.

"Sure, why not. We've got our our fishing licenses on us," the lead kayaker said defensively, seeing Ray's uniform.

"Don't worry, I'm not here to hassle you about fishing. My partner and I just want to ask you a couple of questions. How does a cold beer sound?" Ray suggested.

The two youths were quick to accept the offer. They tied their kayaks to the launch's stern and came aboard. They were both in their twenties, bearded and sunburned. The one who had spoken first introduced himself as Henry Daniels. He was as voluble as his companion was tightlipped.

"I thought Dr. Maschner's research group would still be out here digging. Have you seen them?"

"You mean the archeologists? They were just leaving when we got here last week. We talked to them a little. They said they were heading back to Sitka for supplies," Daniels answered.

"...you guys have been here in Tebenkof all week?" Ray asked.

"Well, not in Explorer Basin the whole time. We started out on the other side and worked our way around to here. We spent a couple of days in Petrof Bay, and last night in Thetis."

"You didn't happen to see any other boats here other than the archeologists, did you?" agent Dolon asked.

Something about the other man made Henry Daniels nervous. He wore no uniform, but he was obviously some sort of investigator. Henry was carrying a small amount of pot in his kayak. He was a teacher and coach at Sitka high school, and even a small drug related infraction could jeopardize his job.

"We've only seen two other boats the whole time we've been here. A fishing boat came in one day for a few hours, and another day we saw a sailboat come out of Thetis Bay," the hirsute educator answered.

"Did you get the name of the sailboat? Can you describe it?" agent Dolon asked, more animated than

Ray had seen him the entire trip.

Daniels and his companion had not been close enough to get the name of the boat, but from their description, it had clearly been Conrad Slocum's double-ended cutter.

It was obvious his original reservations about Conrad Slocum had been right, Ray thought. He found himself wondering whether the agent had shot Tadlock in the process of making a drug bust, or for more personal reasons. But if the shooting had something to do with the smuggling, why did he let Charlie Jackson go free? The personal connection Slocum had to David Stuckrath was the thing that linked him to the deaths of both Daise and Tadlock. And the only motivation that made sense, Ray began to comprehend, was revenge for David Stuckrath's son's death.

Ray realized he had been seriously in dereliction of duty not to have informed sergeant Tenax of his findings immediately. He might have been able to prevent this second death. But another part of Ray balanced the relative worth, from what he knew of the two men, of Tadlock and Slocum. Ray found he was not sorry Tadlock was dead, and after all—strictly speaking—Tadlock had ultimately been killed by the mountain lion, not Slocum, as the evidence seemed to prove. Ray also found himself wondering about agent Dolon's reaction. He seemed almost joyful over the discovery of his fellow agent's possible involvement.

"How about another beer gentlemen?" Ray offered.

"Sure, why not. We're on vacation, after all," Daniels answered. "So, is this about those gun shots we heard?"

"You heard shots?" Ray prompted.

"Yeah, two of them—coming from over towards Thetis Bay. The first one sounded even farther away. Is somebody doing some poaching out here?"

"Yeah, it seems that way. Somebody shot a mountain lion," Ray responded.

"See!—I told you I saw a cougar! Now do you believe me?" Daniels companion declared, punching him in the shoulder.

While paddling on their second day in Tebenkof Cove he had briefly sighted the animal on the shore, but by the time he had called his partner's attention to it, the animal had vanished back into the forrest.

"I'll be damned. I guess you weren't just seeing things. Mountain lions on Kuiu—what the hell?"

"Yes, over in Gedney harbor. We've just come from there. ...already cleaned up the mess, so there is really nothing to see, and we would appreciate it if you guys wouldn't tramp around the area or tell anyone who might come in here about it for now," Ray cautioned the young kayakers. "Another investigator may need to look at the site again, so the less disturbed the better."

The men finished their beers and the kayaking couple paddled away to their nearby camp. Ray conned the launch out into Chatham Sound and pointed the bow north towards Juneau. The sun, though not yet set, was blocked by the peaks of Baranof Island to the west.

The waters were a deep Persian indigo. A cool northwesterly breeze buffeted the boat and raised a short steep chop on the sound, giving them a bumpy ride for much of the voyage.

"I guess your partner Slocum must have shot Tadlock trying to bust him and Charlie for that ephedrine," Ray speculated.

"I don't recall saying anything about Slocum being my partner," Dolon replied.

"Come on, I'm not a complete idiot," Ray retorted.

"Well, I really should not comment on that," was agent Dolon's terse reply.

He had returned to his original reticent demeanor. Ray made several more attempts to draw him out, but it was as though they were strangers again. Jack Dolon seemed to fade out gradually, until Ray feared that he would look over at last and find nothing at all where the agent sat.

They arrived sleepily in the Auk Bay marina north of Juneau very early the next morning.

"I can take things from here," agent Dolon said, once they had disembarked from the launch. "I'll call the troopers. They'll send a team to get the bodies and evidence."

Ray knew that the coroner and evidence experts would have to do their research before his office could take possession of the cougar. In any case he was tired and only too willing to let Dolon take over. Ray drove away slowly with his head full of unanswered questions.

After the Fish and Game officer left, Jack Dolon took the evidence bag which contained the disarticulated legs of Tadlock and put it into the trunk of his rental car before calling the state troopers to collect the rest of the gruesome cargo. Once the troopers left he went home and climbed into bed, setting his alarm for nine AM.

After the short sleep, two cups of strong coffee and a light breakfast, he called his supervisor, Richard Head.

"I have something you might find interesting," he said.

"You found out where Slocum is?"

"I still can't help you with that, but we did find one of the other smugglers, Grant Tadlock. A mountain lion killed him," Dolon said.

"Yeah, so what. He was a minor player. Why would I be interested in him—let alone a mountain lion?"

"You might be interested in what happened to him before the cougar got him. It seems Slocum shot the man and left him so the cougar could finish him off. Not very sporting of him, and not exactly by the book," Dolon said. "I figured you would want to know, and I thought you might like to have a look at the evidence before the local coroner got it."

"I take it back—that is an interesting development. Good work Jack. If what you say is true, we don't want that information in the wrong hands. I look forward to hearing your full report when you get back to

Seattle."

After his morning absolutions agent Dolon did some shopping, picking up a shipping box and some dry ice. He packed Grant Tadlock's lower limbs and the ice into the box and took it to the Juneau airport, where he sent it via air freight to supervisor Head's personal post office box in Seattle.

CHAPTER 34

More Deceptions

Two weeks later sergeant Joe Tenax called Ray Standers at his office.

"The coroner has finished with your cougar. You can pick up your cat any time," the officer said.

"That's great! Everybody here is excited to see the animal. We hope to figure out where it came from. Some of the temps were worried they would get laid off before they got a chance to study it," Ray replied. "What did the coroner come up with on the gun shot wound?"

"Oh, you mean the slug that killed the cat? It was definitely from Tadlock's rifle—ballistics match."

"So that's it then, case closed?" Ray was taken aback. The sergeant had said nothing about Tadlock's bullet-splintered leg.

"Yep, we're all done and the animal is yours. Might not smell so good, but I'm sure your guys won't mind that. ...not everyday you get to dissect a mountain lion—especially a man-killer," Tenax replied.

"By the way, the coroner asked me if there is any chance you could look again for Tadlock's legs. Jack Dolon's report said the legs were not present, and were most likely dragged away by some scavenger. The coroner asked me if there was any chance we might find them with a more thorough search of the area."

Ray at once realized why agent Dolon had encouraged him to go home before he turned over the bodies to the troopers. He had obviously disposed somehow of the evidence that would have proved Tadlock had been shot before the cougar killed him. Ray was tempted to say something to the sergeant, but thought better of it. Whatever agent Dolon was up to—it was something he wanted no part of. His first thought was that the agent was protecting his fellow operative, but as Ray recalled Dolon's pleasure at discovering that Slocum had fired the shot, that line of reasoning made less sense. Once again Ray found reason to dissemble.

"I don't think there is any point in sending anyone out there again. We covered the area pretty thoroughly, and my guess is some animal—probably a bear or wolf—drug Tadlock's legs way out in the brush somewhere. I suppose it's not impossible that somebody might find traces someday, but I would bet the bones are pretty well scattered by now," Ray lied.

"Well okay, if that's what you think. It does not seem important enough to waste any time or resources on. I've got bigger fish to fry. We know Tadlock died from the cougar bite so that wraps it up as far as I am concerned—legs or no legs. It jibes pretty well too with what Charlie Jackson had to say about things for the most part."

"What do you mean, 'for the most part?'" Ray

asked.

"Well, when he was booked and interrogated the first time he insisted there had been another shot fired after Tadlock left the boat. But ballistics showed only one round had been fired from his rifle, and the coroner confirmed the cat had been hit with one bullet, and that single shot had passed through the animals gut and lodged in its hind leg. So naturally we asked Charlie about that again. He said he must have been mistaken, and for some reason that line of questioning really seemed to upset him. Dolon said he also interrogated Jackson separately after the arrests, and Jackson said nothing to him about a second shot. Charlie's story still seems a little odd to me, but then Charlie went half crazy after we caught him with the contraband. We actually had him under suicide watch for the first week, until he calmed down."

After they hung up Ray thought about the sequence of events. As near as he could tell agent Dolon had interfered twice in the investigation. First, when he had withheld evidence from the coroner, and later, when he must have somehow convinced Charlie Jackson to contradict his initial testimony about the second gunshot. Ray wondered what Dolon had said to Jackson to get him to modify his story. He did not have long to wait for his answer.

A few days later Ray was surprised to encounter Charlie Jackson gill netting for coho salmon in the the waters of Lynn Canal fjord just offshore of the small town of Haines, some seventy miles north of Juneau. As their boats rocked together in the gentle seas and Charlie kept an attentive eye on the line of floats that marked his set, 'Good Luck Chuck' explained to the Fish and Game officer that he was now the happy owner of this, his very own used but well-maintained fishing boat, recently purchased "with a loan from a friend" who "preferred to remain anonymous." Fortuitously he had been paroled just in time to take advantage of the last of the commercial salmon fishing season, while his erstwhile partner, Jim Lothar, still languished behind the locked doors of Lime River Penitentiary, Charlie smirked.

After their pleasant gam Ray wished the fisherman well. He motored slowly southwards over nearly flat seas toward Juneau. The afternoon was crisp with the promise of autumn in the air. In the distance Charlie's boat, enveloped now by a gluttony of gulls and framed by the steep glacier mantled mountains of the narrow fjord, receded behind him.

Suddenly Ray shook his head and laughed out loud, though he was traveling solo, and there was no one to share in his sentiment. He was glad to see the fisherman back in his proper element, and he was even more grateful that he too was again doing what he loved and was best at. He was no better a detective than Charlie was a criminal, and it seemed now that both their lives, after an instructive but ultimately fruitless detour, had been set to rights by men much more suited to such enterprises.

CHAPTER 35

David And Cindy

At a mere eight stories high the eighty year old office building would not have been notable in a more populous city, but in Bellingham—a moderate sized college town in the far northwest corner of Washington state—it qualified as one of the tallest of the downtown structures. The building stood high enough that the upper floors enjoyed spectacular panoramic views of the city and its environs; Mt. Baker and the snow-frosted peaks of the North Cascade mountain range to the east; Bellingham Bay and the San Juan Islands to the west and south. From his office on the seventh floor David Stuckrath could even check on his sailboat, swinging from her anchor a mile or so distant as the seagull flies, through a small telescope perched on a tripod next to the large double-hung window.

The small office contained two ponderous mahogany desks, a filing cabinet, bookcases, and several mismatched wooden chairs. Every square inch of surface area was covered with legal tomes, periodicals, and files. There was no anteroom. Clients simply knocked at the age-darkened oak door, where a small sign with the words, "Informed Jury Advocates" hung, and were let directly into the office. David Stuckrath sat at one of the desks. A thick file of legal papers lay open upon it's scarred and gouged surface. His daughter, Cindy, was at the other desk, keying diligently at a computer while her father spoke.

"I have been thinking about how to deal with the Riley case," he said.

"I'm listening—I've got to finish with this today, though," his daughter answered, without looking away from the screen.

"Well anyway, you know we have got a standing court order against communicating with the jury now that they have been selected, and I don't intend to go to to jail again for trying to hand out pamphlets on the courthouse steps. This time we need to be smarter, or at least more devious."

"Yeah, and I don't want to have to bail your ass out of jail again either, Dad. That money could be better spent other ways," Cindy remarked, still typing.

"...so anyway I had the idea that we could probably find out the email addresses of at least some of the jury and paste in the link to the F.I.J.A. (he was referring to the Fully Informed Jury Association, an organization with which they were affiliated) website or a pdf of the jurors handbook. Technically we would not be giving the jurors direct information on jury nullification rights—we would just be giving them a link to the information."

"I'm not so sure the courts would agree with you

on that, Dad. You would still be violating your orders against communicating with the jury."

"Maybe we could get someone else to do it, then. The court order only names this office and me personally."

"...you got anyone in particular in mind?"

"It so happens I do. Do you remember the father and son I told you about—the ones I met in Spruce Cove—the Spencers?"

"No, Dad, I don't." Cindy looked up briefly, then returned to her task.

"Well, maybe I didn't tell you about them after all. Anyway, the old man, Bob—he's over ninety, but still pretty sharp—was very sympathetic to my situation there even though his son disapproved. He sided with me against Daise and was not afraid to speak his mind. I have stayed in touch with him ever since that time. I just got a call from him yesterday, in fact. He wants to help us out. He could email the jurors as a private citizen with no connection to us or the F.I.J.A."

"He'll get in trouble for it. There is bound to be at least one juror who will report him," Cindy commented, while her nimble fingers still clicked away at the keyboard.

"He won't care about any legal threats. I don't think he is a man who can be easily intimidated. I doubt the court will take action either, considering how old he is. If they do go after him it will only help our cause with the free publicity that would come of it."

"Well, if you think it's okay. Somehow we need

to make sure this jury knows about their rights before they go into session, and the judge and prosecutor will be doing everything they can to keep that knowledge away from them, as usual."

"I told him I'd think about it and call him back. He told me not to think too long or he might be dead! He's got a sense a humor all right. I'll call him tonight after dinner."

"Hey Dad, do you ever wonder what a strange coincidence it was that judge Daise and Grant Tadlock both died within a few days of each other?" Cindy asked, out of the blue.

"What got you thinking about that?"

"It was that article in the paper I read this morning—you know—they shot that mountain lion over near Winthrop. Poor thing was skinny and starved, and it had killed some rancher's chickens."

"I read that too. Cougars are still expanding their range—if they can't find deer they'll go after domesticated animals. But back to your question—yeah, I always thought it strange too. I'm not one for believing much in karma—plenty of people get away with bad things and go on to live long healthy lives—but it seemed like poetic justice at the time, and still does," David said. He was not about to voice his suspicions about Conrad to his daughter, or anyone else.

David thought back to his last evening in Spruce Cove with Mike Schwindel and Sam Thornton. He recalled their conversation and speculations about the judge's fate, and his own puzzlement over Conrad's odd behavior.

He read of Tadlock's death weeks after the event. His voyage south through the unpopulated fjords and channels off the British Columbian coast had taken more than a month, and during that time he had stopped at only one small town to pick up groceries and fuel. It was only after he arrived at Vancouver that he happened across the article headlined: "Alaskan Man Killed By Cougar," while browsing periodicals in a downtown bookstore. His feelings had been mixed at the time—joy and relief that his son's killer was dead, and sadness that the man had killed a rare Alaskan Mountain Lion. He remembered Conrad's tale of seeing a cougar in the mountains above Spruce Cove.

David had not seen or heard from Conrad since he had sailed away from Spruce cove and his Alaskan past. After he arrived in Bellingham he had called Karen to get Conrad's phone number, thinking to visit him in Seattle now that he was only an hour and a half distant by freeway. Surprisingly, Karen did not have a current phone number for Conrad either. Apparently it was unlisted or unavailable. The phone number in David's address book was a decade old and long out of service. There was no response either when, on a visit to Seattle, he rang Conrad's apartment. Karen was only able to supply him with a post office box number, where she had sent their holiday cards each year. In the end David had given up the idea of contacting him. He figured Conrad must be off again on one of his secret errands, and would get in touch if and when he was ready to.

As the afternoon advanced, a lively spring breeze drove puffy flocks of white cumulus clouds before it in the brilliant lapis blue sky outside their cozy eyrie. At last Cindy turned from her computer terminal and stretched, arching her back and lifting her hands to the ceiling.

"What do you say to an afternoon sail? We've done enough for today, and the weather does not get much better this time of year," David suggested, observing her fidgeting.

"Sure Dad. I could really use some fresh air."

They sailed back and forth across Bellingham Bay, informally racing the few other sailboats out that weekday afternoon, and trying out several different sail combinations in the somewhat erratic winds typical of the season. When evening came they lowered sails and drifted for a time, eating a light dinner of sandwiches and beer before heading back to their anchorage. The breeze blowing from the shore smelled of blossoms and buds and the rising saps of the newly leaved trees.

As they gathered in the mainsail the mercurial wind reversed directions. A gust sent them scrambling to gather in the loose ends of the billowing fabric.

"Marshall is teasing us over that messed up tack," Cindy said when they had finally secured the contumacious canvas.

They had gotten into the habit of speaking of their brother and son as one of the immortals—as though he had claimed his place as a deity in their own private pantheon. It was their way of keeping his memory alive. Their greatest mutual but unspoken fear was that they would somehow forget him—his facial expressions, the cadences of his speech, his physicality and the sheer force of his emergent manhood. For this reason they included him in certain of their activities, especially when sailing, as children will sometimes include an imaginary friend in their play.

"...but he definitely approved of our textbook anchoring technique," David observed.

"Maybe so, but he thinks we don't have enough scope out."

"Well, he might be right. Better safe than sorry—we are anchored a little deeper than we were before."

David let out another twenty feet of chain. They locked up, rechecked the lines and furled sails, and together lowered the dingy from the deckhouse of *Lethe* into the water.

Sailors have always been a superstitious tribe, and the modern mariners only more self-consciously so. Many prefer not to start an important voyage on a Friday, and boaters still christen a vessel with elaborate rituals and formalities, often referring with careful deference to the ancient deities and mythical personifications of the elemental forces of nature. The loving and playful inclusion of Marshall in their afternoon sail was not so very different in character from the veneration of the Nereids by the ancient sailors of Greece. It was not difficult for father and daughter to visualize, as the two rowed back to shore under a nacarat sunset, the comely Nereid, Pharusa, 'she who speeds the ships,' at play with her new consort in the swell of the waves that rolled across the bay and out into waters beyond.

EPILOG

Karen

It had been over a year since her son's death. The blustery winds of spring were chilly still, but carried with them the scent and promise of warmer weather to come. Karen Stuckrath bicycled slowly home along her usual tree-lined route leading from the university, where she worked part-time, to the quiet residential neighborhood and her tiny rented studio apartment. It was mid-afternoon, the traffic was light, and most of the students had yet to be released from their educational bondage for the day.

Karen liked her new job. She was research assistant and secretary to a well-respected history professor who was writing a book focusing on the early Russian presence in Alaska, California, and Hawaii. The old lecturer was so impressed with Karen's deportment and her experience of living in the north, that he had hired her on the spot during her job interview. She had found her new life almost unbearably lonely at first, having long ago lost touch with most of her old friends from her youth in the Northwest, but after a few months at her new routine she was befriended by two women of similar age and interests whom she saw sporadically for coffee, conversation, and occasional walks. She had even become close enough to one of her new acquaintances to reveal to the sympathetic divorcée the events which had led to her present bereft state.

Although it made her loneliness somewhat more bearable to have a confidant, Karen mostly still lived to hear from her daughter. She called her every week, and sometimes more often, as much to hear her voice as anything. Cindy had made the long drive south from Bellingham to Eugene on two occasions to visit her mother, and they had begun slowly and tentatively to repair their relationship. The news that Cindy was working with David for the common cause of justice for victims of the drug war filled her with conflicting emotions. She was gratified they had been able to work through their grief and rekindle their relationship through their new mission, but jealous of the day to day interaction it afforded them.

As she rode through the quiet streets she thought about the email she had printed out which, though only a single page, seemed to add disproportionately to the weight of her backpack. The message from David was several days old but she still had not answered it. He wanted her to join him in Bellingham. He believed they could work through their grief together. "At least consider a weekend visit," he begged. He still loved and missed her. He was sorry for leaving her, and wanted to make up for it all somehow.

He had called too, and she had listened to his

pleas and felt moved, but for some reason she could not bring herself to respond to his entreaties.

It wasn't that it was such a great life she had created for and by herself here, though the experience had boosted her self-confidence. She did feel some loyalty to the old professor, but not enough to completely explain her reticence. Was it that she really did believe he should have supported her wish to spirit Marshall out of Alaska? It was still difficult for her not to speculate on what Conrad's reaction might have been had he and David's roles been reversed. She knew without a doubt he would have never allowed Marshall to go to prison. (She had not spoken again to Conrad since that morning many months ago in the Juneau harbor, and had no idea where he might be.) Yet she bore just as much responsibility herself. She could have insisted on a jury trial in spite of David and the lawyer's protestations, or escaped to Canada herself with her son.

Karen was aware that David had achieved some sort of catharsis during the time he held the judge captive in Spruce Cove. She was equally convinced Conrad had meted out his own kind of vengeance and justice to the two most responsible for Marshall's death. But for her there could be no such release, nor could she imagine ever achieving any kind of emotional absolution or resolution. Before her stretched a forlorn future devoid of real hope or joy, and dominated by the constant ache of loss which she supposed would only be dulled eventually by the passage of enough time.

So the letter lay, somewhat crumpled and soiled

from its days in her backpack, still unanswered and for now unanswerable, though she could not bring herself to throw it away.

Several blocks further along she turned the last corner onto her own street. It was a pleasant enough avenue, lined with mature maple trees and modest but well maintained homes. The sight of the small pink and gray forms on the street at the intersection interrupted her musings. The opossum had made it half way to the opposite curb before being struck. It lay on its side with its halo of pink joeys scattered round the inert and slightly inflated body. The immature young so abruptly ejected from the warmth of their mother's protective pouch resembled the large shrimp or prawns Karen used to buy from the local Juneau fishermen each summer, when her family had lived in Alaska. They had been a special favorite of Marshall's. Karen bicycled past the tragic tableau, the crisp spring breeze blowing rivulets of tears across her cheeks and into her streaming hair.

* * *

ABOUT THE AUTHOR

Author, playwright, and musician Michael Rostron was raised in Oregon and spent over twenty years in Alaska. He now resides in Northwest Washington state, just a few miles from the Canadian border. His website can be found at mikerostron.com

CPSIA information can be obtained
at www.ICGtesting.com
Printed in the USA
FFHW012025100219
50481929-55725FF